Catherine Cookson, who writes here as
Catherine Marchant, was born in East
Jarrow and the place of her birth provides
the background she so vividly creates in
many of her novels. Although acclaimed as
a regional writer – her novel THE ROUND
TOWER won the Winifred Holtby Award
for the best regional novel of 1968 – her
readership spreads throughout the world.
Her work has been translated into twelve
languages and Corgi alone has 30,000,000
copies of her novels in print, including those
written under the name of Catherine
Marchant.

Mrs Cookson was born the illegitimate
daughter of a poverty-stricken woman,
Kate, whom she believed to be her older
sister. Catherine began work in service but
eventually moved south to Hastings where
she met and married a local grammar school
master. At the age of forty she began
writing with great success about the lives of
the working-class people of the North-East
with whom she had grown up, including her
intriguing autobiography, OUR KATE. Her
many bestselling novels have established her
as one of the most popular of contemporary
women novelists.

Mrs Cookson now lives in Northumberland.

Heritage of Folly

Catherine Marchant

CORGI BOOKS

HERITAGE OF FOLLY

A CORGI BOOK 0 552 10030 7

Originally published in Great Britain by
Macdonald and Jane's (Macdonald & Co.) (Publishers) Ltd.

PRINTING HISTORY
Macdonald and Jane's edition published 1963
Corgi edition published 1975
Corgi edition reprinted 1978 (twice)
Corgi edition reissued 1979
Corgi edition reprinted 1979
Corgi edition reprinted 1980
Corgi edition reprinted 1982
Corgi edition reprinted 1984
Corgi edition reprinted 1985

Corgi Books are published by Transworld Publishers Ltd.,
Century House, 61-63 Uxbridge Road, Ealing, London W5 5SA,
in Australia by Transworld Publishers (Aust.) Pty. Ltd.,
26 Harley Crescent, Condell Park, NSW 2200, and in New
Zealand by Transworld Publishers (N.Z.) Ltd., Cnr. Moselle
and Waipareira Avenues, Henderson, Auckland.

Made and printed in Great Britain by
Hunt Barnard Printing Ltd., Aylesbury, Bucks.

Heritage of Folly

I

It was after the bus had left Morpeth and had passed through Ulgham and Widdrington that the landscape changed. The farm-lands now gave place to bare, scree-covered slopes with small fields bordered by drystone walls. Here and there when the road dipped into a sheltered valley the earth seemed to promise softness, but the promise was not kept. The whole tone of the land was cold and lonely, and this, Linda thought as she gazed through the bus window, was but a reflection of how she was feeling inside. Her heart was cold with fears of what lay ahead, and she was lonely as she had never been lonely before.

In a short while the bus would reach Surfpoint Bay and she would meet her future employer. This alone would have filled her with some apprehension had she been on time, but she was arriving two hours late. Her train having been held up owing to fog, she had lost the bus that would have got her to her destination at two o'clock.

She hoped he wouldn't be annoyed, it was important that she got off to a good start . . . a good start was everything. What if she made a mess of things? She closed her eyes on this thought and her father's voice became loud in her ears, saying, "A waste of money sending her to an agricultural college . . . a waste of money keeping her at school until she was eighteen . . . a waste of everything. Look at her. Does she look cut out for farm work? A land girl! Never heard tell of such nonsense."

But for once in her life her mother had had her own way and she was given the chance to shape a desire into hard reality. And farming was hard reality; even the short stays on the farm which her uncle managed in Crowbrough had taught her that much.

Before proceeding for a two-year course at an agricultural college it was essential that she have a year of practical training on a farm. The farm in Crowbrough did not offer her this as it was given over wholly to the breeding of Galloway cattle, but the owner had been instrumental in getting her fixed up on a farm in Northumberland. And with her mother's blessing and her father's prophetic warning of failure she had early this morning left London; and now the journey was nearly over.

The stage . . . a model . . . or even a shop and I could have understood it. Her father's voice was still going on, and she moved impatiently on the bus seat and almost exclaimed aloud, "Oh, be quiet." If only the interview was over . . . that was really what was worrying her, the first meeting with her employer. Perhaps this was because she knew that Mr. Batley would have preferred a male student. And there was the letter he had written to her; it had been stiff, but then it was a business letter and you couldn't get much idea of a person from a business letter. Well, she told herself, there wouldn't be much longer to worry now, for the journey was almost over, in fact they had arrived. When she shivered she admonished herself strongly, "Don't be silly, he can't swallow you."

The light of the November day was fading and it wasn't until the bus was running on the flat at the bottom of the hill that she realised that what had appeared to be a cluster of houses was in reality only two. Both grey-stoned, they stood tall and stark, dominating about twenty chalets. When the bus drew to a stop, Linda, standing on the platform, saw that the larger of the two houses was an inn, The Wild Duck, and outside it was standing a small, very fat woman, a white apron round her middle and her arms bare to the elbows. Near her stood a little girl of about seven. There was no sign of a man of any sort waiting.

"Kept fine for you." The woman spoke to the driver who had now alighted from the bus and was stretching his arms above his head.

"Aye, it's all right here, Mrs. Weir," he answered, "but it was as thick as clarts when we left Newcastle."

"No!" Her eyebrows slid up her smooth brow.

"Aye, Mrs. Weir, it was." The conductor endorsed his mate's statement.

During this exchange Linda stood aside and looked about her, but she had only time to notice the great expanse of sand with white-collared waves rolling on to it when the woman said, "And you, me dear, you're for Batley's, aren't you?"

"Yes, I am." Linda brought her eyes eagerly to the woman.

"Well, he was down here for the last one and of course you weren't on it."

"My train was late, I lost the connection. . . . is it far to the farm?"

"Well, it all depends what you mean by far. Ten miles is nowt to some folks, then to others a mile's enough."

"Is it ten miles?" Linda could not stop her eyes from stretching in surprise.

"No, it's only me way of putting things. Look, you could do with a cup of tea, I bet. Come along in. Yours is ready for you, lads," she nodded to the conductor and

9

driver. "You know your road. . . . You come this way, Miss."

Linda followed her into a little parlour, so warm, shining and comfortable that for a moment she wished she had reached her journey's end and could sit here and relax and not think or worry about employers or farms or futures.

As Mrs. Weir poured out the tea she talked. "Now if he's not here within the next ten minutes your best plan is shanks's pony. You'll do it in twenty minutes or so and get there afore it's really dark. . . . Oh, I know what. Katie'll climb the knoll and see if the car's coming over the cliff. Katie!" Mrs. Weir's voice filled the house, and when the child came running, saying, "Yes, Auntie?" Mrs. Weir said, "Go, climb the knoll and see if Batley's wagon's coming along the top. Be careful now."

"Yes, Auntie." The child was away, and Mrs. Weir explained, "There's steps up the cliff just beyond the house. Her legs are young, she can do it. You can see along the top from there." She handed the cup to Linda and almost without drawing breath she went on, "You don't look cut out for the part. Would never say you were a farm girl if I had to put a name to you. You're thin. You could do with a bit of this." She thumped her stomach.

This quick change in the conversation made Linda smile and she said, "I'm much stronger than I look."

"Well, you'll need to be to stick farming. And up there an' all. Wild it is up there. Bad enough down here, but we're sheltered a bit. Cut you into slices up there. You know Ralph Batley?"

"No."

"Oh, thought you might."

It was on the point of Linda's tongue to say, "Tell me,

10

what's he like?" but she checked herself. Women were women all the world over, and this woman, as kind as she was, might inform him of her enquiries the next time they met. She didn't want that to happen.

A few minutes later Katie came panting into the kitchen saying, "I can't see the car, Auntie."

"Aw well . . ." Mrs. Weir turned to Linda, "it looks like he's been held up or he might be thinking you're not for coming the day, or his jeep's broken down . . . and that'll be no surprise . . . anything could have happened to stop him."

"Yes . . . yes." Linda was on her feet; the picture that Mrs. Weir presented was sending her spirits down to zero again. By this time of the day she should have met her employer and known, at least to some extent, what he was like. But here she was, darkness not far off and the meeting with him still to come.

"My man's taken the van into Amber, or he would have run you up there like a shot, but my advice to you is to start off now . . . not that I'm hurrying you, mind. If the lines weren't down I'd ring up and that would bring him, but the day afore yesterday we had a fair storm here, took part of the cliff away and a couple of poles an' all. They should be right by the morrow but the morrow isn't the day, is it?"

Mrs. Weir was leading the way to the door again and now she said brightly over her shoulder, "But I can tell you one good thing—your luggage has come: a trunk and two cases . . . that was it, wasn't it?"

"Oh, have they? That's good. That's something, anyway." Linda found herself laughing as she looked down into the big moon face of Mrs. Weir. "And they've gone up?"

"Aye. He took them back this afternoon with him."

The fact that her luggage had arrived at its destina-

11

tion cheered her somewhat and she took leave of garrulous Mrs. Weir and Katie with the promise that she would surely look in on them again soon. They had come to the end of the second house with her, which was a shop but which was now shuttered, and Mrs. Weir's voice sent her on her way crying, "You can't go wrong, keep to the road."

She walked quickly to the end of the sea wall, which formed a sort of promenade, and there she turned and looked back. Mrs. Weir and Katie were still standing watching her and when they waved she answered their salute gaily. She liked these people. . . . Oh, she did.

Once she had left the promenade the road branched away from the sea and steeply upwards. At one point it was just a broad cleft cut out of the rock, and she wondered how a car could ever get through it. As she walked hurriedly out of the gully, the road widened and quite suddenly, as if she had been propelled there by a lift, she found herself on top of the cliff. There to the left of her lay the sea, deep green to where, in the far distance, a strip of fire edged the horizon. It was like an echo of the afterglow, and although it was breathtakingly beautiful and demanded that she stand entranced for a moment in awe-filled admiration, it also told her there was need for hurry. It had not taken her more than five minutes to reach this point and if the journey to the farm was, according to Mrs. Weir, a twenty-minute walk, then if she wanted to get there before it was really dark she must put a spurt on.

It was at this point that she was confronted with a problem that almost made her retrace her steps back to the inn. Mrs. Weir had said, keep to the road, but which road? Before her the road divided itself into two; one side, she noticed, and not without a slight shudder, wound its way perilously near the edge of the cliff, and it was bordered on its right side by a wire fence with a treble row of barbed wire for good measure running along its top. This undoubtedly was to keep the cattle from going over the cliff. But surely it couldn't be the road. She looked towards the other branch. This looked really nothing more than a lane, yet there was the print of car wheels on the rough grass that bordered it, whereas on the cliff path the rocky surface showed no indication of it having been used by a vehicle. Anyway, she considered, no one in their right senses would take that cliff path. As for bringing a farm vehicle along there, you wouldn't do that unless you wanted to commit suicide. Without further hesitation she found herself taking the road to the right and after only a short way she felt that her choice had been the right and sensible one, for it broadened out into a sort of carriageway which was apparently kept in reasonable repair, for she saw that here and there the potholes had recently been made up with broken rock.

Exactly twenty minutes after she had left Mrs. Weir she was still on the road and there was no farm in sight. Just a little tremor of panic rose in her from the region of her stomach. Soon it would be quite dark, she hadn't a torch, she was feeling cold, and her light case had taken on a lead-like weight now. There was only one thing she was thankful for at the moment and that was she had been wise enough to put on her flat-heeled shoes. The path now was winding steeply downhill and she had the impression that she was descending into the cove again at Surfpoint Bay, but knew that this was impossible for this path had led away from the cliffs and the cove. Wherever she was she was well inland. Then, rounding one sharp twist in the path, she saw the light. The relief that surged through her brought her to a halt and she found that she was biting her lip to stop its trembling.

She was here, she had arrived. There below her lay the farm, with lights shining out from the farmhouse itself. She could only make out the dim shape of the buildings but she knew in her heart that it was a beautiful farm. She had to stop herself from running the last few yards down the hill.

Walking somewhat sedately, she left the cliff path, crossed over an intersecting road, through a white gate, up a broad-flagged path to some still broader steps which led on to what looked like a terrace flanking the house, and to the front door. It was a massive door of weathered oak, its blackness intruding into the fading light.

As her hand went up to the knocker she heard laughter coming from somewhere within the house and a woman's voice shouting a name. "Rouse! Rouse!"

She lifted the knocker and tapped rather timidly on the door. The knock seemed to cut off the woman's laughter and there followed a period of silence before the door was opened.

The woman was standing with her back to the light and Linda could not make out her face distinctly; she only knew that she was tall, as tall as herself, and thin, even thinner than she was, and she was dark, as dark as she herself was fair.

"Yes?" The word was a question that seemed laboured with surprise.

"I'm ... I'm Linda Metcalfe."

The woman moved slowly forward now and peered into Linda's face. And then she said, "Are you looking for someone?"

The sickly feeling that was creeping through Linda now told her without further words what had happened. She had come to the wrong farm.

"What's the matter?" A deep, thick voice came from behind the woman, and the voice seemed to suit the man now standing in the doorway. Then as Linda was about to speak he switched an outside light on, and as she blinked and looked into his heavy red face she stammered, "I . . . I'm afraid I've come to the wrong place."

"Yes? Where are you making for . . . the Bay, Surfpoint Bay?"

"No, no, I've just come from there. I was on my way to Fowler Hall Farm and I must have taken the wrong turning."

Although the couple before her neither moved nor altered their expressions, Linda was vitally aware that her words had come as a shock to them. How long the silence continued she did not know, but it was broken by another male voice from somewhere in the house, calling, "Where are you?"

"Come here a minute." The woman spoke over her shoulder but without taking her eyes off Linda, and when into the scene came a young man whose thinness, colouring and height proclaimed him to be the woman's son, she said to him, "This young lady's lost her way, she's making for . . . up there." The last two words seemed to cause her some effort, and she accompanied them with a heavy sidewards lift of her head.

The young man was standing not more than a foot from Linda now and over his dark, bold, appraising gaze there fell, like a sheet, a look of startled surprise.

Again silence enveloped them all.

"What made you take this road? The road you wanted lay along the cliff." It was the elder man speaking, his voice rough and harsh, and when Linda answered, "It didn't look safe somehow," there was a quick exchange of glances between the three people opposite her.

Then the woman seemed to take charge of the situation. "You'd better come in," she said, "until we see what can be done. You can't get there in the dark . . . not alone." On this she turned and walked into the house and the men stood one on each side of the doorway waiting for Linda to pass between them, and as she did so she had the oddest feeling, which made her want to lower her eyes as if from their naked virility.

Once past them she entered a glass-partitioned lobby, and from there stepped into a large hall which was evidently used as a lounge. Immediately she saw it was a beautiful room, so beautiful that she hesitated to walk into it in her outdoor shoes. Red rugs on a light oak floor, flanked by white walls, the white broken here and there by flashes of scarlet, heavy velvet scarlet curtains, a great fire burning in an open fireplace and, fronting it, a deep couch. But dominating all this was the staircase. Bare oak, it wound its way out of the hall to the right to form a balcony flanking the end wall. The whole was like an expensive Christmas card, but strangely out of place with its owners, at least with the two men. It was the woman, Linda thought, who would be solely responsible for this room, for like her it was colourful yet dignified. The woman was wearing a red wool dress and her black hair was straight and pulled tightly back from her forehead, and like her own hair it was long and dressed almost in the same style, lying in a bun on the nape of her neck.

"Sit down . . . will you have a cup of tea?" The woman looked towards the table set with tea things standing to the side of the couch, and Linda, taking the seat indicated on the sofa, replied quietly, "No, thank you, I had some tea in the village . . . at the inn."

"Why couldn't Weir have taken you up?"

"He had gone out with the car." Linda looked up at the elder man.

16

"He would. . . . What're you doing in these parts . . . you've no connection with the Batleys, have you?"

"No, I'm going to study farming. I'm going as a student for a year with Mr. Batley."

The three pairs of eyes were on her again and she turned hers from the older man to the woman and then to the son, but brought them back quickly to the man again as he exclaimed, "God in heaven!"

What was behind this remark she didn't know, and she hadn't time to ponder, for at that moment the woman turned to her son and said, "You'll have to run her up in the car."

"Wh-a-t!" The younger man's whole expression was one of protest. Then as if realising the effect of his attitude on the uninvited guest he turned to Linda and said hastily, "I'm sorry, but you see . . ."

"Rouse! Come here a minute." The woman was walking away across the wide hall towards a doorway. But the young man didn't follow her until his father jerked his head sharply, then very reluctantly he moved away across the room in his mother's wake.

Now the man came and took his position on the hearthrug with his back to the fire. He was dressed in kneebreeches, tweed coat and slippers and he joined his hands under the tail of his coat before he said, "You know what you're in for? Farming in this county, particularly this end of it, is tough."

"I like being out of doors. I'm used to all weathers."

"You may be, but there's weather and weather; we don't just get weather here." His eyes were moving over her now, from her mushroom-coloured, small fur hat right down to her feet. And he seemed amused at what he saw for he began to chuckle. It was a low, rumbling chuckle, it was a spiteful sound and it brought the colour flooding up into Linda's face. And then to her amazement he threw his head back and laughed. He laughed until the tears sprang from his eyes.

Linda had risen to her feet. She was embarrassed, hurt and angry, but more angry than anything else, and when the woman came hurrying into the room again, this must have appeared evident to her, for after admonishing her husband with a sharp "Stop that, John!" she turned to Linda and said, "He's not laughing at you, don't take offence."

Linda was standing stiffly looking at the man, and now he returned her gaze and spoke to her in an enigmatic way, but the meaning of his words she fully comprehended. "He was wanting a cart-horse and he gets a year-old filly," he sneered.

"John!"

The word was a command, but he flapped his hand at his wife and ignored her as he added, "Fowler's Folly, indeed!"

Up to now Linda had liked everybody she had met on her journey through this county, but now the pleasant mood of the day had changed and to her surprise she found that the emotion she was feeling was akin to hate and the strength of it both startled and shocked her. She could only give herself one word to express this man's character and that was spiteful. He imagined her employer had let himself in for a bundle of uselessness and he was revelling in the thought. Well, he would see. She felt that she wanted to do something, and at this very moment, to demonstrate her capabilities, yet she knew that if the opportuniy had presented itself she would have failed dismally , for here was a man who could use a sneer, a laugh or a sarcastic remark with devastating effect.

"My son Rouse is going to take you up."

Linda turned to the woman but did not answer her, for she found that she was trembling with her anger.

"You know what this might lead to." The man was speaking to his wife now . . . his voice without laughter was brittle . . . and she answered without looking at him as she led Linda towards the front door, "He'll drop her at the top gate."

The woman led the way across the terrace, down the steps and along the garden path to the road, where stood a small open car with the son, Rouse, already seated at the wheel. He did not get out and usher her into her seat, it was the mother who opened the car door and indicated that she should get in. Then when she had banged the door closed again she gave no word of farewell, merely inclining her head in a nod before the car spurted forward.

Linda, her anger still bubbling in her, sat silent, and she had been in the car some minutes before her companion spoke. As he gave a swift turn to the wheel to round a sharp bend he said abruptly, "Our name's Cadwell." Then after a moment, during which Linda made no reply, he added, "May I ask what yours is?"

"Linda Metcalfe." Her tone was not conducive to further conversation. She didn't intend it should be.

On the bend they ran into a strong wind and she heard him repeating her name as if he was calling across a valley, and as he shouted, "I'm Rouse, as I suppose you've already learnt," she did not answer, for at this stage she was having her work cut out to get her breath and hold on to her hat at the same time.

Down in the sheltered valley there had been little wind, but now they were climbing up steeply into it and at one point the car slowed to a crawl in low gear. Then suddenly as she felt herself pushed forward she knew they were out of the valley and on high, exposed, level ground again. At one time she thought she recognised the main road on which she had travelled towards Surf-point Bay in the bus, but she couldn't be sure, and she reasoned against this. If Fowler Hall Farm was only twenty minutes' walk from the Bay surely the car should do it in a matter of minutes.

On and on the car went now and no words passed between them. Then after she had been on the road for what she felt must be fifteen minutes at least, she sat up straight and asked, "Where are we going?"

"Fowler Hall, Batley's place. That's where you want to go, isn't it?"

"Yes, but I understood it was only a short walk from Surfpoint Bay."

"Yes, it is, but not this way. Don't worry, I'm not trying to kidnap you or anything in that line."

"I wasn't suggesting that you were." Her tone was cutting, and now the dark eyes flashed sideways at her and she saw he was laughing at her. After a moment he asked evenly, "What part of the country are you from?"

"Sussex."

"Oh, Silly Sussex by the sea?"

This remark she considered was too stupid and she didn't deign to answer it.

With a sudden jolt the car came to a halt and he turned slowly towards her and said, "That was an inane thing to say. The fact is I've never been to Sussex, only heard that saying somewhere."

This touch of humility in him changed her feelings toward him somewhat and she said with a softening of her tone, "If you've never been there, it's a pleasure you must give yourself, it's a wonderful county."

"Yes, I've heard that an' all. . . . Well, you've arrived."

Linda peered about her, but there was no house within the radius of the headlights, and when she stood on the road she was somewhat appalled to find herself confronted with nothing more than a five-barred gate, a field gate.

"Where is the house?"

As she spoke a fierce gust of wind pulled at her hat and swelled her clothes into a bell about her legs, and as she pressed down the skirt of her coat with one hand and clung on to her hat with the other, his hand came on to her arm and steadied her. Then after a moment he led her towards the gate and, pointing into the darkness, he said, "Over there, those are the farm buildings. Can you see that flicker of light?"

So faint was the light that she would not have noticed it had he not focused her attention upon it, but just as she caught sight of it, it disappeared.

"The house is beyond. It looks as though there's someone in the yard. You'll be all right. There's a cart track leads round this field, it will take you right into the yard. . . . Have you a torch?"

"No . . . well, not with me."

"Here . . ." he put his hand into the pocket of his duffel coat and pulled out a torch, "take this."

"Oh, thank you."

He unlatched the gate but stood with it in his hand before opening it, and then he said, "Well, good luck."

Again Linda felt kindly disposed towards him for he sounded, unlike his father, as if he really did wish her good luck. She held out her hand, saying "Goodbye, and thank you very much for helping me."

The fingers that closed round hers were hard and the grip was tight. "I want my torch back, mind." He was smiling.

"Of course, I'll leave it at your house."

He released her hand as he said, "No, don't do that." Then he added quickly, "Not because you wouldn't be welcome; don't judge us on how my father reacted today, I'm only saying this for your own sake. . . . It'll be better for you not to have us on your visiting list."

"Why? Aren't you friends with Mr. Batley?" She asked the question pointedly.

"Huh! You'll find out soon enough. . . . But don't you fret, I'll get my torch back. I'll look out for you."

His tone had changed and its quality was slightly too familiar and she wanted to say, "Please don't. I'll send it through the post," but she let it go. "Goodbye," she said again, "and thank you."

He said nothing further but pushed the gate open and she passed through it, and when a few minutes later she turned the corner of the field, she saw that the car was still but with the headlights pointing in the opposite direction now, and in a way she felt comforted that he was waiting until she reached the farmyard.

Her torch picked out a dark huddle of buildings and then an archway, and before she passed through this she turned her eyes across the field again but there was no sign of the headlights now. As she entered the farmyard she wondered for a moment if there were dogs about . . . she was very fond of dogs but dogs weren't usually very fond of strangers . . . and when almost immediately she heard the sound of muffled barking which indicated it was coming from somewhere indoors, she sighed thankfully.

She flashed her torch around the familiar sight of a farmyard and noticed with pleasure that it was clean. She'd heard tell that some of these out-of-the-way farms could be shockers. From a door to the right of the yard came a chink of light and with her heart now thumping heavily against her ribs she made her way towards it and after only a moment's hesitation she lifted the latch and pushed open the door.

She was looking into a single cow byre. The smell that met her was warm and sweet, like incense, and there before her on a heap of fresh straw lay a small Galloway cow. The animal was on its side and kneeling on the ground stroking its face and talking to it was a man with his back towards her. The inflection of his voice was rising and falling in gentle murmur. He was talking as if the animal was a child, a sick child, saying, "There, there. There, there. It's all right, it'll soon be over. There, there. It won't be long now, take it easy . . . we'll have her on the mat before you in no time. Is that you, Michael?"

He did not turn round, and Linda found she could not answer him one way or the other.

"Did you find Uncle Shane?"

At this point she coughed and the sound brought him sharply round on his hunkers. She saw his mouth drop open in surprise before he jerked himself to his feet. He was standing at the front of the byre staring at her as if he thought she was not real, and just when she felt she could not stand his concentrated gaze for a second longer, he passed his hand over his eyes and slowly down his face.

"I'm sorry . . ." the voice came from between his fingers where his hand was resting against his mouth, "it went clean out of my head . . . with Sarah here." He jerked his head in the direction of the cow.

"That's quite all right." She felt a wave of relief as she moved slowly forward into the light towards him. This then was Mr. Batley. He was quite different from the picture which she had created of him and which had taken on something of a sinister quality since her meeting with the Cadwells. He wasn't as old as she had thought, under thirty-five. He was tall, very tall, perhaps six foot two, and his breadth owed nothing to flesh. As she looked into his face she could not help being struck by the sparseness of flesh on it. There was something about his face that gave her the impression that he might, sometime recently, have passed through a grave illness. His hair was dark but not of the black darkness of the Cadwell men. What caught her attention immediately were his eyes, the eyes that were hard on her again. They were grey, clear and without warmth. They did not seem to belong to the man whom she had heard talking softly to the cow. She knew that in his look there was something of the same ingredient as had been in Mr. Cadwell's, and in a wave of anxiety she recalled Mr. Cadwell's words: "He was wanting a cart-horse and he gets a year-old filly."

To disabuse him of this impression and put herself immediately in the picture, she looked down at the cow and giving silent thanks for the little knowledge of cattle she had picked up on the Crowbrough farm she said, "You stock Galloways then?"

"Yes." He was still looking at her.

"Is it her first?"

"Yes." This question brought his attention to the animal again, and he turned and was about to kneel down beside her when he twisted his long length round and as if speaking his thoughts aloud demanded, "But how did you manage to get here? Didn't you go to the house?"

"No, I came across a field from the roadway."

"Who brought you up there? Mr. Weir?"

"No." As she returned his gaze something within her warned her not to mention the name of Cadwell, yet she couldn't see how else she could explain her arrival, so she prevaricated by saying, "I went to the wrong house. They . . . they brought me to the gate."

There came upon them a silence that she recognised, it was the same kind of silence that had followed the name of Batley when she had spoken it to the Cadwells. He was standing stiff and straight now, looking at her.

"What was the name of the people who brought you?"

She swallowed once before answering, "I think it was Cadwell."

Was it hate she watched spring into his face, or pain, or fury, or all three? But in an instant he was transformed before her eyes, and she had to tell herself firmly that it was her imagination and that he was not menacing her.

The cow at this moment gave a cry, and its moving uneasily on the straw had the power to bring his attention from her. Her heart was racing as she watched him close his eyes then swallow hard before turning away and on to his knees again.

She stood helplessly watching him for some moments as his hands moved over the animal, then more out of nervousness than a desire to help at this stage, for she had never seen a calving, she heard herself saying, "Can I . . . can I do anything?"

So long was he in answering her that it would appear he hadn't heard her or that he could not bring himself to speak. Then the words seemed to be squeezed through his lips as he said, "You'll . . . get . . . messed . . . up."

"Oh, that doesn't matter." Her relief sounded in her voice, and the next minute she was pulling off her coat and hat and hanging them on a nail at the side of the byre. His eyes flicked towards her as she stepped on to the straw, but they were raised no further than the skirt of her soft blue woollen dress.

"There's an apron there." Again his words came reluctantly as he thrust one hand out behind him indicating the corner of the byre.

Following his directions she took from a nail a large

piece of clean sacking, and when she had tied it around her waist she again entered the box.

"Go to her head. Keep your voice low, keep talking to her, her name's Sarah. . . .She's not easy."

As he finished this staccato information she was vitally aware that he was still consumed by a turmoil of feeling. He rose and went to a steaming bucket just outside the byre and plunged his arms up to his elbows into the white-coloured liquid, then taking a file from a tray standing on a shelf, he began methodically and quickly to clean his nails before he came again to the animal.

Kneeling on the straw Linda touched the cow's head, but when she began to talk to the animal the sound of her own voice seemed to embarrass her and she was hesitant. Then suddenly self was forgotten, submerged before the miracle that was taking place.

She was talking softly and rapidly to Sarah now and fondling her head as if she herself had reared her, and the man delivering the calf was her Uncle Chris. "There, there, Sarah, you'll be all right. There, there, that's a dear. It's nearly over, good . . . dear Sarah." Then she looked to where her employer was holding across the palm of his hand two quivering little hooves, the forelegs of the calf. She could only see part of what he was doing but she knew by his actions that he was rolling back the bag of skin that enveloped the calf. It was as if he was pulling the baby out of a stocking. Sarah squirmed, and he said to her in a voice that Linda could not associate with the glowering man of a few minutes ago, "Gently, Sarah, gently, gently."

At this point the byre door was thrust open and a thick Irish voice cried, "Begod! Ralph, has it come upon her? I was away up at the . . ."

"Stay still, keep quiet."

The command had more power than any shouted

order. It was soft yet grinding, as if every word was being strained through steel filings.

Linda watched an old man with grey hair approach the byre on tiptoes and by his side a small boy of not more than seven or eight. The eyes of both the old man and boy were fixed on her and not on the progress of the birth.

The old man's mouth had dropped into a gape, and when he finally closed it it was to mutter, "Mother of God!"

"Uncle Shane!" It was another command, still soft, and the old man whispered back quietly, "All right, Ralph, all right, I'll hold me whisht."

Sarah's body looked a contortion of pain and Linda could feel the strain under her hands. Pity for the animal swelled in her so much that she had to crush her teeth into her lower lip to stop herself from moaning in sympathy.

"Keep talking." It was an unusually quiet request.

Unselfconsciously now she looked down into the soft, melting, pain-filled eyes of Sarah, but her voice was unsteady as she talked to the animal.

An oath from Ralph Batley brought her head up, and as she looked in concern towards him the old man whispered low, "What's wrong, Ralph?"

After a moment the reply came. "The head's turned back."

"Aw, Holy Mother, will it be a vet job?"

There was no answer to this and, fascinated, she watched her employer gently inserting his arm up to the elbow into the cow.

Quickly and softly she talked to Sarah now. Stroking the animal's sweating face and forgetting herself and those about her entirely, she poured out endearments, saying, "Darling, darling. There, sweet . . . there. All over, all over."

Suddenly Sarah gave a very human sigh and, when her body began to sink in and her muscles relax and she sighed deeply again, Linda sighed with her and her sigh released a smile. Then with her forearm she wiped the sweat from her own brow.

"Oh, bejapers! What a beauty. She's a beauty, Ralph."

Ralph Batley now silently motioned Linda to her feet and out of his way, and when she had obeyed him she watched him wipe down the new baby with a wisp of straw before placing it near its mother's head, and when she saw Sarah's black tongue come out and lovingly lick her daughter, she experienced a wondrous feeling of happiness. She had witnessed her first calving. She couldn't explain it but there would never be another calving like it.

She was loosening the apron from about her waist when she became aware that the boy and the old man were gazing at her fixedly. Methodically she dusted the straw from the sacking before hanging it up on its nail again, and taking down her coat and hat. Then shyly she turned and faced the pair and after returning their scrutiny for a second or so she smiled, and almost immediately her smile was returned by the old man. But the boy's face remained solemn and full of enquiry, not untouched with wonder.

"Tell me, how did you come? Did Weir bring you?" The old man was standing near her now, his eyes shining up at her like beams through the rough stubble of hair that covered most of his face.

Before Linda could make any reply Ralph Batley's voice cut in sharply from just behind her shoulder, saying, "This is my uncle . . . Mr. MacNally, and this," the hand came past her and rested on the boy's head, "this is my nephew, Michael." Before she could acknowledge the introductions in the conventional way or otherwise he went on, "Take Miss Metcalfe up to the house, Uncle, I'll be there in a moment or two."

"Aye, Ralph. Yes, I'll do that. Will you come along now?" The old man backed away from her, one arm extended in a courtly gesture as if she was some personage he was ushering into a banquet. She felt inclined to laugh. She liked this old man. From first impressions she didn't think she would get many laughs from her employer, but this old man seemed to be bubbling with a peculiar sense of joy, and she found her heart reaching out to him as if it was aching to come within the orbit of such warmth.

The boy Michael was going ahead of her towards the byre door, when Ralph Batley's voice crying sharply, "Michael!" brought him round, and whatever signal he received from behind her he immediately stood to one side and allowed her to pass out through the door which Shane was now holding open for her.

In the yard the wind tore at them, and as the old man steadied her with his hand on her elbow he yelled, "Have you long come? I've been away up in the top field, the fence is flat."

"No, I've just arrived."

"Then you haven't been in the house at all?" His voice was high with surprise.

"No."

She could feel his bewilderment and it came over strongly as he said, "I wondered about your case there. By the way, pass it over here." He put out his hand for it, and she did not protest that she could carry it, but let him take it from her.

"Did Weir bring you up? You didn't say."

"No, Mr. Weir was out."

"You couldn't have got here afore dark then?"

"No, I lost my way and I arrived at another farm. The name . . ." She paused, then went on, "The name was Cadwell." She gave this information briefly.

The old man came to an abrupt stop and his hand came off her arm and she was forced to stand with her head and shoulders pressed back against the wind while he turned to the boy and said, "Michael. Here, take hold of this case and go on up." He pushed the case and the lamp into the boy's hands, then added, "Away with you now." And it wasn't until the child had moved off that he said quickly, "Don't tell me that a Cadwell brought you up here?"

"Yes, the young man, Rouse, I think his name was."

"You didn't tell him that . . . Ralph, back there?"

"Yes, I'm afraid I did. I didn't see any reason not to." This wasn't strictly true but Linda could not explain how it had been impossible for her to withhold the means by which she had arrived here.

"Name of God!"

"What have I done wrong?" There was a tremor of apprehension in her voice. "I didn't know that Mr. Cadwell and Mr. Batley were at loggerheads, it was unfortunate that I should go there. I wouldn't have had this happen for the world, I'm terribly sorry if I've caused—"

"That's all right, that's all right, you weren't to know, girl. Now we must go in. . . I don't know how Maggie will take this . . . his mother. Come." He took hold of her arm again. "I'll take you round to the front door, she'd never forgive me for taking you in by the back way. Visitors must always come in the front door."

Linda did not protest that she did not come within the category of a visitor, for she was now too disturbed and distressed with the thought that even before she had reached her destination she had gathered up the threads of a feud and trailed them along with her to this very house, and this fact was bound to have a dampening effect upon her reception.

They were walking along a broad, flagged terrace now and the wind was meeting them head-on, and when they reached the porch they both stood panting for a moment, before the old man said, "I'll take off me boots, Maggie would brain me if I went in with me boots on." Then bending towards her he whispered, "Wipe your feet, there on that mat. Wipe them hard. Mud you know, it treads in."

Very like a child, and feeling at this moment not far removed from one, she did as she was requested, while she watched him hop from one stockinged foot to the other over the cold stone flags to the door. Then when he opened the door it was immediately made plain to her why her feet should be as clean as possible, for the floor on to which she stepped was shining. It was polished as she had never before seen a floor polished, except in an advertisement. But her attention was lifted from the floor to the hall which opened out before her, for in size and shape it was an exact replica of the hall of the Cadwells' house. There was the same large, open fireplace. There was the same winding staircase but going off to the left with the balcony running from it along the entire length of the far wall; yet for all the similarity the hall was as different from the Cadwells' as chalk from cheese, for it had nothing of its elegance or charm. This room, Linda saw at once, was used as a general room. Being so, it recalled to her mind Mrs. Weir's parlour, yet because of its size it lacked the cosiness of that small room. A long black oak refectory table ran lengthwise down the hall. Standing with her back to its head was a woman. She was of medium height with greying hair and had two patches of red high on her cheek bones. Her eyes were round, brown and bright, and her expression checked Linda's progress.

The Cadwells had looked at her each in their own way. Ralph Batley's appraisal had shown her his surprise, and she did not think that it was of a pleasant nature to him. The old man Shane had greeted her gleefully, the boy with wonder; but this woman's look was different. Linda was conscious of her gaze sweeping her from head to foot. It seemed as if she was being called upon to make a quick decision and was finding the progress difficult. The boy Michael had evidently prepared her to some extent, for he was standing by her side biting at his thumbnail, looking up at the same time from under his brows towards Linda.

"Well, she's come, Maggie." Shane's voice was high again. "Found her way here in the dark."

The woman was now coming towards Linda, her eyes still holding her gaze.

"I'm sorry you've had to find your way. When you didn't come at two he thought maybe . . . anyway, he couldn't leave the calving." The woman's voice was soft and thick and pleasant, but before Linda could reassure her that it was perfectly all right, she had turned on the old man, crying, "It's your fault. Where d'you think you've been, you could have gone down."

"Now, Maggie, whisht a while, I was up in the top field with the railings as flat as a pancake. You wouldn't have had me leave them and the cattle get through, now would you?"

"Oh." She moved her head impatiently then turned to Linda saying, "Well, come in, come in. Here, let me have your coat. You'll be frozen."

As Linda took off her coat Shane, tripping towards the fireplace like an aged gnome, said with evident pleasure,

32

"She's got her hand in already, Maggie, she's been help-ing with the calving. Now what d'you think of that? It's come, it's a fine heifer although her head was back."

"Helping with the calving?" The woman held Linda's coat across her hands and looked up at her incredulously, and Linda, going hot with what she knew was to come, said hesitantly, "Apparently I came in the back way, I saw the light in the byre."

"You came in the back way? From the main road?"

"Yes."

"Oh." She nodded at Linda, a smile now softening her face. "Mr. Weir brought you?"

"No."

"No, Weir didn't bring her." They all turned their eyes towards a door under the balcony through which Ralph Batley was entering the room. It was evident that he had heard his mother's question, and as he came slowly across the hall he said to no one in particular, "She took the wrong road." Then throwing a cold, grey glance at her, he added, "Didn't you, Miss Metcalfe?"

"Yes, I did."

Even to herself she sounded on the defensive. It was as if she had committed a crime by taking the wrong road. She watched him reach up to the high mantelshelf and take a pipe from out of a wooden rack, then knocking the bowl into the palm of his hand he turned to his mother. But his eyes remained on the pipe as he said heavily, "She forked right at the cliff end."

Linda was now looking at Mrs. Batley, but Mrs. Batley was looking at her son. Her brown eyes were wide and unmistakably there was fear in them.

Ralph Batley turned from his mother's gaze to the fire now and lifting his foot he thrust it into the heart of the blazing logs. A shower of sparks sprayed around the chimney and fell on to the gleaming copper kettle that stood to one side of the hearth and on to the great black-leaded kettle resting on a stand near the bars. Then taking a home-made spill from out of a bunch that filled a rack on the brick wall and putting it towards the blaze he said, "Our neighbours were kind enough to bring her to the top gate."

With a feeling of utter helplessness Linda watched the older woman's eyes come towards her again, in their depth such a look of pain now that she wanted to cry out, "What have I done?" but her attention was drawn to Ralph Batley, for he was giving her evidence as to the extent he was disturbed for he was attempting to light an empty pipe. Realising this he threw the spill into the fire and thrust the pipe into his pocket, and as if to cover up his mistake his tone and manner changed and he said with a poor attempt at lightness, "I'm forgetting, you haven't met my mother."

It seemed a little late for a formal introduction, but she forced a smile to her face and inclined her head towards the older woman.

Mrs. Batley's response to this was to say quietly, "You'll be wanting a wash, will you come up?" She turned about and walked across the hall, Linda's coat still on her arm, and Linda, picking up her case, followed her up the stairs, along the balcony to the far end. There Mrs. Batley opened a door, saying over her shoulder, "I hope you'll be comfortable."

Linda moved into the room. Then turning quickly about she looked at the older woman appealingly and said under her breath, "I'm sorry, Mrs. Batley, I seem to have done something wrong. I'm sorry."

Mrs. Batley stared at her for a moment, then stepping into the bedroom and closing the door behind her, she continued to look at Linda for some seconds before she said, "I'm sorry too, my dear. I'm sorry you had to start like this. One thing I'll ask of you, keep away from the . . ." she paused here as if the name was too painful to utter, then brought out, "the Cadwells." She shook her head back and forwards in small movements as she went on, "If you want to work here and in peace, don't even mention their name. And another thing I would ask you, do your best for him, will you? I'll have to say this quickly for I wouldn't like him to think I was talking, but you see he never wanted a woman on the place, he was against it. But I was for it, and you're not quite what I expected." She held up her hand in a gesture of appeal. "No offence meant, but you don't look exactly cut out for this life. Still, time will tell. . . . Come down when you're ready." She turned about and went quickly out of the room, leaving Linda staring at the closed door in bewilderment.

Her mind was in a whirl. Unintentionally she had stirred up a hornets' nest and naturally she was getting stung. Then everyone she had met since coming off the bus had told her in one way or another that she was unsuitable, at least for the part she hoped to play on a farm. And now, Mrs. Batley's words, "He didn't want a woman on the place."

Slowly she turned and looked about her, and what she saw was pleasing and held some comfort, for there was a wood fire burning in the grate, the furniture was old-fashioned but solid and shining. The bed was a single brass one, with large knobs dominating each corner. On it was a patchwork quilt but a patchwork with a difference for the patches had been made into a design which spoke of countless hours of labour. The floor was bare wood and again highly polished and before the hearth and by the side of the bed were two clippie rugs, and in the corner near the black-faced wardrobe stood her trunk and two cases. This then was her room. It was comfortable and homely. And this house was to be her home for the coming year. She should be bubbling with happiness but all she wanted to do was sit down and cry.

She did not unpack but merely washed herself and combed her hair. She used little make-up at any time, but tonight she was more sparing with it than ever. Yet fifteen minutes later when she went quietly down the stairs it could have been that she had come down dressed for a ball, for all their eyes turned and watched her approach.

The table was set now with a white cloth and was laden with food and she said apologetically, "I hope I haven't kept you waiting."

"No, no, we're just going to start. Come and sit down." Mrs. Batley took her seat at one end of the table and indicated a chair to the right of her. On her left sat Uncle Shane and next to him Michael, and at the head of the table Ralph Batley took his seat.

"Say your grace." Mrs. Batley's head dropped forward as she spoke, and Shane and Michael's followed suit, but as Linda's head moved downwards she knew without looking at him that her employer's remained erect.

"Bless us, O Lord, and these Thy gifts which we receive through Thy bounty, through Christ our Lord, Amen. . . . Now would you like bacon and egg pie and a bit of ham, or this salted pork?" Mrs. Batley pointed to a large flat dish.

"You have some of that, Maggie salts it herself." This was Uncle Shane speaking, his fork pointing to the dish.

"I'll have some bacon and egg pie, please. Yes, and a little pork . . . thank you."

Linda had always considered that she had a good appetite although she may not have shown it in her figure, but she could not attempt to eat half of the dishes that were offered to her. There was little talking during the meal except at one stage when Mrs. Batley asked, "Have your parents ever been in farming?"

"No, never . . . except my uncle, my mother's brother, he manages a farm in Sussex."

"What is your father?"

"He's an accountant."

"An accountant?" Mrs. Batley made a small motion with her head, and Shane said, "An accountant. Now there's a fine job for you, you don't soil your hands at that. No going out in the rain, hail and snow and getting the skin whipped off your nose. What possessed you to go in for this?"

"I'm fond of animals and I've always spent my holidays with my uncle and aunt, on the farm."

No one made any comment on this but Ralph Batley must have moved on his chair for the leg squeaked on the polished floor and Mrs. Batley put in quickly, "Well, if you've all had sufficient you can make a move to the fire."

"I'll help you to clear."

Linda's help was accepted by Mrs. Batley without comment, and carrying a tray of dishes she followed the older woman to the door through which Ralph Batley had entered the hall and into what she found was a large kitchen.

Michael trotted back and forward carrying plates, and each time he entered the kitchen he cast his eyes shyly towards Linda, which she found both endearing and amusing.

When some time later she was standing at the sink drying the dishes that Mrs. Batley had washed and was searching in her mind for something to say to break the awkward silence that was hanging over them, Mrs. Batley said softly but with startling suddenness, "Were you inside the house?"

"You mean . . . you mean the Cadwells'?" Linda's voice too was quiet.

"Yes." Brs. Batley's hands moved rapidly in the water.

"Yes, I was in the hall."

"Oh, you were." The older woman flicked her hands downwards into the sink with a violent movement, and with a harsh bitterness but still under her breath she said, "And I suppose you're comparing it with ours? We haven't got a hundred-pound carpet or a Parker-Knoll suite, nor all the fal-dals."

Linda looked at Mrs. Batley, who was now thrusting the china noisily into the cupboard. She was not hurt at the attack, rather she found herself pitying this woman, and she lied as she said softly, "I didn't notice how the place was furnished. All that I can remember about it is that the hall is somewhat similar in shape to yours with the stairs and balcony at the end. . . . But one thing I did notice and that was the floor and furniture, they didn't gleam as yours does."

Even if this latter had not been true she would have been bound to say it, for the woman before her, she felt, needed comforting. There was a loneliness emanating from her that touched some chord in Linda's own heart, for in spite of her youth she, too, knew what it was to feel lonely. The love in her own home had been so divided that it had never been able to bear fruit. Because of her father's jealousy her mother's affection towards her had only been doled out at opportune times. Her father, she had realised long ago, was a man who should never have had any family for he claimed the undivided attention of his wife. It had been painful to her to realise that her parents' life together was easier when she was out of the way, for her father was a different man when her mother did not show her any undue attention. You had to taste loneliness before you could recognise the form it took in others.

All Mrs. Batley's movements were quick and jerky, and her voice was of the same pattern, and now, taking off her apron and flattening down her hair from its centre parting with both hands and making no reference to Linda's flattering remark, she said, "Come along and sit down."

As she spoke Ralph Batley came into the kitchen. He looked neither at his mother nor at Linda but went straight to the back door and, lifting his coat off it, he thrust his arms into it, and he was on his way out when his mother said, "Will she do?"

For a moment Linda had the awful sensation that the question referred to herself, but when the reply came, "She'll do all right," she was forced to smile. It was the calf they were speaking about. It had yet to be proved whether she herself . . . would do all right.

For the first time Linda saw a flicker of a smile pass over the older woman's face as she turned to her and said, "That's one mercy." She said this as if the calf was a precious addition to the stock, not just another head to be counted.

In the living-room Shane was sitting with his feet stretched out to the blaze but he heaved himself up with rare courtesy on her arrival, saying, "Sit yourself here, it's the best chair in the house."

"No, no, I'll sit here next to you."

"Do what he says, he's getting selfish enough."

On this Shane MacNally turned on his step-sister, saying, "Now, now, Maggie, tell all me sins but don't pin that one on me. I wouldn't be where I am this day if I could claim that quality." The old man's jocular tone was tinged with sadness and Mrs. Batley said briskly, "Sit yourself down, man, and stop being sorry for yourself."

"Aw, Maggie." He was laughing again.

Mrs. Batley was busy now setting up a framework to the side of the fireplace and Linda saw it was a half-finished rug. She watched her bring a carrier bag from a cupboard under the stairs and drop it on Shane's knee, saying, "Get yourself busy, that'll keep you out of mischief. I've run out of clippings."

"Oh, I'll help, Gran. I'll roll the balls." The boy scrambled from the rug where he had been reading and took up a position, not next to the old man but to the side of Linda's feet. It wasn't the best position for catching the strip of cloth that Shane was cutting, and every now and again he had to lean his elbow on the floor and reach across her to grab at a fresh strip. He was methodically rolling the cloth into a ball when he spoke to her but still without looking at her. "I lit your fire," he said.

"Did you? That was kind of you, it was lovely to see a fire in my bedroom." Linda smiled gently down on his bent head.

A short silence followed, broken only by the sound of the progger as Mrs. Batley thrust it through the hessian. Then the boy's voice came again, scarcely above a whisper now. "That was my mummy's room."

"Michael, leave that be and get on with your reading." The command came from Mrs. Batley, and the boy, his head drooping, said, "Yes, Gran," then crawled slowly across the floor to the mat and lay down on his stomach. But he didn't pull his book towards him again. His elbow dug into the mat, his head resting on the palm of his hand, he lay gazing into the fire, and Linda's eyes went wonderingly to him. So she was in his mother's room. . . . Where was his mother? At this moment her thoughts were lifted from the child as her employer once again came into the room. He was in his shirt-sleeves and wearing slippers now, and when the firelight fell full on his face it lent to it a warm colour. Linda found herself thinking as she looked at him that he could be good looking, almost handsome, yet he wasn't, his face was too stiff, too expressionless. Except for that moment in the cow byre when he had almost frightened her with the look in his eyes, his expression was fixed, embedded in a cold reserve.

Before he took his seat in the winged leather chair against the chimney wall he glanced down at the boy on the rug, then lifting his eyes quickly to his mother he tapped his cheekbone.

Linda had not guessed that the boy was crying, for from taking up his position on the mat he had not moved, not even his head. She had been watching him. But Ralph Batley apparently knew the signs.

Now she saw Mrs. Batley nod quickly towards Shane and Shane look towards the boy. Following this the old man coughed and pulling himself slowly up in his chair he turned towards her and said in an off-hand way, "Have you been about at all in your time . . . travelled much?"

Linda shook her head. "Not a lot, I'm afraid. I've been to France twice and Italy, but I have usually spent my holidays on the farm as I said."

"Ah, it's a pity. Now there's me, I've travelled the world. I've been a bit of everything, cowboy, pirate, aye and sheriff. Aye, I have that, I've been a sheriff. I nearly hung a man once, I did an' all, and I nearly got hung meself into the bargain, for the fellow I was going to hang got away and if I hadn't had the fastest horse in Mexico it wouldn't be me here this night telling you."

Although the old man was nodding at her and looking

her full in the face he did not seem to be seeing her, nor did he seem to notice the boy as he turned from the fire and looked towards her. Yet she knew it was precisely for the boy's sake that he was talking. But as he went on she found herself becoming enthralled with his tales. She did not know whether to believe what she was hearing or not. Some of his exploits were of the giant-killer type, yet she felt there must be an element of truth in them. Mrs. Batley was prodding at the canvas and her face looked relaxed, Ralph Batley was sitting smoking now, leaning well back in his chair, his gaze directed into the blaze. The expression on his face was a curious one, it wasn't only that he looked miles away; it was as if the essential part of him, the soul of him, was lost.

When Shane at last brought his tales to an end the boy had been sitting at his feet for some long time, and the old man looked down at him and said, "Aye, Michael, if that mule hadn't gone lame on me and I'd reached that plot of land and staked my claim, I'd have been the richest man in the world this night, I would that. There now," he leaned back in his chair, "I've talked meself as dry as a fish . . . and just look at the clock." He pointed. "Time's up."

"Is it bed?"

Although the boy did not speak with the Irish twang he used the same idiom as the old man and Shane laughed as he replied, "Aye, bed it is, and that's where I'm going an' all, for me eyes are asleep in me sockets and if it wasn't that I knew me road I'd never find me way upstairs." He slapped at the boy's cheek with a gentle slap, and as Linda looked at them a warmness enveloped her, there was something so endearing about them both.

"Wash your hands and face and have your milk." Mrs. Batley spoke to the boy while still prodding away at the mat and not until the child returned from the kitchen did she leave the frame. Then saying to him, "Bid good night," she walked slowly towards the staircase.

"Good night, Uncle." Linda watched the boy support himself on the arm of the leather chair then reach up and plant a kiss on the side of Ralph Batley's cheek. The salutation was not returned but Ralph Batley's hand came onto his head and ruffled his hair as he said quietly, "Good night, Michael."

Now the child was standing in front of her, looking up at her from under his eyebrows in a manner she found characteristic of him. "Good night, Miss," he said shyly.

"Good night, Michael."

From where she sat she watched him and his grandmother go up the stairs side by side, and her eyes followed them along the balcony until they were lost to her sight. She turned now to find that Shane's eyes were on her, and his wrinkled lids blinked rapidly as he met her gaze. Pulling himself to his feet now he said, "Well, I'll bid you good night an' all."

"Good night, Mr. MacNally."

"Oh, bless us and save us, don't MacNally me, Shane is me name. If you want to give me a title then call me uncle."

It was impossible not to be happy in this old man's company and she smiled widely and freely at him, saying again, "Good night," and adding now with a little stress, "Uncle Shane."

"That's more like it." He jerked his head at her before turning towards the fireplace. "Good night, boy."

"Good night, Uncle."

It seemed impossible that anyone could refer to the grim-faced man sitting deep in the big chair as a boy, yet perhaps only ten years or so ago he had been and looked a young man, a handsome young man that anyone could refer to as . . . boy, and not be so very far out.

When Shane reached the top of the stairs he met Mrs. Batley and Linda heard their low exchange of "Good nights", and on entering the hall again the older woman did not go to the mat frame but, turning towards the door that led to the kitchen, she said across the room, "I'll make a drink."

On this Ralph Batley rose heavily from his chair and, passing Linda without a glance, began taking out the pegs that held the rug on the frame. Then he rolled it up and carried it across the hall to a cupboard under the stairs.

When he returned to the fireplace he did not resume his seat, but after knocking his pipe out, he kicked at the logs as he had done earlier in the evening, and stood, his back to her, staring down into the fire.

She sat waiting for him to speak; he must talk to her some time, talk about her appointment and tell her what was expected of her. Apart from the few remarks he had made to her in the byre and when she had first come into the room, he hadn't opened his mouth to her. Perhaps he was waiting for her to speak. She searched in her mind trying to make a choice of words with which to begin, but her mind seemed to have gone blank, and she was thankful when at this moment Mrs. Batley returned to the room bearing a large brown jug in one hand and a tray in the other. When she had placed the jug on the hearth she said, "Let it brew a while," then she folded her hands one on top of the other on her stomach and for the first time that evening they became still, and looking at Linda she said, "Well now, I'll bid you good night an' all. I'll give you a knock at seven. Good night then, and I hope you sleep sound."

Linda rose to her feet, saying, "Thank you, I'm sure I

shall, Mrs. Batley . . . good night." She would have given anything to have added, "I'm coming up, too," but she knew they were being left together purposely to talk.

"Good night, son."

Ralph Batley turned quickly now from the fire, his hand lifted in a protesting motion. Then as his mother turned away as if she had not noticed the gesture the hand dropped heavily to his side.

It was too much. He might be hating the situation but he needn't show it so plainly. She was turning from him when he said, "Sit down."

Reluctantly she faced him. He was pointing to her chair, and when she had seated herself again he took up his position, not in the seat close to the fire but in a chair to the left of her and slightly behind hers.

The fire crackled, the steam rose from the brown jug, and still neither of them spoke. How long the silence lasted she did not know, but her apprehension was overcome by a feeling of sudden and utter weariness helped considerably by the heat of the fire, and now, try as she might, she could not keep her eyes open. In this moment nothing seemed to matter very much. Even her employer temporarily lost his significance. Her lids had dropped and in another second she would have fallen fast asleep had not the peremptory question of "Well?" brought her eyes straining wide.

As she turned her head and blinked at him she saw him rising from the chair and she said quickly, "Oh, I'm sorry."

"You're tired, we can talk in the morning." His voice was neither concerned nor harsh, it was merely making a statement.

"No, no, I'm not really, it was just the fire." She got to her feet.

"We go to bed early anyway."

She made no move but stood looking at him, straight into his eyes, and he returned her look steadily for some seconds before he said, "I don't think you'll like it here, the country is rough and the weather is vile, besides which the work is hard. I have only one man besides my uncle, and," he paused before adding, "as for entertainment, it's nil."

She would not allow her eyes to waver from his and her voice was steady as she replied, "I've worked long hours on my uncle's farm for a month at a time, and I don't mind isolation. As for entertainment, I manage a good deal of the time to entertain myself." She knew that the last was not strictly true for if there was one thing she loved above all else it was to dance.

"You're very fortunate to be so easily satisfied. You must have acquired a great deal of wisdom in a short time."

His tone was sarcastic and made her chin lift, and to hide her feelings and prevent her making a cutting retort in reply she was turning from him, when he said, "I'm sorry. I also forgot to say that we're raw and uncultured up here."

So quickly did she turn her head to look at him that she found him off his guard for a moment. His face had suddenly relaxed and there was a sadness about it that reminded her of the expression on Michael's face when his grannie had stopped him talking about his mother, and he had turned to the fire and cried silently in his loneliness. It came to her that this was the dominating factor she had found in the few hours she had been in this house—loneliness. The loneliness that was deep within Mrs. Batley and would not allow her hands to be still for a moment, the loneliness of the boy who was forbidden to talk about his mother, the loneliness of Uncle Shane living on dreams, and the loneliness of the man before her. She had felt his loneliness from the first, although she had not been able to put a name on it right away.

She had an almost uncontrollable urge to put her hand out to him in comfort. Her voice was low when she said "Good night" before turning quickly from him and going up the stairs.

As she reached the balcony and glanced sideways down into the hall, she saw that he was just moving away from the foot of the stairs. Parallel with her now, he walked towards the fireplace as she walked towards her room at the end of the balcony.

Once inside she did not immediately busy herself by getting ready for bed, nor yet by unpacking her luggage, but slowly she sat down on the rug before the fire, and staring into the dying mushed wood she asked herself what awful thing had happened between the two families she had met within the last few hours to create the hate that existed between them. Feuds weren't infrequent between farmers over land and rights of way, she knew. Also there could be jealousy over stock. But the feeling between the Cadwells and the occupants of this house was something different. It was something deep and menacing. The loneliness that she had sensed in each of the Batleys was not a separate thing, it was a rope binding them together, and in her mind's eye she saw the rope stretching across the cliffs and down the valley and into the heart of the Cadwells' house, the house that was almost a twin to this one, so much so that evidently it had sprung from the same idea, from the same plan. And people didn't build alike in hate. It was usually friendship, deep-linked friendship and admiration that brought about a similarity in dwellings, and only some deep wrong could have forced the houses and their occupants apart.

She did not know who was in the right and who was in the wrong, but already in heart she knew where her sympathies lay. . . .

2

It must have been around four o'clock in the morning that Linda awoke with the feeling that she was cold. When she had got into bed she had been as warm as toast, in fact she had felt there were far too many clothes on, but now she was so cold that she could well imagine that she was lying out on the hillside under canvas with only one blanket covering her. This then was what they meant by . . . weather . . . and weather. Sometimes the dawns in the south had been cold but nothing compared with this. She put her head under the bedclothes and curled herself into a ball. Almost immediately she heard the distinct sound of someone moving about outside and she lifted her head from under the clothes, struck a match and looked at her watch. It was only half-past five. He was certainly about early, perhaps something had gone wrong with the calf. As she thought of this she heard the creak of a door opening on the landing and then the padding of footsteps going down the stairs, accompanied by a soft cough. Surely that couldn't be Mrs. Batley, not at half-past five in the morning!

She heard no more after this until a knock on her door and a voice saying, "Are you awake? It's seven," brought her upright in bed.

She murmured, "Yes, yes, I'm awake," and realised with a start that she must have fallen into a deep sleep in spite of the cold.

The comfort that the room had held last night was gone. Her breath hung on the air, the water she washed in was icy cold and she guessed that she had never dressed so quickly in her life before. The whole proceedings from start to finish did not take more than ten minutes. At the speed she had dressed she made her bed and left the room tidy, and as she stepped out on to the landing the hands of the big old grandfather clock, which stood against the wall to the right, had not reached a quarter-past seven.

Although her only desire was to get near the fire she stopped at the head of the stairs and looked down into the hall. The fire was blazing, the black kettle was singing on the hob, the long refectory table was laid for breakfast, and in the far corner of the room Mrs. Batley was on her hands and knees polishing vigorously at the floor.

The older woman looked up as Linda came down the stairs, and she paused in her rubbing for a moment to say, "By, you're early down!"

"Early?" Linda, reaching the foot of the stairs, looked about her. "I should say I was very late. You look as if you've got a day's work done already."

"Well, not quite." Mrs. Batley was rubbing vigorously again. "It being Sunday I don't rise until half-past five or thereabouts. Other mornings I'm up at five."

"My goodness." Linda's tone spoke her admiration.

But Mrs. Batley thrust it aside saying, "Oh, there's no merit in that, I can't sleep after five, I never have been able to, it's what you've been used to." She paused, then added, "But I meant you were quick down. Breakfast's not till half-past seven, but pour yourself some tea out if you want it." The rubbing went on.

Then as Linda stood in front of the fire, thinkful for the glowing warmth on her back and the hot tea sliding down inside her, Mrs. Batley asked, "You warm enough in the night?"

"I was until about dawn; it was rather chilly then."

"Yes," Mrs. Batley nodded her confirmation, "it gets nippy between four and five."

It was just as Linda finished her tea that she heard the back door open and voices in the kitchen. Instantly she made out Shane's merry voice and the deep, restrained voice of her employer. But she was surprised to hear Michael's voice and she was thinking, "Poor child, to be got up so early," when Michael, running into the room, disabused her of the opinion that he had been made to rise with his elders, for he shouted excitedly to his grandmother, "She's lovely, Gran, and walking about, and Uncle Ralph says I can give her a name."

He was opposite the fire now and, becoming aware of Linda, he pulled up sharply. Turning his eyes full on her but looking not at her face but at her legs, he exclaimed in high pleasurable tones, "What long legs you've got; they're just like the calf's."

"Michael!"

Michael's voice was cut off abruptly and he looked towards his uncle. Ralph Batley was standing within the doorway and he added curtly, "Sit up to the table."

On this the boy's head drooped slightly and he turned about and took his place at the table, and as Linda looked at the pathetically narrow little back she felt a momentary anger against her employer. What right had he to squash the child like that; it had been the same last night. One couldn't say that the boy was afraid of his uncle, but he obeyed him mutely as if he was some kind of personal god.

For a moment she forgot her apprehension at the coming talk with her employer, a talk that was inevitable for she must know the extent of her duties on the farm, and she was filled with an urge to oppose him in defence of the boy and so she said, on a light note, "Wait until you put on breeches, Michael, and you'll find your legs will grow three inches right away."

Michael screwed quickly round on the chair and was about to speak again when Ralph Batley said, but quietly now, "Go and help your grannie fetch in the plates."

"Yes, Uncle."

As the boy slid swiftly off his chair Shane came breezily into the hall exclaiming, "Did I hear talk of breeches? Oh, hello there." He beamed across the room towards Linda. "Did you sleep well?"

"Yes, very well, thank you." Linda returned his smile, and he went on, "Did I hear you say that breeches make your legs longer? Well, I can vouch for that meself, I can indeed, for without me own here," he slapped his thigh, "it would look to all appearances as if I was hobbling about on me knees."

Linda laughed outright and Shane laughed with her, and at the peak of his laughter he looked at her breeches much as Michael had and commented, "I'd say you've got fine legs for a horse." Then his head went further back and he cried, "You know what I mean."

"If we can stop discussing Miss Metcalfe's legs for a moment, Uncle Shane, I think we might start breakfast, the porridge is on the table."

There was no anger in the words. It would have been better if there had been, the cut they made in Linda would have been less deep. She felt as if she was actually shrinking under her employer's gaze. His grey eyes looking at her now held that cold, impersonal look she remembered from last night, as if there was not an emotion yet created that could bring warmth into them. When his gaze dropped from her she did not go to the table and take her place, but she went into the kitchen to assist Mrs. Batley and also to give herself time to regain her composure before sitting down to breakfast opposite to him.

The meal was passed almost in silence and, as last night, Linda was amazed at the amount of food that was consumed. The house itself might be without its luxuries and modern conveniences but the amenities of the table were certainly not neglected, in fact they were even lavish.

When the meal was over and she went to help clear the table Mrs. Batley said quietly, "That's all right . . . leave that to me . . . I would get out."

Taking this broad hint she hurried upstairs and, snatching up her duffle coat, she was out on the landing within a matter of seconds. Undoubtedly it was her speed that brought her within hearing of the conversation, for Uncle Shane's low, rumbling murmur came to her from the hall saying, placatingly, "Hold your hand a while, man. Think of the saying the iron fist in the velvet glove . . . although mind, I'll admit, when I saw her standing there with the firelight on her she looked for all the world like some picture in a magazine trying to entice you away to Switzerland for the winter sports."

"Exactly."

That one word brought Linda's hand tightly across her mouth. Exactly! It spoke volumes. There came back to her mind Mr. Cadwell's words, "He's wanting a cart-horse and he's getting a year-old filly." But why couldn't he wait and judge her on her work and not go totally by appearances. . . . Well, she would show him that she was no year-old filly.

Her attitude of mind was expressed in the squaring of her shoulders as she marched noisily to the top of the stairs, but as she descended them and watched the two men walking towards the kitchen door her courage wavered and slithered downwards and she warned herself: Go steady, go quiet, don't get off to a bad start.

When she reached the kitchen Shane was saying, "I'll go off to the top and run another wire along them spiles." He did not speak to her, but as he went out of the door he jerked his head sideways towards her, and even with such a mundane action he had the power to convey warmth, and this heartened her. Whoever was against her, Shane was for her.

"You'd better start by seeing the buildings." Ralph Batley was buttoning up his coat and he did not look at her as he spoke, and knowing his feelings towards her, she found difficulty in even emitting the syllable "Yes."

The side door of the house led on to a paved square. It was bordered on two sides by a dry-stone wall but opened out onto grassland, and as she stepped from the shelter of the wall her eyes darted about her in amazement for she had the impression that she could see to the ends of the earth, so open was the land before her.

There, some distance to the left, she glimpsed the sea sparkling under the hard winter sun. But her employer had turned sharply to the right and she turned, too, keeping just slightly behind him. Now they were in the farmyard, and as her torch had indicated last night, she saw it was not only as clean as farmyards go, but scrupulously so.

"This is the main shed." He opened the door and stood somewhat reluctantly aside to let her pass, and now he was behind her speaking in rasping, low, gruff tones as if determined to get it over and done with. "We have eighteen milkers, all Ayrshires."

She looked at the empty byres and asked in surprise, "Are they out?"

"Yes, of course. They're hardy. They need to be up here."

She closed her eyes for a second. Would he never stop emphasizing that everything had to be hardy to exist on this farm?

She had seen the parlour system of milking and the latest modern machinery. Here nothing was modern, but even so she wanted to exclaim on the beautiful condition of the byres . . . they were spotless. She wanted to remark on the cards in their little slots attached to the posts, each bearing the name of a cow, but she couldn't bring herself to say a word.

He passed her now and walked down the length of the cowshed to enter the dairy. Here the cleanliness was almost of clinical standard. The urns were gleaming, the wooden table taking up one wall was the whitest she had ever seen. A marble slab along the farthest end of the dairy held an array of patters and wooden rollers all laid ready to hand. No attitude of his could stifle now her admiration and she exclaimed, "Why, this is lovely." And to her it was lovely, for such cleanliness touched her as poetry or music would touch another.

"My mother sees to this." He was away ahead of her again, and as she followed him she thought, I might have known, yet she questioned: Where on earth does she find the time with all that housework and cooking to do?

She was now walking behind him through a narrow open passageway and into another yard, a stockyard. Here, hemmed in by three high walls, were about a dozen head of Galloway cattle, all, with the exception of two, very good specimens. These two had bare patches on their rumps which they were endeavouring to enlarge by rubbing their haunches against the corners of the hay feeder in the centre of the stockyard. The sight of them enjoying this recreation brought Ralph Batley striding towards them, and hitting out right and left with the flat of his hand, he thumped their rumps, crying, "Away out of it! Away, Judy! You too, Beth."

For the moment Linda entirely forgot her employer. Here were twelve Galloways, fine animals—they looked as good as any her uncle had charge of—and she was to work with them for the next year. Perhaps she would help to bring their calves into the world as she had helped with the one last night. She became lost in the happy thought, and she gave evidence of it when she spoke, for, quite unthinking, she voiced her opinion of the feeder by placing her hand on it and saying, "They'll always rub on this kind. My uncle got rid of his. You wa . . . ant . . ." Her voice trailed off as she was suddenly made aware of what she was saying by Ralph Batley's narrowed gaze fixed on her. And now she stammered in apology. "What I meant was they're apt to rub against this." Her fingers fluttered over the sharp corner of the feeder. And she went from bad to worse by quoting some information she had picked up from her uncle. "I suppose it's because their skin gets irritable when they're fed too much pro . . . tein." Again her voice trailed away. Her eyes dropped from his and miserably she was turning about when his voice held her.

"Do go on. I have the wrong type of feeder, I am feeding too much protein. . . . Do go on, there's a lot I would like to learn about this type of cattle."

Her body made a quick jerk and she was facing him, but she did not raise her eyes, nor even her head as she said stiffly, "I'm sorry, it's not my intention to try to teach you anything, I've come here to learn. What . . . what I said was . . . not meant . . ." Her head was drooping lower again when his next remark, and the tone of his voice, whipped it upwards as he said, "Well, I hope at this juncture we're not going to have any tears."

Her teeth were clenched so hard that her jaw bones

seemed locked as she stared back at him, glared back would be a more correct definition of the look which she now gave him, and her voice showed her anger as she said, "I am not given to crying. You needn't be afraid, Mr. Batley, you will not have to contend with tears in my case."

Their eyes were hard held, nor did they speak for some seconds, and only her anger was sustaining her to look back unflinchingly at this man who she was telling herself at this moment was worse than a dozen Mr. Cadwells rolled into one.

"I would not waste your energy in giving way to temper, Miss Metcalfe, you'll need it all for your work." He swung away from her, and she drew in a deep breath and let out a long-drawn "Ooh!" Last night she had had it in her to feel sorry for him. She felt then that he was lonely, sort of lost. But at this moment she wished she had never set eyes on him.

He was holding the gate open for her and she stalked past him.

To add to her discomfort, he said, "We're not going that way." He was standing at one end of the passage and she at the other. Again she drew in a deep breath. And now, when she saw that he was amused in a cynical kind of way, she felt really furious.

Through door after door she followed him, and she made no comment on anything he said until they came to a great barn. Garaged just within the entrance stood an old Jeep, and in a far corner, lying half-way in a straw-filled box, was a Collie dog. One back leg, Linda saw, was bandaged up to its hock, and a front paw was also bandaged. But even with this handicap the dog tried to hobble towards its master as he moved forward. She watched Ralph Batley gently lead the sick animal back towards the kennel again, saying in much the same tone as he had used to the cow last night, "There, there, now. Take it easy, Jess."

For the moment forgetting her own feelings, Linda found herself kneeling down by the dog and asking, "What happened?"

"A trap."

"A trap?" she repeated. "Oh, the poor thing." She stroked the dog's head, and as she was licked vigorously in return she remembered that she had seen no other dogs about the place, which was odd, and this caused her to ask, "Have you only the one?"

"Yes." She felt him straighten up, and she was still looking at the dog when he said, "We had another, it was poisoned a fortnight ago."

"Oh no!" She turned her head slowly and looked up at him, and was not surprised now by the grimness she saw on his face.

In the stillness that followed, her mind swung to the Cadwells but she dismissed the thought. They didn't look the kind of people to stoop to petty cruelties like that, poisoning a dog and setting a trap. Likely it was someone after game of some kind. . . .But you didn't lay poison to catch game. She shook her head at herself.

Ralph Batley was speaking now from where he was standing near the Jeep, and after giving the dog one last tender pat she got to her feet and went towards him.

"We fill up out of here every day or so." He pointed to where the bales of hay were stacked deep in the barn, which she saw had two floors for at least half its length, the upper floor being accessible by means of an open ladder set against the right-hand wall. "The feed goes into the corrugated hut at yon end of the main byre, it's easier to get at these dark mornings. . . . Well," he turned towards the entrance of the barn, adding, "I think that's the sum total of the buildings. Now for the land."

She was walking abreast of him now, and as they approached the end of the barn she noticed a flight of wooden steps going up to a door in a brick building. This building was attached to the end of the barn and as he had not taken her into this place she looked up and remarked casually, "Is that the granary?"

He did not follow her look, nor did his eyes turn from their forward gazing as he said, "No, the grain is kept in an off-shoot of the house."

"Oh." She did not press the matter and say, "Well, what do you keep up there?" Later on she would take a walk up the steps to the loft and find out for herself.

They were going in the direction of the house again when he stopped and said, "There's the bull. . . . And Sep Watson. You'd better meet them both." He was talking over his shoulder to her as he continued, "As for the bull, I'd give him a wide berth for the moment. Later on, when he gets used to you about the place . . ." His voice trailed off as he opened a gate, and she thought, Well, he does think there will be a later on, that's something.

When she first saw Sep Watson standing next to the bull within the strong-walled bull box she was immediately struck by the incongruous similarity between them, for the man had the same points as the Galloway, his body was heavy and his legs were short. His face, too, was short, in his case with a compressed look, and seemed to spread downwards into his thick powerful neck. And to make the similarity almost uncanny his ears were pointed sharply outwards. They were for all the world like "cocky wee lugs" as the ears of a good Galloway were termed. But whereas these points might make a prize bull they, on the other hand, made for a repulsive man.

"This is Miss Metcalfe, Sep." The introduction was made in a flat, almost inflectionless, voice.

The man left the animal which he was grooming and came slowly towards the iron barred gate. He did not open it but looked over it, and for no reason she could explain, for his tone was very civil as he said, "How do?" she felt the blood rushing to her face.

"How d'you do?" She inclined her head stiffly.

"Miss Metcalfe will give you a hand with the milking this afternoon, Sep."

"Aye, all right." The man looked at Ralph Batley and nodded.

"You can show her the ropes."

"Aye." Sep Watson now turned his glance on Linda and added with a grin that showed a set of surprisingly large white teeth, "Pleased to, Miss."

"Thank you."

There was nothing offensive in either the man's words or manner yet Linda was experiencing a feeling of panic, the thought of standing near this man somehow terrified her.

"Here Leader!" Ralph Batley called the bull towards him, and it came shambling heavily forward, pushing Sep Watson aside in the process, which only caused the man to laugh. "Good fellow! There's a boy." Ralph Batley fondled the animal's head, and like some great dog its tongue came out and slobbered him. It was evident to Linda that her employer was very proud of this animal.

When with a final pat he turned away she followed him, and they continued as before in the direction of the house, but when they came to it he did not turn right or left but kept straight on, and it seemed to Linda as she walked rapidly by his side that their destination could be the horizon, for in front of them there lay nothing but the sea and the cliff edge, and Ralph Batley walked almost to the brink of it before he stopped. Looking down she saw that from his very toes there started a line of

60

steps. They were cut out of the solid rock and dropped steeply down the face of the cliff until they reached the cove below. And the sight of the crescent of dry sand, with the jagged walls of rock on each side stretching out into the water to form a sheltered harbour, brought from her an involuntary exclamation of delight, for she could see herself in the late hot evenings of the coming summer plunging into the cool waters of the lovely little bay.

The exclamation or something in her face must have conveyed her thoughts to Ralph Batley, for immediately he said, "Don't be misled with what you are seeing, that small stretch of sand down there is the only innocent thing connected with our cove."

Refusing to have her dreams entirely shattered, she remarked somewhat dreamily, "It looks beautiful to me."

"It's the worst piece of coastline for miles; you'll see what I mean when the tide's out."

"But the boats." She pointed to where a sailing dinghy and a small cruiser were bobbing on the sunlit water some distance from the shore. "How do they get in and out?"

"They don't—at least so little that it makes no odds. The dinghy we have to edge carefully between the rocks to get her through the gap out into the open sea. The cruiser can only get out through the gap at certain periods when the tide is coming in and the weather calm. But she's rotting now and hasn't been out for years."

"What a shame."

He passed no comment on her remark but said, "Don't go down these steps when there's a wind of any kind, there's air currents sliding along the face of the cliff that will lift you up before you know where you are."

She looked at the steps. It was likely quite true what he said, but she also felt he was exaggerating the danger. He was going to allow her no pleasure to look forward to. The weather here was tough . . . the life was tough . . . and now the scenery was not only tough but spelt danger. All of a sudden she found that she could laugh at his tactics, and this fact acted like a tonic. If she could laugh at him she would not fear him, and not being afraid of him her work would be much better. She had the inclination to whistle but checked it.

They had now turned from the cliff edge and were going, she realised, in the direction of Surfpoint Bay and the road she should have taken last night. But they had not gone more than half a mile along the cliff top when the open land suddenly ceased and she saw the barrier of wire fencing. It was topped with barbed wire similar to that she had noticed last night, beginning at the cliff edge. She just stopped herself in time from exclaiming, "Is this the Cadwell boundary?"

Yet once again he seemed to read her thoughts, for without looking or indicating the fencing with even a motion of his hand, he said flatly, "This is the extent of our land."

The distance between the wire fencing and the edge of the cliff at this point was about thirty feet, but at the other end she knew that it was not more than fifteen feet and by the looks of things it would become narrower with each storm, for at the far point the cliff was evidently crumbling away. Instinctively she knew that the land here had not always been fenced in. At one time there had been a good road leading down into Surfpoint Bay. There must be virtually a right of way along the cliff top, and this had been left, but only barely. For the moment her curiosity got the better of her and she wanted to probe the reason why this should be and so she said, "Wouldn't it be a quicker way to take the milk down if you could use this road?"

"I do use it."

62

She looked at him, her eyes wide, and then she remembered the little girl down at Mrs. Weir's being sent on to the cliff top to see if Mr. Batley's car was coming. He was mad, he must be stark staring mad to take the jeep along this road . . . and the cliff crumbling. She shuddered, and then she asked quietly, "What about the back road?"

She was daring his anger she knew in referring to her acquaintance with this road, for it would remind him of how she had come to the farm. But his voice was still impersonal as he replied, "It's four miles or more that way and time counts."

The subject was closed. He turned abruptly about, and now he led the way across fields that hadn't the appearance of fields to her mind for they were studded with crops of rock, and again fields that were but the steep sides of fells. Some of the sloping land was scree covered and showed the tracks of sheep. She was about to broach the subject of sheep when quite suddenly they came upon a valley. It was deep and wide and showed immediately to be good grass land, at least the best she had seen so far. When her eyes ranged down it to the left there was an unbroken vista right to the horizon . . . that meant the valley opened out on the cliff top . . . but when she turned her gaze upwards through the valley she saw the gleam of wire . . . the boundary again. Why was this valley, this pleasant, sheltered valley that was surely an asset to the Batley farm, cut off by a boundary running across what was apparently its middle—for far beyond the wire fence she could see the hills rising on either side.

She brought her gaze from the land and glanced at Ralph Batley, and although she was certain that his bitterness against the Cadwells was not primarily concerned with land, she could gauge his feelings about this particular matter from her own at the moment, for she felt incensed that the only decent pastureland she had so far come upon was mostly denied to the Batleys and evidently owned by the Cadwells when the location pointed the other way.

Beyond the valley the land rose steeply and the hills took on the appearance of small mountains, and whenever she reached the top of a rise there to the left lay the sea and the jagged coastline.

At one point they came upon a flock of sheep, well over a hundred she reckoned, all black-faced Cheviots. They were skirting the scampering animals when Ralph Batley, pulling up sharply, cried, "No, no, not again!"

The words had a desperate sound, and she followed his gaze towards where a sheep was trotting on the outskirts of the flock. She knew very little about sheep but it did not require much knowledge for her to realise what it was he was dreading. Foot-rot, which showed itself first in lameness—and definitely that sheep was lame. Yet on this rough ground it could have got its hoof caught in a cleft.

He was hurrying on now, and she was surprised that he made no attempt to round up the lame sheep. She was behind him when they climbed yet another hill, and just as she reached the top she saw him cup his hands to his mouth and call, "Shane! Uncle!"

There in the distance was the old man wiring staves together. He turned on the hail and waved his hand and, dropping the railing, came hurrying over the distance.

When they were still many yards apart Ralph Batley shouted, "Do you know one's lame?"

Shane, stopping in his tracks, exclaimed, "No, begod no! They were fine and well yesterday, I looked them over in the valley."

"They're just beyond the rise and one of them's limping badly."

Shane was now close to them and his old hairy face showed his concern as he said, "In the name of God, man, how could they get it. The land's as clean as a new pin and we went over them foot by foot more than two weeks ago."

Linda watched Ralph Batley rubbing his hand roughly up and down his cheek. His gaze was now pointed away from the old man towards the sea, and she wondered if she was hearing aright when she thought he said, "There are such things as wishing." And she knew that she hadn't been mistaken when Shane turned on him with surprising roughness as he cried, "Be your age, man. Who's talking like a mad Irishman now? I'm the one who thinks up spells and omens and witches' wishings. If it's only a witch doctor we have to contend with then we'll fix him, never fear."

There was a moment's silence, then the old man gently put out his rough hand and, gripping his nephew by the arm, shook him almost playfully saying, "Come on now, come on."

Linda watched Ralph Batley turn his eyes slowly towards his uncle and she knew a moment's curiosity and surprise not unmixed with sympathy when she heard him say, "They've only got wishing left, they've used up every other device."

"Well, you're strong enough to stand up to that. Come on now, come on. If the worst comes to the worst we can round up the whole flock and dip 'em again."

A short while later, walking with her silent employer back over the fells, Linda attempted to sort out her feelings. She realised that her main feeling at the moment was surprise and this was caused by the thought that this stern, taciturn man should need any reassurance whatsoever, for he seemed not only a law unto himself in his own domain, but over-brimful of self-confidence.

Then there was her curiosity; this, she knew, was a natural desire to get to the bottom of the reason for the feud that existed between the families of the Cadwells and the Batleys. And last, and she would have said least, the grudging feeling of sympathy this man evoked in her. On the face of it this last emotion was utterly absurd, for at the moment her employer looked and sounded as if stood as little in need of sympathy as did his own bull.

Linda had not been working with Sep Watson for more than an hour before she discovered a number of things about him. Apart from the knowledge that he was a married man and had five children and lived in a cottage four miles across the fells in the direction of Longhorsley, she found that he was a talker. But in spite of this she realised he was also a very good worker. Although his movements were slow and heavy the work seemed to dissolve under his practised hands. But her main discovery was that Sep Watson did not like his employer.

The first indication she had of this was when she was standing looking at a particularly nice cow and Sep Watson's elbow gave her a quick dig in the back and his voice, issuing from the corner of his mouth, whispered, "Look out, no standing around, here's God Almighty comin'." When, in the next moment, Ralph Batley entered the cowshed and she heard Sep Watson's servile tone as he answered him, she thought to herself, He's a crawler.

When Ralph Batley had left the cowshed without even a glance in her direction, Sep Watson, busy again with the milking, turned his slanting glance on her and remarked, "You don't want to let him get you down. Take my tip, 'Yes sir' him and 'No sir' him, and then go your own way. If you're cute you'll manage it."

As Linda looked down into the horrible grinning face she realised that this man already accepted that she was on his side of the fence . . . she was a worker and so was naturally opposed to the boss. Then with his head pressed into the side of the cow and his face hidden from her he mumbled, "He's always got my goat, right since he was a lad."

"Have you worked here since you were a boy then?" Linda's repulsion was for the moment overcome by her curiosity.

"Aye, on and off, like. I take a spell away for two or three years some place else, but I always come back. I worked for his father. Oh, his father was a lad. Huh!" He jerked his head upwards now on a laugh. "By! he was. He could carry more drink than four dray horses. Aye, those were the days, things used to happen then. The old boss and Jack Cadwell—he's got Crag End Farm—they were up to all larks. They were pals . . . just like their fathers afore them, them that built the houses . . . but they were always fightin' and gamblin'." His head went further back still and he gazed upwards towards the roof of the byre as he said, "I'll never forget the day he gambled the south side away, right from the cliff top round to the valley."

Linda's eyes were stretched wide as she repeated, "He gambled the land away?"

"Well, sort of. Jack Cadwell had always wanted the valley stretch but Batley would never sell an inch of ground. But over the years he piled up a tidy sum to Jack Cadwell in borrowing, and one night they had a big drink up and they played cards for it. If Batley won he would be cleared of his debt and keep his land, if he lost the land would go to Cadwell to pay for the debt. It was as easy as that. You've only to look at the cliff top to know who won."

"It's fantastic."

Slowly Linda lifted the pail of milk from the man's side, and he repeated, "Aye, it's fantastic, but that's nowt. Oh, my! if you knew the history of this family it would make the hair in your ears waggle. It would make a book, aye, it would that, but if anybody read it they wouldn't believe it. No, they wouldn't."

Linda carried the milk into the dairy. So that was it. The fact that part of the land had been gambled away in a drunken orgy was enough to embitter anyone.

She could understand her employer's attitude a little more now. Yet, as Sep Watson suggested, it was far from being the real cause of the bitterness. She was filled with curiosity and wished that the cowman was other than he was and she could talk to him, even question him, but such was the effect the man had on her that she knew she would never be able to bring herself to question him with regards to her employer and his family. Yet she also knew she would be unable to close her ears to his prattle, for she might live in the Batley house for the next year and be no nearer to the deep sorrows that affected them . . . they were not the talking kind, even Uncle Shane with his kindliness would be restrained, she felt, in discussing the family's affairs.

It was just as they were about to finish for the night that the man supplied her with yet another bit of information. It concerned Michael. The child had been trailing her footsteps for most of the afternoon and he only left her side when his grannie's voice hailed him from the house. From just inside the door of the cowshed Sep Watson watched the boy running across the darkening yard and he remarked in an undertone, "Taken to you, hasn't he?"

When Linda made no comment he went on, "He wants a mother." Then he laughed a deep, thick, quiet laugh, and his voice was quiet too as he continued, "Not that you look the mother type to me. Well, you know what I mean. I can tell you I got a bit of a gliff when I saw you. You don't look cut out for this ramp, although mind, I'll say this, you're not dim."

"Thank you."

Linda's voice was small and cold and it brought another quiet, deep laugh from him. Then as he pulled on his coat he said, "It's any port in a storm with Michael, and it's natural, I suppose, all bairns should have a mother. Like animals, they need a bit of snuffling now and again. But there, he wouldn't have got much snuffling from his own mother, she wasn't the type to snuffle.'

He turned and looked at her now, knowing that he had whetted her curiosity, and he stood waiting, and in spite of her feelings towards him and her intention of never questioning him about her employer or his family she could not restrain herself from asking, "Is she dead?"

"Dead? No, she's very much alive. She was always alive she took after her old man. She was his favourite and lad mad since she could walk. She hooked Lance Cadwell, he was the middle one of the three sons. Old Cadwell nearly went up the lum for he had somebody else cut out for Lance, somebody with money. The match was hopeless right from the start and within a year or so they were divorced. Young Patricia married again when the child was around six, but the new husband didn't take to the lad and he took bad . . . the kid, nerves, so he was packed off here." He jerked his head upwards and exclaimed, "Oh, you don't know the half of it." Then putting his hand out swiftly and chucking her under the chin he said, "You're interested, aren't you? You haven't been able to make the set-up out. I know. We'll have to get together one of these days and I'll tell you the whole history, eh?"

Linda had darted back from him, and on this his squat face seemed to expand further as he grinned and exclaimed softly, "There's one thing I've found out about you . . ." he paused, holding her eyes for some moments before finishing . . . "you've got a lot to learn. . . . Good night."

When he went through the door Linda leaned against the wall and closed her eyes. She was no fool. That last remark hadn't meant that she had a lot to learn about farming. She knew what he meant by it and the thought terrified her, the man terrified her. It was just the essence of bad luck that her co-worker had to be a man of Sep Watson's make-up and mentality.

"What's the matter?"

"Oh!" She nearly leapt from the wall.

"What is it, are you feeling ill?" Ralph Batley was standing close to her, his face not a foot from her own, and she had to take two great gulps of air before she could bring out, "No, no. I'm not ill."

"Then what is it?" He was looking at her with a slightly mystified look, and then she saw his eyes move swiftly in the direction of the door and it was some seconds before he spoke. "Was it Watson?" he asked. "Did he——?"

"No. No, it wasn't. It's nothing."

On no account must she say anything against the cowman. She knew within a little how much her employer relied on this man, for he was a very efficient worker, and should she infer anything there would undoubtedly be trouble. Yet, she told herself and rather ruefully now, the trouble wouldn't be for Sep Watson, but would more than likely descend on her own head. She knew that her employer, to use his own words, had never wanted a woman about the place, so it was natural that should any trouble ensue between her and the cowman he wouldn't get the blame. Yet as she raised her eyes to Ralph Batley's face there came a small doubt into her mind, for his expression for once had lost its hardness, and the curve of his mouth was softened as he said, "Manners in general around here are apt to be rough, but should Watson at any time say anything to you that you don't like, come straight to me . . . you understand?"

She nodded slowly, then said, "But he didn't—he . . ."

She was silenced by his uplifted hand and he accompanied this gesture with, "All right, all right, we'll leave it at that." Then after a moment he ended, "Now go in and have something to eat. You can tell my mother that my uncle and I will not be in for some time and not to wait for us. You can also tell her it isn't rot . . . it was just one lame."

"Oh, I'm glad." She smiled at him, then quickly lifting her duffle coat from a hook, she put it on and pulling the hood about her head, she went out and across the yard and into the house.

It was close on seven o'clock before Ralph Batley and Shane came in, and at the sound of their approach Mrs. Batley threw down the sock that she was mending and hurried towards the scullery. Linda, from where she sat to the side of the fire, listened to her voice talking low and rapidly. But two words only could she make out, and these were, "Say nothing," and as the words came to her she looked down on the boy lying sound asleep within the circle of her arms.

After tea the child had edged himself off the mat and to her feet, and brought with him his books and his engine. Next he had knelt at her side with his elbows resting on her knees. His following move was to sit on the edge of her chair and in such a position that it had been natural for her to put her arm about him. It was when his grannie was out of the room that he had sat on her knee. He had not looked at her as he took up this position but had talked rapidly, explaining the pictures in the book he held close to his face.

On entering the hall Mrs. Batley's step had been checked, and over the distance she had looked at them. Then without making any comment at all she resumed her seat and took up her darning, and in some subtle way Linda knew that the older woman was hurt at the sight of her grandchild being cradled by a stranger. It should be her daughter who was sitting here nursing the boy.

Shane was apparently obeying orders when he entered the room for he said nothing but, "Ah, well, I'm glad that's over for I'm as hungry as ten bullocks." Studiously he avoided even glancing in her direction. But when Ralph Batley entered the room he did look at her, yet she could gauge nothing at all from his expression, for his face was wearing the blank look which seemed to be habitual to it.

Michael stirred within her arms and snuggled closer to her, but Linda sat without moving. She was very much aware of the two men to the side of her eating their meal. She was also aware that although Ralph Batley from his position at the table had a view of her and the boy, he never once now looked in their direction.

Mrs. Batley was at her darning again. After some time had elapsed and there came the sound of a chair scraping the floor as it was pushed back from the table, she said, without raising her eyes, "Would you carry him up?"

When Ralph Batley's figure shut out the glow of the

fire as he bent above her, Linda kept her eyes on the relaxed and sleeping face of the boy. Then as she gently passed the child over to him there was a moment of contact when their hands touched, but it was only a moment, for she felt his recoil as if he had been suddenly stung. The action was like a slap in the face and she found herself flushing as if with shame.

Mrs. Batley followed her son upstairs and Linda sat stiffly in her chair, staring towards the fire and she did not raise her head to look at Shane when he came and stood by her side. One kind word and she would cry. She had emphatically denied earlier that she was given to tears, but it had been a long and trying day and she was very tired, and now, because a man had drawn his hand sharply from contact with hers, she was feeling hurt, as she had never been hurt in her life before.

Uncle Shane gave the kind word. With his hand gently patting her shoulder he said, "The child's taken to you, it's a very good sign." Then after a silence during which his hand became still he added, "And he's not alone, no, not by a long chalk. In spite of what you might think, you've started well on your first day." The fingers gave another gentle pat as he ended, "Aye, you have that."

It was too much. Linda with head bowed rose swiftly from the chair and under pretence of clearing the table, she hurried with some dishes towards the kitchen, and there, because the lump in her throat threatened to choke her she put her face under the cold tap. She had found in the past when her father's biting remarks had become unbearable, that cold water had a very steadying effect on keeping her tears at bay. Whatever happened, Ralph Batley must be given no opportunity for further comment on tears.

3

Following on a long and good night's rest, because she had retired early the previous evening, Linda found that the fears and hurts of yesterday had sunk into their right perspective and the day ahead even had a certain glow about it. This was brought into effect when Ralph Batley bade her good morning in a voice that was quite pleasant . . . and gave her, what with a little stretch of imagination could be termed, a smile. It was as if he were trying to make up for his involuntary action of last night.

She had not as yet let the thought of Sep Watson enter her mind, and when she reached the bacon-and-egg stage of the breakfast she was engulfed in a happy feeling, and it was at this point that the knock came on the back door.

That a knock on the door at this time of the morning was an unusual occurrence was made evident when she watched every head at the table move upwards. She knew that the cowman did not get here till eight o'clock; later, he had informed her, if the weather was bad. But as if her mind touching on him had conjured him out of thin air, there he was, his breadth actually filling the hall doorway. He looked agitated and his breathing spoke of his having run hard.

Both Ralph Batley and Mrs. Batley had risen together and they were halfway across the hall towards him when he said, "It's the sheep, they're out, some . . . some on

Fenton Moor and t'others . . ." there was a pause in his speaking and he took a deep breath before bringing out, "t'others are in Cadwell's."

The next few moments were uncanny, at least to Linda, for no one, not even Michael, made any comment. Not a syllable was spoken as they all scrambled, one after the other, into the kitchen and flung on their coats.

Last night she had left her duffle coat among the others, and now she was thrusting her arms into it as she ran out into the cold, drizzle-filled morning, Mrs. Batley at her side.

She had not gone far when the older woman's hand gripped her arm, pushing her forward as she said, "You . . . you go ahead, lass, your legs can carry you."

Without any comment Linda sprang forward. She was a good runner and she liked running, and in a short while she came up with Shane. He was gasping and panting and he pointed ahead to where Ralph Batley's bounding figure was disappearing down into the hollow, and yelled, "Follow him. I'll make for the moor."

Slithering and stumbling she dropped into the valley, then climbed the other side just in time to see Ralph Batley once again disappear from view. The direction he was taking was new to her, and soon she found herself on a narrow, winding path that seemed never ending. Suddenly she came upon outcrops of stone like miniature cliffs and for a moment she could imagine she was on the beach. Still running swiftly she rounded them, to pull up abruptly in startled surprise. She was close to a sunken main road and there, like a tableau before her, were three men—Ralph Batley and the two Cadwell men. Ralph Batley, with his back to her, his feet astride and his hands held stiffly by his side, gave some indication as to what his expression was like. Out beyond him, over

75

the fence, in the roadway she could see the bouncing heads of two horses and the upper part of their riders. The two Cadwell men were vibrating with anger. Yet this word was not quite strong enough to express the older man's emotion, for his face was convulsed with a dark rage as he pointed to the Batley boundary and cried, "Don't tell me that you know nothing about this! That wire's been cut, and in several places. It doesn't need a blind man to see that. Sheep don't bite through wire. Your bloody vermin have got the rot and you think to pass it on to mine. Nearly every blasted one of them's lame, look at that." He pointed his crop down the road.

"That's not rot, that sheep's lame." Ralph Batley's voice sounded unnaturally quiet as he went on. "And if every one of them had rot their combined stink couldn't come from anything more putrid than what I'm looking at now."

In a flash the horse's forelegs were brought from the ground and it was swung round to mount the bank. In another second, with his mouth spewing oaths and his crop raised to strike, the elder Cadwell man and the horse would have been upon Ralph Batley but for a voice screaming, "Stay! Hold your hand there."

Linda, who had been transfixed by the scene, had not noticed Mrs. Batley's arrival. She watched her now advance to the side of her son and look down on the Cadwell man. The horse was now standing in the ditch frothing and prancing and bouncing its rider, giving the impression that Mr. Cadwell was boiling in his own rage. He was not looking at Ralph Batley now but at Mrs. Batley, for she was speaking to him in what sounded to Lnida under the present circumstances a very odd way. Her voice held neither fury nor anger, rather the tone seemed to imply despair. "So you've started again," she said.

"Has he ever stopped?" The words came grinding from between Ralph Batley's lips.

"No. Nor I won't until I finish you off, you bloody upstart." Mr. Cadwell turned his fiery gaze on to Ralph Batley again. "Farmer. Huh!" His head went back on a mirthless laugh. "Why don't you go back to your garret and play at making your dolls? Or have you decided to play with live ones now?" His eyes swung to where Linda stood at the other side of Mrs. Batley, and after raking her for a second with his sneering gaze he ended, "But mind she's not pinched from you an' all. That would be a laugh, wouldn't it?"

In the instant that Ralph Batley swung himself up and forward over the broken fence his mother threw herself on him, screaming, "No! no! I tell you no." Her hands breaking his spring brought him doubled up over the wires, and for a moment he could not extricate himself from the barbed thongs hooked in his clothes. As he hung there Mr. Cadwell let out a bellow of a laugh and cried, "That's just how I'll see you end up, like your old man, bent and broke."

"Shut up! Shut up, will you! Shut that vile mouth of yours." Mrs. Batley was on the edge of the bank now, glaring down into the face of the Cadwell man.

Rouse Cadwell, who had so far not spoken, now brought his horse round to his father's side and said, "Come on, that's enough."

But Mr. Cadwell was not to be led away so easily and he cried at his son, "I'll go when I see their scum off me land."

Mrs. Batley, drawing in a shuddering breath, now turned to her son and in a voice full of pleading she beseeched him as she stared up into his frozen countenance, "Go on, lad, no more now. For God's sake, no more now. Get them off . . . please." She shook his arm as if bringing him out of a trance and ended softly, "For my sake."

With pity swamping her Linda watched her employer move away. It was as if he could not trust himself to go down the bank near the Cadwell men. Her eyes followed him as he jumped the fence further down, then cross the road and go through an open gate into the Cadwell's field to where, in the distance, she could see the broad bulk of Sep Watson rounding up the sheep.

When Mrs. Batley spoke quietly to her, saying, "Can you get those off the road?" she immediately slithered down the bank. She had to pass close to the horses but she looked at neither of the riders.

There were only two sheep in the roadway, but as sheep will, they proved difficult and were determined to go in any direction but the right one, and each on his own side of the road. When finally she got them together they would not be persuaded to return straight up the road but seemed bent on entering the field again through the wire fence.

When she saw the horse and rider coming towards her she thought, "Oh, the devil, he's doing it on purpose to make things worse." But when Rouse Cadwell, having passed her, brought his horse broadside to the road and the sheep scattered away before it, she turned and looked at him in surprise. His face was unsmiling but it no longer showed anger. She turned her gaze quickly from him, but as she scrambled out of the ditch and on to the road again, his voice brought her eyes back to him as he said quietly, "Don't let this upset you, it's all part of a pattern." Then bending forward and his voice dropping low, he added in an aside, "Don't forget that torch."

At the same moment that she turned away from the horse and rider she saw up on the far bank behind the fence the bristling figure of Ralph Batley. He paused for only a second, but it was long enough for him to look straight at her. His face was livid, and she wanted to call out, "I wasn't talking to him."

The sheep had now bounded away and being unable to get past the elder Cadwell man and his horse, they scrambled up the bank and through the torn wire and into their own domain, seemingly unnoticed by either Mr. Cadwell or Mrs. Batley, for when Linda reached them it would seem that they were aware of no one but themselves. Mrs. Batley was speaking in a quiet, intimate sort of way that puzzled Linda. She was saying, "Jack Cadwell, you'll know no peace until you can forgive. You're so important to yourself you can't imagine you're not important to everybody else, too. Nobody must let you down or they'll suffer for it. Well, hasn't there been enough suffering all round? Aren't you satisfied?"

"I'll never be satisfied, Maggie Ramshaw, and you know that."

He was calling Mrs. Batley Maggie Ramshaw. Although she could not make head or tail of what was being said, she knew that the beginning of this conversation lay far back in the past.

Mr. Cadwell now turned his horse about and joined his son, and they stood like two dark sentinels while Sep Watson and Ralph Batley drove the sheep out of the Cadwell land, onto the road and over the wire gap into their own field. And when this was accomplished Mr. Cadwell, looking up to where Ralph Batley stood once more on his own land, cried, "Let it happen again and I'll impound every damn one of them, or better still, I'll shoot your rottin' vermin."

Ralph Batley made no reply, perhaps because his mother was holding tightly to his arm.

Not until the Cadwell men disappeared from view did Mrs. Batley release her hold, and then with a great intake of breath and indicating the fence with a weary sweep of her arm she said, "Now let's get this up."

Ralph Batley did not immediately start on the repairs, but after looking at the fence he beckoned Sep Watson towards him and asked, "How did you know they were out?"

"Well, it was like this," Sep Watson looked from his employer towards Mrs. Batley, "you know old Badger Mullen? Well, he must have been on the prowl last night, he was passing our way around seven and he knocked and said there were sheep on the road and he fell into them in the dark."

"How did you know they were ours?" Ralph Batley was looking intently at his man.

"Well, I didn't." Sep Watson's tone was now slightly huffed. "But I thought I'd better not leave anything to chance, knowin' how things are, so I got on me bike and away I came. It was gettin' light then I saw the gap, and when I rode over the moor I saw they had reached there an' all."

"This was no break-through, that wire's been cut. And they would never have got into Cadwell's if the gate hadn't been open, it's got a slip catch on, it would have to be lifted. . . Was Badger Mullen drunk?"

"No, he daren't make the home brew now, not in any quantity anyway. He was as sober as me."

Ralph Batley bit on his lip and turned his eyes away from the man and gazed ahead thoughtfully for a long moment, and then he said, "Well, you'd better go and see what Shane's up to."

"Aye."

"Come back here as soon as you get them in."

"Aye." Sep Watson's face looked dark as he passed Linda, and he muttered something to her which she could not catch.

Ralph Batley had his head bent and he was pulling at the twisted wire of the fencing as he spoke to her. "Bring me a coil of wire and the cutters and as many staves as you can carry along with them. You'll find them all in the workshop. If you can find Michael he'll help you . . . and a hammer."

She ran all the way back to the farm. When she had collected the required articles and there was no sign of Michael she set out laden like a donkey. But her load was so unwieldy that every now and again she had to stop and readjust it. When finally she returned Ralph Batley was alone, and as she dropped her burden, one piece after another, on to the ground he turned and looked at her. Then, making an impatient movement with his head, he exclaimed, "I didn't mean you to bring all that amount."

"Well, this is what you asked for and I couldn't find Michael." Her own tone had a slight edge to it, and he glanced again at her sharply. "You could have made two journeys," he said.

"It's done now."

For the next half-hour she worked with him, helping to repair the fence, and there was hardly a syllable exchanged between them except, "The hammer there," or "I'll have that piece of wire."

Next followed an inspection of the whole boundary line bordering the road and the moor, and it was well in the middle of the morning when they again returned to the farm.

Mrs. Batley was standing at the kitchen doorway. "Come in," she said quietly, "and have a drink, it's ready."

They stood, each in his own way, before the fire in the hall, drinking the hot cocoa, and the scene had the same uncanny feeling upon Linda as had the one earlier when the news that the sheep were out was received without a word. No one was making the slightest reference to what had transpired. If it wasn't for the grimness on Ralph Batley's face and the deepened sadness in his mother's eyes, Linda could have imagined that she had dreamt the whole thing.

If the Batley family as a whole chose to ignore the happenings of the morning, Sep Watson certainly made up for their reticence, for from the moment Linda joined him in the cowshed after lunch he talked of nothing else, and he vented spleen particularly on his master.

"Not a damned word of thanks. No 'thank you, Sep, for racing your guts out and coming to tell me the sheep had broke through.' Oh no, his lordship is not expected to do things like that. . . . Did you hear him go at me as if I'd done it, as if I'd pushed the bloody things through to Cadwells'."

He stood confronting her, standing squarely before her in the gangway of the byre, an empty pail in each hand, and he did not wait for her to answer, but clashing the pails together with such a clang that she actually jumped aside, he continued, "He'll go too far one of these days and I'll leave him on his backside. I've done it afore, and he can't get anybody up here for love or money . . . you're only here 'cause he couldn't get anybody else." He bounced his head at her on this, then turned from her and into a byre.

Linda would have liked to take him up on this last, but she warned herself, "Say nothing, let him go on."

And he went on for most of the afternoon and without interruption, for Ralph Batley did not put in an appearance. Linda surmised he must be doing the circuit of the rest of the boundary fencing, making sure there were no weak spots. Yet if this morning the wire had been cut it could be cut again.

On one of her journeys from the dairy to the byre with the pails, Sep Watson stopped milking for a moment and, turning his great flat face upwards to her, he asked, "What did Cadwell say to the missis?"

Linda remembered every word, every pregnant word that she heard pass between Mr. Cadwell and Mrs. Batley, but she was certainly not telling this creature what she had overheard, so she replied tartly, "I didn't hear anything, I was on the road busy getting the sheep in most of the time."

"By! I'd like to have been there when they were at it, it would've been worth hearin'." He pursed his thick lips and jerked his head. "That's the first time they've been face to face for nearly three years to my knowledge. Every time they meet he pays her back, knocks a bit off, so to speak."

"Pays her back? What are you talking about?"

"Love's young dream, of course. You wouldn't think as things are now that Jack Cadwell and the missis . . ." he jerked his head in the direction of the house . . . "were thick at one time, would you?"

Linda's face showed her distaste for the man and disbelief of his words. Recognising this, he straightened up his short body and said, "You don't believe me, do you? Well, it's true. She ran the hills with him when she was young. You wouldn't think to look at her now that she was a spritely piece and a looker in her way, but she was . . . and she had money. Aye," he rubbed the bottom of his nose with the back of his hand and gave his characteristic thick laugh as he went on, "it was bad enough to lose her, but to lose her money an' all and to his own pal, Peter Batley, well, it was more than his stomach could stand. But they did it quick like, away to a registry office one morning and he could do nowt about it, not on the surface he couldn't. But he's paid her back ever since."

Linda was staring down into the cowman's face, but she wasn't seeing it, she was seeing Mrs. Batley's pain-filled eyes, her work-stained, restless hands, her face that rarely smiled. The Batley history that had baffled her from the moment she stepped into the house was taking shape. At least she had its beginnings—Mrs. Batley, Maggie Ramshaw the girl that was, had thrown over Mr. Cadwell for his friend, Peter Batley. Whether her choice had been for the best Linda could only judge of what she knew of Mr. Cadwell. Peter Batley had evidently been a heavy drinker; very likely, too, a weak character, but whatever he had been, Linda felt glad that the girl Maggie Ramshaw had chosen him rather than Jack Cadwell.

Sep Watson was still talking as he worked away at the milking. "She had a tidy sum. Her father and mother died one after the other and left her with Brookside. It was a farm bigger than this 'un, and she sold it, and there she was with a nice packet that Jack Cadwell was just waiting to spend. And then, bang! . . . she's Mrs. Peter Batley. Oh, boy, I remember how the countryside rang that day. There was bets laid on as to how long Cadwell would take to finish Batley off, with the fists, that was. But nobody thought he would do it the clever way, make him drink himself to death. . . . Here, where you goin'?"

"I'm going to take the feed over."

"What about the milk?"

"That's the last, surely you can take that in yourself."

"He said you had to help me, he said you had to stay here and help me."

Linda stopped on her way to the door, and although she couldn't see the man she called back to him, "Then you can tell him that I haven't done my job properly, can't you?"

She received no answer to this, but when she heard the scuffling of his feet as he rose from the stool, she turned about and hurried out and towards the big barn. At the moment she could stand no more of Sep Watson's prattle. Her mind was repeating over and over again, Poor Mrs. Batley, poor woman. Because she jilted him, if jilted was the word, that Cadwell man had tortured her for years. Sep Watson had said yesterday that Mr. Cadwell was furious when his son had married the Batley girl. Under the circumstances she could just imagine his fury. To be baulked of money coming into his family for the second time, and from the same source, would be more than just a blow to his pride. But the business of Patricia Batley marrying Lance Cadwell must have happened more than eight years ago, for Michael was turned seven, yet Sep Watson said the last time Mrs. Batley and Mr. Cadwell had met was three years ago. What had happened then? In her mind's eye she saw the face of Ralph Batley and she sensed that whatever clash had flared up again between the two houses was in some way directly concerned with him. There returned to her mind, as it had done a number of times today, the enigmatic sentence that Mr. Cadwell had thrown at Ralph Batley. "Why don't you go back to your garret and play at making your dolls?" And he had referred to herself as a live doll. Whatever the meaning of it, it had filled Ralph Batley with fury.

When she reached the barn she saw that she would have to get the hay from the upper storey, and this was going to be no easy task on her own. But knowing that she would have to accomplish it herself, for she had no intention of going and asking Sep Watson's aid, she pushed a hand trailer close to the ladder, her intention being to topple the bales of straw from the edge of the platform above down on to it. When she had climbed the ladder and reached the floor on the upper storey, she gazed around her with interest. It covered a very large space, and not having the height of the ground floor, it had the appearance of being twice its size. She saw immediately that there wasn't only hay stored here but a number of other things, boxes and crates, all empty as far as she could gather. She walked down a gangway between the hay and the crates, and when she reached its end she found that although the bales of hay were stacked to the end of the barn, there was a passageway between the last crates and the wall. The light was dim up here, but through a chink between two warped boards just below where the side of the barn joined the roof, she saw what appeared to be a door. On closer inspection she found that it was a door. She was thinking that it was a funny place to have a door when she remembered the outside brick building attached to the end of the barn. Of course, this door, too, would lead into it. She hadn't yet had time to investigate it from the outside, and so she turned the handle, but the door did not open. Thinking it might be stiff she put her shoulder to it and pressed forward, but she could make no impression on it. And then she realised that the door was locked. Why? Oh, well, perhaps the outside door would be open. When she had finished loading up she would run up the steps and try it. Likely it was some sort of a storeroom, she was thinking, when a voice from behind her seemed to hit her in the neck and knock her forward.

"Interested?"

She placed her two hands flat against the door for a moment before swinging round, and she could almost have cried with relief to see that the man facing her was Sep Watson and not her employer. As much as she disliked this man she almost welcomed him at this moment.

"Oh," she laughed shakily, "you gave me a start."

"Aye, I seemed to. . . . You trying to get in there?"

"Yes, I wondered if it was another storeroom."

"No, it's not another storeroom and it's locked." He pointed to the keyhole. "It's always kept locked; nobody's been in there for three years."

Three years again. She looked at him, waiting for him to go on. He didn't go on immediately but stood looking at her, a smile on his flat face, and she knew he was savouring the power of his knowledge, keeping her on tenterhooks. Although she wanted to know, and badly, why that door was kept locked, she had no intention of asking him or even waiting until he decided to tell her, and she was moving away from the door, keeping close to the wall of straw so as not to come in contact with him, when he said, "Bet you'll never guess what that place was?"

In spite of her good intention she stopped and looked at the man as he leant forward, his face now one oily grin. "Boss's love nest."

Although she did not move she felt her whole body swiftly recoil. And he felt this too for, the smile wiped from his face now, he said sullenly, "You don't believe me, do you? You're a disbelieving little puss, you are. But that's what it was. Him and his lady love spent days in there, and not another soul near them. She had her own key and I've seen me bump into her first thing in the morning, aye, around seven in the summer time when I come early. Mind you, I didn't blame him for that for she was a luscious piece. He used to keep on an extra man in those days so's he could have more time for his larking."

Linda felt as though she was going to be sick, literally sick. She must get away from this man and his evil chatter. She pressed past him and was at the beginning of the alleyway between the hay and the crates when she was brought to a sudden breath-checking halt, for there, just stepping off the top of the ladder at the other end of the barn, was Ralph Batley. His step was slow and measured as he walked towards her, but before he had covered half the distance Sep Watson had pushed past her and hurried to meet him, and he began immediately to talk, his voice so low that she could only catch a word here and there. But the fragments of two disjointed sentences coming to her brought a sharp exclamation of denial from her. "You're lying" she said. "I wasn't sneaking about."

"You were." The cowman turned towards her as she came up with them. "I followed you up; you were trying to open the door."

She glared back at him for a moment then switched her eyes to Ralph Batley's face. "I did try to open the door, but I wasn't sneaking. I came up here to get the hay, and saw the door. I thought it was a storehouse or something."

"Or something!" Sep Watson's chin jerked upwards, and he turned from her and addressed his employer again in the oily tones that he kept especially for him. "She's done nowt but question me since she come. She's as nosey as you make 'em."

"Oh, you . . . you lying beast. I've never asked you a single question. Oh——!"

"No? What about yesterday in the byres? Couldn't get the pails back quick enough before you started."

"That's enough!" With a movement of his head Ralph Batley indicated that the cowman should get going, and not until he had watched his lumbering figure descend the ladder and disappear through the barn door did he turn towards Linda.

Again sustained by her righteous indignation she had

no fear of him, and she spoke rapidly in her own defence, unintimidated by his steely gaze. "I don't care whether you believe me or not, but I've never questioned him, so there."

"I believe you."

She was not only taken aback by this statement but by the quality of his voice. For it was quiet; she could even think it was kind and reassuring, and belied the look in his eyes.

"Talking is Watson's mania, if he hasn't anyone to talk to he talks to himself." There could even be the suspicion of a smile on his lips, and as she looked at them her breathing became steadier and on a great intake of breath she dropped her eyes from his face and said, "Thank you."

She was moving away when his hand came out but did not touch her, and he said, "You would like to know what I keep in the room at the end of the barn?"

She felt the blood rushing not only over her face but over her whole body. It was as if she had been caught red-handed in a misdemeanour and she stammered, "It . . . it doesn't matter, I'm not interested. It was only that I thought it was a storeroom, as I told you." She had an impelling desire at this moment to get away from him. She did not want to hear his translation of . . . a love nest.

"Oh, I can tell you what it is." His voice now had an airy note. "I haven't got a dead body stored away there or anything like that. It's a studio. Before I was a farmer I was a sculptor."

A sculptor. She found herself looking at his hands, and to her further embarrassment he made a strange, disparaging sound in his throat, then placing his hands together he examined them as if he hadn't seen them for some time. Having turned them first one way then another, he said, "I suppose I was born a farmer and sculpturing was only a dream that interrupted it." It was for the moment as if he was thinking aloud. Then flinging his hands quickly downwards as if throwing off the dream, he looked at her and said rapidly, but still in a quiet tone, "I want you to promise me one thing. Should Watson molest you in any way, you will come and tell me. Don't be put off by thinking you will be depriving me of a good man. They're never so good but there are better. He's likely told you already that he can't be replaced. Don't believe him. . . . You promise me?"

"Yes." She inclined her head slowly with the affirmative. They looked at each other for a moment longer, then the strange interview was over. She turned from him and went towards the ladder, and as she descended the first rung she saw that he hadn't moved from where she had left him.

It was only as she reached the barn floor that she remembered the reason why she had gone up to the loft: it was to get the feed. She was looking at the trailer that she had placed ready to take the bales when Ralph Batley descended the ladder. He passed her without any further word, but even when he had left the barn she did not immediately get on with the job. A sculptor, and that was his studio. But why was it locked? He had evidently worked there at one time. She remembered Mr. Cadwell's strange words that morning about Ralph Batley living in a garret and playing with dolls. It was evident that he had been away from the farm at one time for a period of years, but when he had returned he had still kept up his work, for there was the studio. But why had it been locked for three years, and what had happened to the girl? She found her mind dwelling on the girl. What had she been like? Luscious, Sep Watson had said. What had gone wrong? She couldn't guess, and she would likely never know, for she would hear no more chatter from Sep Watson. Her mind coming to Sep Watson she felt a thread of fear spiralling through her. Ralph Batley had said that should the cowman offend her she should go and report him. There was never a good but there was a better, he had said. That had only been to reassure her, for good farmhands were difficult to come by and a man would think twice before taking a post on this bleak hillside. It would have simplified matters if there had been accommodation for a worker and his family, but there was none. But she knew if she was not to report the cowman she must avoid him at all costs, and this was going to be difficult to say the least.

She sighed somewhat wearily. Worrying wouldn't get the work done, and she could see no further use in speculation. She began loading the trailer with the bales of straw. Because of their size and the weight of the trailer she could not trundle more than two at a time across the yard to the storeroom, and it was when she was making her fourth journey in the growing dusk that Shane came on the scene. Back bent, putting all her weight into the job, she did not see him until his voice crying, "Hold your hand a minute, what're you up to, pushing that load? Where's Watson?" brought her up straight and she smiled at the old man. "Oh, I can manage quite well, Uncle Shane. They're not very heavy, just awkward," she said.

"Awkward, be damned! That's no job for you." She could see that he was angry. "Leave them where they are this minute and go an' tell Sep Watson to come out here."

"No, no. Please." Her voice was urgent. "I can manage quite well. He . . . he would have helped, but I didn't ask him. And please, please, Uncle Shane," she put her hand on his arm, "don't say anything to him . . . don't go for him, it isn't his fault."

He stared at her intently for a moment, then pushing her almost roughly aside he took up the handles of the trailer and, saying, "Go and give Sarah her feed, I was just on me way to her," he thrust the trailer ahead.

She lingered rather longer than was necessary in the byre with Sarah and her calf. It was warm in the byre and quiet, and the sight of the little Galloway mother and her spritely baby was comforting somehow. Sarah seemed to have taken a liking to her; perhaps she remembered that the hand that was stroking her back now had gentled her head a couple of nights ago. Anyway, it was a nice thought, and Linda stayed on talking softly to the animal.

When at last she dragged herself away from Sarah and was on the point of opening the door to leave the byre, it was pushed roughly in, knocking her backwards against the wall, and there in the dim light stood the menacing figure of Sep Watson, dressed ready for his homeward journey. He did not attempt to enter the byre, but with the door gripped in his huge fist, his eyes narrowed and his lower jaw jutting outwards, he growled at her, "Think ye're smart, don't you, well, let me tell you: you watch your step, missie, or you won't reign long here. And it's me that's warning you, mind you that." He banged the heavy door back on her and she only just warded off its impact by thrusting out her hands.

He was gone and she was left standing trembling from head to foot. Ralph Batley had said: "If he molests you in any way let me know." At this moment she wanted to fly to him and cry, "I'm scared, I'm frightened of that man."

She stood for a moment longer until she had steadied herself, then went out and across the yard towards the house, and as she neared the back door Michael came running after her, crying, "Wait! wait!" then hanging on to her hand he looked up into her face as he said, "Guess where I've been?"

She shook her head.

"Down to the bay with the milk. Uncle let me drive. Well . . . well, I had my hand on the wheel, anyway. . . . Oh, I'm hungry, starving! Gran's baking." He dashed ahead of her now and burst open the back door, shouting, "Gran! Gran! I drove the car."

When she entered the kitchen she could hear his voice chattering away to his grandmother. There was a smell of baking bread all about her, the air was warm and pungent, and as she let the hood of her duffle coat drop from her head and was about to loosen the button at her neck she blinked rapidly, then went swiftly forward and placed her hands flat on the white wooden table near the stove. A feeling of faintness had swept over her and she felt for a moment that she was going to fall. Her head drooped lower. She didn't know how long she stood like this before she heard Mrs. Batley's voice at her side saying kindly, "What is it, girl?"

She shook her head slowly from side to side, then Mrs. Batley, turning her about and looking into her face, said, "Are you feeling faint like?" But she did not wait for an answer, instead she unbuttoned the duffle coat and, pulling it off Linda, murmured kindly, "Come away in and sit down, it's the heat, it often has that effect on you when you come out of the cold. . . . Out of the way now." She brushed her grandson aside as she brought Linda across the hall to the fireplace. And when she had seated her in an armchair, she said, "The tea's just mashed, have a good strong cup and you'll feel better." Then turning to her grandson, who was standing at Linda's side peering sharply into her face, she said, "You go,

Michael, and rake up your uncles. Tell them tea's on the table. . . . Away now."

Reluctantly, Michael went to do his grandmother's bidding, and she brought the tea to Linda and said, "Here, drink this up, you've had a heavy day."

"No, no, it was just the cold, as you said." Linda sipped hurriedly at the tea.

Mrs. Batley had turned away and was arranging the plates on the table. With her back still turned, she said quietly, "My son told me about Sep Watson."

Linda, in the act of taking another drink from the cup, stopped and looked towards the older woman. "I don't want to cause trouble, Mrs. Batley." Her voice was anxious.

"I know that, girl." Mrs. Batley was still moving the plates. "Sep's a good worker, he knows his job, none better, but he's ugly inside and out. He's always been the same. And you must do as my son says—if he annoys you in any way you must tell us. He can be a nasty customer, Sep Watson. He's just had it hot and heavy and gone home with his tail between his legs."

So that was it. Ralph Batley must have gone for the cowman, that was the reason for him threatening her.

Mrs. Batley moved towards the fire now and, picking up the kettle, said, "I understand he's been talking, and he'll go on talking. Some of what he says will be the truth and some will be his idea of it." She bent forward and screwed the black kettle into the heart of the fire as she asked quietly, "Did he say anything about my son today?"

Although Mrs. Batley's back was towards Linda, it was as if she was being confronted with the older woman's honest round eyes, for she drooped her head forward as she murmured softly, "Yes." She could not lie to this woman, nor did she think there was any need.

"What did he say?"

"I can't ..." Linda shook her head ... "I mean I can't repeat. ..." Nor was it in her to repeat what the cowman had said, and she ended lamely, "It was just about the studio."

"Oh, the studio." Mrs. Batley repeated her words. "Did he tell you why it was locked?"

"No."

"No? Then he was keeping it for another time likely." Of a sudden Mrs. Batley was standing before Linda and looking hard at her. Without taking her eyes from her she pulled a chair forward and sat down and began talking rapidly in a voice little above a whisper. "There's not much time, they'll all be in in a minute. Whatever Watson said it would be something nasty, so I'll tell you the truth and it'll keep things straight in your mind. ... My son should have been a sculptor, not a farmer. He was a sculptor, a real sculptor, but when his Dad died the farm was in—in a pretty bad state." Linda watched the older woman close her eyes as if on a bitter memory before going on rapidly, "He came home and tried to work at both. There was a girl, from the other valley. She was of some consequence in the district and had been on friendly terms with the Cadwell boys, especially the eldest, Bruce, but as soon as she sees my son she goes all out for him." Mrs. Batley's eyes dropped from Linda's now as she added more slowly, "And he for her. The feeling between the Cadwells and us was bad even then, for you see my daughter, Michael's mother, had married the second son, Lance." Linda gave no indication that she already knew this, but continued to look with pity on this woman. "Bruce Cadwell wanted this girl. You see, her people were important, not so much with money as with position, and it would be a feather in his cap if he got her ... the Cadwells are like that, they like

95

feathers." This was the only vindictive note that Linda had heard from Mrs. Batley, who went on, "And because of this girl the fire that had smouldered between our two houses for years burst into flames. It had just been waiting for a match, and it was struck when Ralph and her became engaged."

She spoke her son's name softly, Linda noticed, but never put a name to the girl. Mrs. Batley now drew in a deep breath that lifted her chest upwards, and as she let it out she said, "Then ten days before the wedding she ran off with Bruce Cadwell." It was odd, Linda thought, but did she detect relief in this statement.

Whatever exclamation Linda was about to make was stilled now by the voice and racing steps of Michael coming through the kitchen. Mrs. Batley, holding Linda's gaze for a second longer, patted her knee in silence, then quickly getting to her feet she went towards the table, calling to Michael as he now ran towards her, "What have I told you about those wellingtons, get back and take them off."

"They're coming, Gran."

"All right . . . do as you're bid."

Linda was still sitting in the chair when Ralph Batley and Shane entered the room. Mrs. Batley had talked about her son and the hurt he had received. She had not spoken of her own hurt that went back deep into the years. But one thing Linda gauged from what she had just been told. Although Ralph Batley had become an embittered man because of being jilted by this girl, the break had brought nothing but relief to his mother and, in a way, she was suffering from a feeling of guilt because of it.

Linda rased her eyes and looked towards the tall, spare arresting figure of her employer approaching the hearth and thought, and very much in the idiom of Uncle

Shane, "Why, the girl must have been daft," and on this the colour rushed back into her face. . . .

No one would have guessed during the evening that followed that the day had been full of turmoil right from its beginning, for at times the hall was filled with laughter. Shane had brought out two packs of cards and had invited Linda to join in a game of snap with Michael and himself on the hearthrug. Forgetting everything and letting herself go, she lost herself in the fun. On her knees, her head close to those of Shane and the boy, she waited her chance and did her share of the yelling, until Michael, turning on the old man, cried playfully, "Oh, Uncle Shane, you're cheating, that wasn't yours, it was . . . was . . ." He turned his eyes upwards to Linda and in the quiet that had settled on the room for a second he said, "What's your name? What can I call you?"

"Call me Linda." Linda was smiling warmly down on him and he repeated, "Linda," and then childishly bit on his lower lip and wagged his head.

"Linda," Shane was nodding at her now, "it's a lilting name. . . . And are we all to call you Linda, eh?"

"Yes. Yes, please."

"D'you hear that?" Shane sat back on his hunkers and looked towards Mrs. Batley and his nephew. Mrs. Batley smiled and nodded back to him, but Ralph Batley was not looking at Linda, his eyes were fixed on the fire. It was as if he had not heard Shane's remark. But in the next moment he was forced to turn his attention to the group, for Michael, bobbing up and down on his knees, cried, "Oh, that's what I'll call the calf . . . Linda. Can I?" The boy looked first at Linda and then towards his uncle. Linda had said nothing, and now she waited to hear Ralph Battley's comment. He was not looking at her but at the boy, and he seemed to give the question some thought before he replied, "Miss Metcalfe might not like the suggestion."

He could not have made it more clear that he, at least, was not going to use her Christian name. As last night, when his hand had jumped from contact with her own, the hurt feeling returned but not in its intensity. Last night she had felt hurt and repulsed because she thought that his rejection was personal, but from what she had heard of him today she now surmised that his attitude was more of an armour against all things feminine, and so she was able to answer quite brightly, "Oh, I don't mind in the least. In fact, I shall feel honoured to have the calf named after me." She turned her soft, warm gaze down on Michael, and in an instant the boy threw himself across her lap, wound his arms tightly about her waist and buried his face in her breast. His action left no one in the room untouched. Mrs. Batley, in an assumed leisurely fashion, rose from her chair and, laying down the mending she had been busy with, said, "Well, come along now, time's up."

"Aye, the evening's fled . . . go on now." Shane hoisted the boy from Linda's lap with one hand on his bottom, and he smacked at him playfully as he pushed him towards his grandmother. And when, a few minutes later, having given the boy his wash and his milk, Mrs. Batley escorted her grandson up to bed, Shane rose to his feet and saying to no one in particular, "I'll go and have a look round," he left the room.

Linda was still sitting on the hearthrug, her legs tucked under her. Ralph Batley was still sitting in his chair, his gaze once more directed towards the fire, and in each silence-filled moment that followed Linda became more and more aware of his presence, and, strangely, she sensed that he too, although he did not move a muscle, was very much aware of her for, and her heart sank at the thought, she embarrassed him. She felt his aloofness, forged by his experience, had built itself a steel armour about him, making it impossible for him now to break through. Then, as if to give the lie to her thoughts, his voice asked quietly, "Do you think you're going to like it here?"

She wanted to turn round with almost girlish effusion and cry, "Yes, oh yes, I'm going to love it," but she forced herself to keep her gaze steadily turned towards the fire and answer in a calm voice, "Yes, I'm sure I shall like it . . . that is if I can satisfy you."

This was a statement that could be answered or side-tracked without giving offence. He side-tracked it by saying, "I understand you are very interested in Galloways."

"Yes." She looked at him now. "Yes, I am, very."

"They are breeding them quite a bit in the south."

"Yes, but just certain farmers. It's an expensive business, breeding." She nipped at her lower lip wondering if once again she had trodden on soft ground, but he immediately confirmed her statement by saying, "Yes, you're right, it is. You've got to have a side line to keep going. Have you been to any of the big shows?"

"I went to the Royal Counties Show at Portsmouth in June."

"Mm! did you? I read about that. I hope to show next year at Castle Douglas. I'm taking Great Leader up and a couple of heifers."

She had screwed round on the hearthrug and was facing him now, her hands clasping her knees. She could not see the expression on his face, it was lost in the heavy shadow of the winged chair. But they were talking, really talking, for the first time since her arrival.

"There's a cattle market in Morpeth . . . perhaps you know?"

"Yes, I had heard there was one."

"It's held on Wednesday. I'll be going in but I won't be taking any stock." He did not add, "Would you like to come?" but now fell silent, and for no reason she could understand she felt his sudden withdrawal. It was as if he had said his piece and now it was over, and that was that.

Yet Linda was not depressed by his retreat into silence again. Turning to the fire she sat gazing into it once more. He had talked to her in an ordinary way and he had asked her if she was going to like staying here. She felt warm and strangely content. Sep Watson was once again forgotten. She lifted her arm on to the seat of the chair near her and rested her head upon it. . . .

How long she had been asleep she did not know, but she woke with a start when she heard Shane's voice whispering softly, saying, "She'll be cramped to death lying like that."

"Oh!" She blinked and stretched one arm outwards. "Oh, I'm sorry, I must have fallen asleep." Then as she tried to move she groaned aloud and laughed as she groaned.

As Shane's arm assisted her to her feet she became aware that her hair had become unpinned. It was lying dishevelled on her shoulders, the grips sticking out of it at angles. As she smoothed it back from her face she glanced towards the winged chair. It was empty and there was no sign of Ralph Batley in the room. She smiled at Shane and said, "Thanks," then looking to where Mrs. Batley was stripping the loose covers from the cushions of the big couch, she asked, "How long have I been asleep?"

"Over an hour, I should say."

"I think I'll go to bed."

"Yes, I would." Mrs. Batley turned and gave her a quiet smile.

"Good night, Mrs. Batley."

"Good night."

She did not say Linda, perhaps the use of Christian names did not come easy to her. But not so with Uncle Shane, for when she turned to him saying, "Good night, Uncle Shane," he nodded his kind, hairy face at her as he quietly said, "Good night, Linda girl, good night."

If during the next few days Linda could have discounted the personal tragedies of the occupants of Fowler Hall, she would have said there was an ordered harmonious peace pervading the farm, but knowing something about the lives of the people in the house she had to confess that this feeling was perhaps only within herself. Perhaps it was because of the knowledge that her employer had accepted her that she was feeling as she did. Whatever it was, even the presence of Sep Watson could not impinge upon her present feelings. In any case, the telling off seemed to have had a salutary effect upon him, for he kept his distance, and when he did come in contact with her he was civil, oily civil.

Moreover, she had been heartened by a reply to her first letter home. Her mother said she was relieved and delighted that she liked her work and was settling down ... and Daddy sent her his love. Linda could even believe this letter, for now he had her mother to himself he could be generous. Uncle Chris, too, had written, he said he knew of course that she would like the job. Mr. Ainslie thought very highly of Mr. Batley, that was why he recommended her to him, and she must work hard—she laughed at that. Uncle Chris thought he worked hard but the northern work, like the northern weather, was different, harder, harsher ... different.

And then came market day.

Long afterwards she remembered how she had woken on this particular morning with a bubbling feeling surging through her. Last evening, right out of the blue, Ralph Batley had said to her, "Would you care to come in tomorrow? I don't think it wise for my mother to come with the cold she has on her. I have to go to the bank and also see my solicitor. You could get the shopping if you wouldn't mind doing that."

Mind doing that? She felt like a child going on a school outing, happy, excited, expectant. . . . Of what? Like a child, she did not question.

About fifteen minutes before they were due to leave at half-past ten, she dashed into the house, changed into her ordinary clothes, quickly made up her face, and was on the point of leaving the room when she remembered the torch, Rouse Cadwell's torch. She hesitated a moment before going to the chest-of-drawers. She had no wish to see or speak with Rouse Cadwell or any of the Cadwells, she was firmly and wholeheartedly on her employer's side, but she had borrowed his torch and he had reminded her of it only a few days ago. If she were to run into him then should could give it to him; if she didn't see him she would post it to him from the post office in Morpeth, and that would be over and done with. Quickly she opened the drawer and slipped the torch into her handbag, then ran downstairs.

As on that first evening she had descended the stairs into the hall and brought all their eyes upon her, now the procedure was being repeated. There they all stood as she moved down the staircase, Shane, Michael, Mrs. Batley and Ralph Batley, and under their concerted gaze she gave a self-conscious little laugh and on reaching the last step she smoothed down the front of her coat as she said, "It seems odd getting into these clothes again, I feel I've been wearing breeches for months."

But no one seemed to have any comment to make on this. Ralph Batley turned towards the kitchen door, and his mother, after a long look at Linda, followed him. Michael was hanging on to her arm now, his face very aggrieved as he said, "I wish I could come."

Then Shane, putting his hand on the boy's head but looking at Linda as he did so, said, "You're a bonnie sight, Linda. I wish I had me years afore me again."

"Oh, Uncle Shane." Linda laughed softly at him. Then leaning forward she whispered teasingly, "If you had I would fall for you right away."

"Away with you!" His tone held mock sternness and he flapped his hand at her. "Laughing at a man because he's up in years. Away with you!"

She went away with Michael clinging to her arm. But at the back door the child was restrained by his grandmother saying, "Leave go and behave yourself, boy, you'll rumple her."

Ralph Batley was already at the wheel of the jeep, and as she climbed up beside him he slipped in the gears and she turned and waved to the group standing in the yard. The Sunday School treat feeling was very much to the fore at this moment.

The journey to Morpeth was uneventful except for one thing. Ralph Batley had taken the main road through Widdrington that led straight on to Ashington, and it was in this last town, while held up in a traffic jam, that a voice from a station wagon to the left of Linda said, "Hullo, there, Ralph man." The speaker was evidently a farmer, somewhat older than her employer, and although he was leaning across the wheel looking in the direction of Ralph Batley, Linda knew his eyes were taking her in.

"Hullo, there." Ralph Batley's returned salutation did not sound over friendly.

The man was grinning widely as he said, "Having a day off?"

"Not more than usual."

The remarks flowing back and forward in front of Linda sounded ordinary, but their implications, she knew, were far from ordinary, and later she was to think that this meeting had a great bearing on what followed, for after parking the jeep near the market-place, Ralph Batley turned to her and with a curtness that had faded slightly from his manner during the last few days said, "You have the orders, you'll find the three shops over there . . ." he pointed . . ."I'll be back here round about two."

She knew a dampening of her spirits as she answered, "Very well." Then as she turned from him he spoke again. "About lunch," he said. His voice sounded slightly hesitant now as he ended, "The Earl Grey does a very good lunch." He did not say where she would find the Earl Grey nor add, "Would you like to meet me there?" Perhaps if it hadn't been for the traffic jam and the man with his wide grin he might have said that, but she would never know.

"Very well, I'll try it. Two o'clock, you said?" She tried to keep the disappointment out of her voice. "Good-bye." The next moment she was walking briskly away from him into the throng of people. It did not matter to him that she did not know the town. All that mattered was that since the farmer had chipped him he was not going to lay himself open to the same thing happening again.

It did not take long to give in the orders, the arrangement being that the goods would be packed and ready for her to pick up later. Mrs. Batley's personal requirements at the chemist and the hardware store took a little longer. Her own shopping amounted to buying a box of sweets for Michael and a copy of the *Farmers' Weekly*. And when all this was accomplished the time was not yet twelve o'clock. But there was much to see, and she had not yet been round the market.

It was, she found, the usual type of cattle market, with its pens full of animals and its farmers prodding and pressing the beasts. Leaning over a sheep pen she saw two girls dressed in breeches. They were about her own age and definitely attached to farms. Had she been so dressed she might, through the camaraderie of the attire, have approached them, but she knew that in her present attire, there was nothing to associate her with a farm and she felt somewhat shy of joining them. She became aware that she herself was drawing curious glances.

At one stage when she handled the haunches of a young heifer there was laughter from behind her, and she turned to find two men greatly amused at her action. The look that she levelled on them sobered them somewhat, and as one made a crude remark on how a heifer should not be judged, she was reminded forcibly of Mr. Cadwell comparing her with a year-old filly.

As she moved away a man, detaching himself from another group, exclaimed, "Why, hullo there," and in the next moment she was face to face with Rouse Cadwell.

"Oh, hullo." She smiled. "I was hoping I would see you."

That was not what she had meant to say at all, but she was flustered, for the eyes of the two men were covertly watching her and their grins were in evidence again.

"Now that is nice."

Linda's face became straight, and her voice was flat and emphatic as she said, "Please don't misunderstand me. You asked for your torch, I've brought it." She opened her bag and handed him the torch, and as he took it into his hands he patted it and said jovially, "Nice torch, good torch for bringing her to market." It was as if he was talking to a dog. Then dropping his jocular tone he asked quietly, "Are you on your own?"

"Mr. Batley is with me."

"Oh." His lip pursed and his head bounced gently. Then he said, "You'll be going straight back?" This seemed to indicate his knowledge of Ralph Batley's movements on market-day and suggested that her employer stayed no longer in the town than was necessary. But she did not think of this as she replied, "No, I'm having lunch first."

"Alone?"

"Yes . . . no."

"Well now," his lips were twisted into a little smile, "make up your mind. But I can tell you what you're doing, you're lunching alone, aren't you? You haven't been invited to have it . . . with your master." He stressed the last three words with a deep intonation. "But you shan't have it alone," he went on. "Will you have it with me?"

"No, thank you." Her voice was stiff.

He looked at her in amused silence for a moment, before saying quietly, "Now let's get this straight. You're not a Batley . . . what's happened between them and us has nothing whatever to do with you. Right?"

She did not answer, only looked squarely into his dark, narrow, handsome face as he went on, "You've come to market, you're off duty, you've got to eat, so why not eat with me?"

She paused for a moment before answering in a level tone, "Ask yourself, if you were in his place how would you like your employee to take lunch with a member of the opposite camp, for you are in the opposite camp, aren't you?"

He was looking at her with his head on one side. "You are a very nice girl, you know, besides being a very beautiful one," he said. "Why didn't we think of taking a student?"

"There's no reason why you shouldn't."

"No, I suppose not. But you wouldn't happen twice, would you? You wouldn't like to change over?"

"Don't be silly." Linda's tone was sharp. She pulled the large collar of her coat up around her neck and was in the act of turning away when his hand came out and touched her lightly as he said seriously, "I'm sorry, I was only joking. But do come and have lunch with me. . . . Please. If you don't want to run into Batley we can go some place away from the centre of the town. I can understand your feelings about the matter, honestly I can."

He could be nice, even charming, this Rouse Cadwell. Under other circumstances she might have accepted his invitation and thoroughly enjoyed herself, but not now, not for the world would she do anything that would annoy the Batleys, mother or son. Now her tone was much softer as she said, "Thank you all the same, but I'm sure you understand that it would be better not to. Good-bye."

"Good-bye." Although he held her glance as long as he could he made no effort to detain her, and she walked swiftly away from the market.

The encounter with Rouse Cadwell had shaken her somewhat, for all the time she had been on tenterhooks in case Ralph Batley should appear. She decided to have her lunch straight away, then return to the shops and collect the orders. This would fill in the time until two o'clock. Strangely now she wanted to be away from Morpeth and back on the cliff top, on the wind-strewn farm.

She was approaching the Earl Grey Hotel when she saw a modern Rover car pull up outside. The door was pushed open and Mrs. Cadwell alighted. She was dressed in a gun-metal coloured coat with a large opossum collar. On her black hair was perched a small hat made up of glistening green feathers and small pieces of fur. She looked statuesque, expensive, and not at all like the usual conception of a farmer's wife. She was the antithesis of Mrs. Batley. Why Mr. Cadwell had married this woman Linda didn't know; perhaps she had money. By what she had learned of him he laid great stock by money. Well, whatever the reason, she had not been able to eliminate his first love from his mind.

Without seeing her Mrs. Cadwell cut across Linda's path and walked into the hotel, and Linda found herself not following her but walking straight ahead. She could not go into the hotel and risk being seated near to the Cadwells, for likely Mr. Cadwell would join his wife for lunch.

She walked on for some way, then up a side street she saw a sign hanging over a small window, advertising lunches and grills. The small window, she found on entering the restaurant, was deceptive. The place was of considerable size and contained a number of rooms, all busily attended by efficient-looking waiters. From the hallway she saw that one room was entirely taken up by men. The one next to it seemed to be given over to families, and into this she went and found a seat in a far corner.

The lunch was good but expensive, as much she guessed as she would have paid at the hotel, perhaps more.

She took the meal leisurely, then went up to the ladies' room. It was as she descended the stairs to the small foyer again that she saw Rouse Cadwell for the second time. He was taking up his coat from the hallstand and as he turned and thrust his arms into it they came face to face.

"Well, don't tell me you've been lunching here." His voice held amused surprise.

"Yes . . . yes, I have."

"Now isn't that silly? You in one room and me in another! Don't you think it is?"

"No, I can't say I do."

"Oh, well, have it your own way. Did you have a good lunch?"

"Yes, a very good lunch."

"They are noted here for their steaks . . . did you try the steak?"

"No, chicken."

"Oh, I never have their chicken, they buy the old birds from us and they're tough." He was laughing, and she could not help but smile back at him.

He was opening the door for her as he spoke and she had just passed him and was stepping into the street when she wished with all her heart that the earth would open and swallow her whole, for there, about to enter the restaurant, was Ralph Batley.

Even the night she had first made his acquaintance and the name of Cadwell had brought a look of mad hatred into his face, was nothing compared to his expression at this moment. His ice-grey glance moved once between them before settling on Rouse Cadwell, and, strangely, it was Rouse Cadwell who spoke, and even placatingly as he said, "Now look here, Batley, it isn't——"

Ralph Batley cut him short with words that seemed to be wrenched from some black depth within him: "You try anything on and I'll kill you."

"Listen . . . but——" As Linda put her hand out protestingly towards her employer she felt herself almost lifted off the ground. It was as if he was taking a child by the arm and sweeping it along. She almost cried out at the pain of his fierce grip and she protested weakly as he hurried her away. "You must listen . . . I wasn't. . . . Please . . . please, you're hurting me."

"Shut up."

When he turned into a side lane that was practically deserted Linda cried, "Stop it. Stop it, will you?" She dug her heels into the rough road and dragged on him, and this action seemed to bring him to his senses, for he released her and so quickly that she almost fell. Rubbing her arm now with her hand she muttered, almost on the verge of tears, "I can explain."

She saw that his face was contorted with his anger, and he growled at her, "Don't talk! Shut up!"

He now turned and went hurriedly forward again. After a moment she followed him, but at a distance. The lane brought her into the street where the car was parked, and as she approached it he swung away across the road towards the shops. She made no effort to follow him to help carry the parcels, but climbing into her seat, she sat with her head forward, rubbing gently at her arm.

What she had tried so hard to avoid had happened. He had found her with Rouse Cadwell and had immediately jumped to the conclusion the meeting had been prearranged.

Although she did not raise her head she was aware of him making several journeys between the car and the shops. She could not help but be aware of this, for the boxes of stores hit the floor of the jeep behind her as if they had been dropped from the cliff top.

When at last he took his seat beside her the car seemed to become filled with his fury. The gears were rammed in and the car leaped away. It was as well it was a slack time in the town otherwise they would surely have run into something.

The journey was almost half over when she made a

decision. She must, no matter how he reacted, explain the situation. She must make him listen, for once they got back on the farm he would avoid her so skilfully that to talk to him would become almost an impossibility.

They were not returning by the main road but by a narrow, winding side road that was little better than a track. At one time, when they were bumping across an open stretch of moor, she thought they had left the road altogether. It was at this point that she spoke. Turning her face full towards his iron-stiff profile she said loudly, for it was impossible to speak softly against the noise of the car, "Will you stop a moment and listen?"

The car bumped and jolted but went on.

"Please."

Still there was no response. She turned her head to the front and it drooped as she clamped her teeth hard down on her lower lip. The next second she had swung round and was yelling at him, "Stop, will you! Stop and let me speak."

The car stopped so suddenly that she was flung forward, her brow hitting the windscreen. She dropped back into her seat, dazed for a moment, then turned to him to find him looking at her as if he loathed the sight of her. His face held so much bitterness that she cried out immediately, "Don't look at me like that. I haven't done anything that I'm ashamed of."

"No, of course you haven't." His voice had the terrifying quiet quality about it. "Duplicity isn't anything you would be ashamed of. Why should I blame you for acting according to your lights? You have no standards."

"I did not meet Mr. Cadwell by arrangement." Her voice was high as she cut in on him. "You can say what you like about standards, it doesn't hurt me. But what I'm telling you is the truth."

111

"You just ran into him by accident and had lunch together, that was how it happened, wasn't it?"

"No, it wasn't. I did run into him by accident but I didn't have lunch with him."

"Don't lie to me." He was yelling now. "I saw you in the market . . . you were arranging where you would meet, weren't you? And then you come out of Sprigley's together, and you have the nerve to sit there and tell me you didn't have lunch with him?"

"Yes, I have." She was spitting the words now.

"Oh, don't be such a stupid little fool!"

"How dare you!"

Their eyes were blazing each into the other's, and when he now spoke his lips moved with a curl back from his teeth as he said slowly, "And what about in the lane the other morning when he was whispering to you? Are you going to tell me that a man whispers when he has nothing to say, nothing that the rest of the world might not hear? It all fits in."

"I had borrowed his torch; he was asking for it back."

"Oh," his head went up and he let out a cruel laugh, "oh, this is the limit. Rouse Cadwell is short of a torch!" Now his head was forward again and his face was not more than six inches from her as he said, "what d'you take me for, a damn fool? And don't play the naïve stuff to death. If you can't think up a better lie than that, then I advise you to keep quiet."

"I tell you I'm not lying."

"Shut up."

"I won't shut up, and don't speak to me like that." Now justifiable anger rising swiftly in her, she cried at him, "I have told you the truth. Who do you think you are, anyway, talking to me in this manner. You don't own me . . . why, you would think I had committed a crime. When I come to think of it, I'm a fool. Why should I try to convince you that I wasn't having lunch with Mr. Cadwell. Why? I'm unmarried and I'm free and I can have lunch with whoever I like, and what's more I'm going to. The next time you accuse me of having lunch with Mr. Cadwell there will be more than a grain of truth in it, it will be a fact, I can promise you that."

They were caught up now in a silence. It settled on the car like a weighted blanket. His face had a death-like whiteness about it while hers was suffused with the heat of her anger. Then with the shattering brittleness of cracking ice he said, "I won't avail myself of that opportunity, Miss Metcalfe. I will release you from your agreement and you can leave at the end of the week."

Ignoring the stab that seemed to pierce her clean through her breast, she cried back at him, "I won't wait until the end of the week, Mr. Batley, I'll leave at the earliest opportunity, tomorrow morning."

"Suit yourself."

The gears were rammed in again, the car bounded forward, and in spite of the jolting Linda sat as stiff as a ramrod. She was raging inside. She seemed to have been impregnated with Ralph Batley's own fury; she could not find words within herself to describe him; she only knew that she hated him; she wished she had never met him . . . she couldn't wait until tomorrow morning when she would have seen the last of him.

When after what seemed a never-ending journey the car bounced from a narrow side lane and on to a main road, she realised that it was the same road that led down to Surfpoint Bay and a curious question, one that she could not voice, cried in her head. Why is he going this way? Then within a few minutes she had the answer, for the car turned sharply off to the right and into nothing more than a lane, then right again, and now she found herself being whisked and jolted through the narrow rock passage which led to the cliff path. Her anger was suddenly shot through with fear. Why had he come this way? In his present mood he seemed capable of anything.

As the car came out of the narrow gorge and to where the road divided, the right one leading to the Cadwell's house and the other along the cliff top to the farm, she could not prevent herself from crying out, "Stop! Stop! do you hear? I'm going to walk."

He took not the slightest notice of her and the car swung sharply to the left. For a moment she gazed straight ahead, then, as if drawn by a magnet, her eyes slewed towards the cliff edge, not more than four feet away. As she cast one terrified glance far below her to the beach her stomach seemed to heave upwards. She closed her eyes, and when a few seconds later she opened them the distance to the cliff edge had widened. When they flew past the end of the boundary of the Cadwells' land and on to the open cliff top, her whole body seemed to crumble and she slumped back for a moment against the seat. But it was only for a moment, for this last action of his which seemed to her to speak of unnecessary cruelty brought her rage bubbling upwards again, and when the car came at last to a jolting stop in the yard opposite the kitchen door, she turned on her employer a look that was more than a reflection of his own. Then flinging open the door she jumped out, to be confronted almost immediately by Mrs. Batley.

The older woman was standing in the kitchen doorway and she exclaimed in some surprise, "You're back early . . . is anything . . .?" Her mouth hung open on the words that did not come, and as Linda hurried past her without a word she grasped her arm and asked rapidly, "What is it? What's happened?"

"I'm leaving." Linda was so angry at this moment that her pity and affection—for she had found herself becoming very fond of Mrs. Batley—in no way helped to soften her attitude.

With her hand still on Linda's arm and holding it tightly, Mrs. Batley turned towards her son as he came toward the door now carrying a box of groceries in his arms.

"What's all this? What's happened?"

He did not pause in his step as he said, "Miss Metcalfe has told you. She's leaving, and don't try to stop her. I want her to go and she wants to go. It's mutual."

Mrs. Batley turned her eyes on Linda again, and slowly relaxing her grip, she allowed her to move away.

Linda, almost running, went across the hall and up the stairs and into her room, and dropping down on to the side of the bed she sat rubbing at her arm. He was nothing but a wild, rough brute. Oh, if only she could get her things down to the Bay she would leave this minute, this instant. She turned and buried her face in the pillow, but only for a second. Springing up she walked to the window. She wouldn't cry, no, she wouldn't. He was a beast, a beast, she wouldn't cry because of him.

There to the right of her lay the farmyard. She could see Shane coming towards the house with Michael at his heels. She turned her eyes quickly from them both, she wanted no softening effects. She looked away to her left and over the open ground to the cliff top and down to the sea, where she could just see the far end of the Bay with the ugly, dangerous rocks dotted about it. Well, they could be as dangerous as they liked, they wouldn't affect her, she wouldn't be here in the summer, and thank goodness for that.

The murmur of voices from the hall now penetrated

115

the room, Shane's raised above the rest. Would Shane believe that she'd had lunch with Rouse Cadwell? Well, it wouldn't matter if he believed it or not, she didn't care. The voices died away and she still stood at the window. Then asking herself angrily what she was standing there for when she should be packing, she turned about and went to the wardrobe and began pulling down her clothes. . . .

It must have been an hour later when her trunk and two suitcases were packed that the knock came on the door, and she turned her head sharply towards it before saying, "Yes, come in."

Quietly as if she was a stranger in her own house, Mrs. Batley entered the room, and closing the door softly behind her, she looked not at Linda but at the luggage lying at the foot of the bed. Then coming slowly forward she stood before Linda, and with the sadness in her voice matching that on her face, she said, "I'm sorry about this, heart sorry."

Linda could not bear to face the older woman's eyes, and she turned her head away until Mrs. Batley said, "I'm going to ask you something point-blank. Your answer cannot make any difference now, but I know you'll tell me the truth. . . . Did you go and have lunch with Rouse Cadwell?"

Linda was now looking directly at Mrs. Batley and she could not keep the bitterness from her tone as she replied, "No matter what I say, you'll still believe your son, it's only natural."

"That I won't."

A weighty silence hung between them and then Linda, with a heavy sigh, sat slowly down on the bed again, and after closing her eyes wearily for a moment, she said, "Well, it was like this, Mrs. Batley . . ." and she went on to tell the older woman exactly how her meeting with

116

Rouse Cadwell had come about, right from the night of her arrival when he had lent her the torch, even the whispered words as he bent from his horse in the lane, and then the happenings in the town today.

When Linda had finished speaking Mrs. Batley, after staring down on her for a moment, put out her hand and patted her arm as she said softly, "There's one thing I'm glad about, I wasn't mistaken about you. But there, nothing can be done now; you're going, and as I've said I'm heart sorry." When the hand slid down her arm and the rough, worn fingers pressed the back of her hand as she ended, "I had taken to you, girl," Linda's defence was almost broken.

The next minute Mrs. Batley was moving towards the door, but before leaving the room and without turning, she said quietly, "He's out and won't be in for some time . . . come down and have a bite of tea."

"No, thanks."

"Please." Mrs. Batley still had her back towards Linda, and looking at the drooped shoulders Linda was forced to say, "Very well, then."

Some minutes later, when she descended the stairs and saw below her the big room with the table set as usual for tea, and the fire glowing and the air of homely comfort pervading the whole atmosphere, she felt a wave of regret that this was to be the last evening she would spend in this house, and she knew that she would always remember this hall-cum-living-room with a feeling of home-sickness.

Shane and Michael were already at the table and they both looked at her but did not speak. The expression on Michael's face was one of hurt bewilderment, whereas Shane's expression was so grim that she could hardly recognise him as the kindly old man she knew, for at this moment he looked a reflection of his nephew. She had not been seated at the table for more than a few minutes when Shane got up hurriedly, almost toppling his chair backwards in the process, and as he made for the kitchen door Mrs. Batley, who was coming into the room, said to him, "What's the matter? Aren't you having your tea?"

"No . . . no, Maggie, I have no taste for it. I'll go and have a look round."

Linda saw Mrs. Batley watch him for a moment before coming to the table, and then taking her seat she looked to where Linda sat with an empty plate before her, and she said, "Eat, my dear. Have a little something." She pushed a laden plate towards her and when Linda shook her head she said, "All right then, Michael will put a fire on in your room, won't you, Michael?"

Staring at Linda, the boy nodded. And when Mrs. Batley ended with, "I'll bring you something up on a tray later," Linda thrust her hand across her eyes and beseeched her, "Oh! Mrs. Batley, don't . . . don't."

She could call up anger to fight anger but before this kindness she was melting into her natural self again. And she knew she mustn't do this, her indignation must sustain her until tomorrow when she would be gone from this house. With a muttered "Excuse me" she rose from the table and went swiftly up the stairs again.

Once more in her room Linda could no longer restrain her tears, and she gave way to a passion of weeping that seemed to rend her apart. She had been in this house just over a week, yet during that time she seemed to have experienced every emotion in life, and now her anger was being washed away in the storm of her weeping.

She had to fight for control when a gentle tap came on the door and Michael's voice said, "I've brought the sticks."

Keeping her face averted from him she went towards

118

the window under the pretext of drawing the curtains, then she busied herself with her dressing-case while he slowly laid the sticks on the paper and then the coal, and finally put a match to the fire. His work done, he did not immediately leave the room, and Linda was forced to turn towards him to see him staring at her. There was a lost look in his eyes, it seemed to envelop the whole of his small body, but the lost look was not alone, the childish gaze that was on her was also accusing and he gave proof of this when he said, "My mummy went away, too."

That was all. He turned about and left the room.

The child's few words spoke plainly of the misery that had taken its toll of his nervous system, and Linda felt as though she were sinking down into a well of guilt. His mother had let him down, now she had let him down. She wanted to run after him and say, "Listen, Michael, it wasn't my fault." But did it matter to him whose fault it was . . . she was leaving and that was final. Ralph Batley had said, "She wants to go and I want her to." There was no more to be said.

She heard Mrs. Batley's voice now; it was coming from outside, from somewhere below her window, and she was calling across the yard, "Have you seen your uncle?" Linda did not hear the reply, but after a while she heard Mrs. Batley's voice again and in the distance now calling, "Shane! Are you there, Shane?" And again, "Shane! Are you there?" and as Linda listened the guilty feeling became more acute. . . .

The fire was crackling brightly and Linda, sitting hunched up before it, was now thinking dully about what she was going to do. It wasn't that she was afraid of not being able to get another position, but she was wondering if she should go home until she got fixed up somewhere or stay in the north and seek another post here. She remembered the *Farmers' Weekly* she had bought only a few hours ago. But she had, in her temper, left it in the car, and she wasn't going to venture out of this room any more tonight . . . she couldn't bear the thought of running into Ralph Batley before tomorrow morning, when it would be impossible to avoid him then, for he would have to take her and her luggage down to the Bay. She shuddered at the thought.

Mrs. Batley's voice broke in on her thoughts again. It was coming from the landing this time, and she seemed to be calling down into the hall. "He's not up here, I knew he couldn't be up here."

Linda rose to her feet. Were they looking for Michael? Had something happened to the child? She remembered the look on his face, and she had opened the bedroom door and was on the point of stepping on to the landing when her employer's voice checked her. It was coming from the direction of the stairs, and she heard him ask, "How long is it since he went out?"

"About an hour or an hour and a half," came Mrs. Batley's reply.

On this Linda realised they were not talking of Michael but of Shane. Then Mrs. Batley's voice, holding a desperate note, said, "Oh, don't say he's gone down to the Bay. But I'd like to bet anything that's where he is at this minute. . . . Oh, after all this time to start again. . . . I should have realised it, the way he left the house, there was that look on his face."

"And you're blaming me." The words that Ralph Batley spoke were low and bitter.

"No, I'm not, son, only I'm worried. If he gets bottled up he'll never make his way along that cliff path, you know how he goes on, dancing and acting the goat . . . it's a black, dark night. I'm worried, Ralph."

Linda heard no more but she seemed to see the mother and son looking at each other. Then came the sound of

Ralph Batley's steps running down the stairs, and a few minutes later the back door banging told her that he was on his way to Surfpoint Bay and The Wild Duck.

Softly she closed the door, and with her back to it she waited. When she heard the car start up she could not help but hold her breath. Would he take the cliff path in the dark? When the throb of the car did not become louder but faded into the distance, she knew that he was going by the back road and she closed her eyes and sighed.

Some time later, hearing the chink of crockery from down below, and remembering Mrs. Batley's promise to bring her up a tray, she got to her feet instantly. She couldn't let the older woman wait on her, she had enough to do. Anyway, she didn't want anything to eat at all.

As there was no fear of running into Ralph Batley now, she went hastily from the room and down the stairs and straight to Mrs. Batley's side, and looking from her to the tray she said, "It's very kind of you, Mrs. Batley, but I really don't want anything to eat."

"We've all got to eat, girl."

"But really I couldn't." She put her hand out tentatively and touched Mrs. Batley's arm.

"All right, as you say." The older woman looked wearily ahead for a moment, then turning her eyes towards the large curtained window which faced the sea, she changed the conversation entirely by saying, "The wind's getting up. It's going to be a rough night."

"Yes. Yes, I think it is."

After this attempt at small talk they both stood, uncertain what to say or do next, and as if by common consent they sat down.

The minutes passed. Then, as the noise of the wind dropped for a moment, there came into the room a strange sound: it was of distant hilarious singing. And when there followed the sound of the car stopping in the yard Linda knew that Uncle Shane had arrived. Glancing swiftly towards Mrs. Batley she saw that her face had a grey ashen look, and she was surprised when she did not immediately make for the kitchen, but rising went to the fireplace, and with one hand pressed against her side and the other stretched upwards on to the mantelpiece she stood with unusual stillness gazing down into the fire.

Quickly Linda turned away. She must get upstairs before Ralph Batley entered the house. And what was more, she couldn't bear to see Uncle Shane drunk. As she hurried across the hall she heard Shane's thick voice crying from the kitchen, "Leave be! Leave be!" and she had her foot on the first step of the stairs when he came with a shambling run into the room crying, "I'll not be baulked, nor preached at. I'm a man, amn't I?"

If Shane saw Mrs. Batley he took no notice of her, but seeing Linda about to ascend the stairs he came at her with a rollicking rush, crying thickly, "Aw! me darlin', there you are. There's me bonny lass. Come away. Come away. Come on, let's have a dance, a farewell dance." He had pulled her down from the third step when Mrs. Batley's hands came upon him, dragging him away. But he would not release his hold on Linda and she found herself once more in the middle of the room. She had a glimpse of Ralph Batley standing in the doorway. But even as she saw him he disappeared back into the kitchen again, and Mrs. Batley cried, "Sit down, Shane. Sit down! Do you hear?"

"Aw! Maggie, give over, will you, you're always worryin'. Let's have a sing-song, eh?" His voice breaking into song, he yelled, "To the toot of the flute and the twiddle of the fiddle-o, Hoppin' up and down like a herrin' on a griddle-o."

It should have been laughable but it wasn't. Linda was filled with a deep sadness as she looked down on the old man. He was sitting now, but he still held tightly to her arm, and when Mrs. Batley struck at his hand, crying, "Leave go!" he said to her in a hiccupping whisper, "Whi . . . sht, Maggie! Linda here and me are goin' to have a party . . . a farewell party."

"Leave go of her, Shane, do you hear? Leave go this minute."

"Don't be vexed with me, Maggie. Don't be vexed with old Shane . . . a man's got to do somethin' when he sees his world going wrong and he cannot put it to rights. Well, a man's got to do somethin', so he closes his eyes. . . . I've close me eyes, Maggie."

"Leave go of her, will you?"

"Aw! she doesn't mind old Shane, she doesn't." The old man was looking up into Linda's face now, his voice low, thick and sad. "She's a girl after me own heart for she's got spunk. Aye, she has that, for all her gentle ways she's got spunk, and I'm going to tell her why I've got drunk this night, I am, I am. And she'll listen to old Shane, won't you, me dear?"

"Yes, yes, of course, Uncle Shane." Linda's voice was scarcely above a whisper. She was cut to the heart at the sight of the old man. For all his jovial ways he'd had a bearing, a dignified bearing; there had been about him a suggestion that he had not always spent his days doing odd jobs on a farm. But now all dignity was stripped from him and it hurt her deeply to see him only as an object of pity.

She was not aware for the moment that Mrs. Batley had left their side until she heard her voice speaking urgently in the kitchen, and the next moment Ralph

Batley was in the room. He was standing opposite to her at the other side of Shane. Putting his hand under his uncle's armpit he gave a hoist as he said curtly, "Come along."

But Uncle Shane was not to be moved so easily, for looking up at his nephew, he laughed as he cried, "Oh, there you are. There you are again, my pig-headed paddy. Aw! . . . aw! . . . " He pushed roughly at Ralph Batley's chest. "Leave me be, will you? I'll go when I'm ready. Don't annoy me, for you know," he wagged a solemn finger now up into his nephew's face, "I'm agen you this night, aye, I am that. Not that I don't love you, I love you like a son, an' always have done, and I've bled for you, aye, I have. When that loose slut got her claws into you I bled for you . . . and I got drunk that night, didn't I? . . . paralytic. Now, now! Leave go of me, I won't rise until I'm ready." He thrust Ralph Batley off while he still retained hold of Linda's sleeve, and he cried at him now, "Every man gets a second chance, and you got yours, and what did you do? You closed your eyes, like me the night, only with a difference."

"Are you coming or have I to make you?" Ralph Batley's voice was quiet, so quiet that Shane, pretending that he didn't hear him, turned towards Linda and, blinking his heavy eyelids and smiling widely up at her, said, "Oh, me darlin', when I first saw you kneelin' near that wee cow when her labour was on her, I thought of the mother of God, I did that. For your beauty is like gold . . . leave me be!" He tried to thrust off Ralph Batley's hand again as he cried, "I'm not going up, I want to talk to her . . . for isn't she off in the mornin'?"

With a jerk Shane was brought to his feet and Linda found herself free. Ralph Batley was now propelling the old man forcibly from behind towards the stairs, and Shane, making one last effort, hung on to the knob of the

124

balustrade until his fingers were forced off by Mrs. Batley, and he was borne up the stairs like a child, his arms flaying widely, his voice still yelling. Helpless in his nephew's grip, he made the undignified journey across the landing, and when his bedroom door banged on them his voice was heard for a moment or so longer, and then there was silence.

The silence descended on the whole house, and it seemed to Linda that it would go on forever when a small voice from the balcony said, "Gran, Gran."

Slowly Mrs. Batley raised her head and looked upwards to where Michael was standing in his pyjamas, peering through the banisters, and she said wearily, "Its all right. Go back to bed, it's all right."

Linda watched the small figure turn reluctantly about and disappear from view, and then she looked towards Mrs. Batley, whose face was now greyer than ever. And when the older woman, catching her glance, said, "I'm sorry you've been subjected to this," she could say nothing, for she was being weighed down with the sense of guilt again and the feeling that Uncle Shane's lapse lay at her door. She wanted to say something comforting but she couldn't. The silence swallowed them and became unbearable and so, saying quickly now, "Good night, Mrs. Batley," she turned and went upstairs.

Poor Uncle Shane . . . the pity of it. But she wasn't to blame. How could she be? She had known him only a matter of days. She endeavoured to recall now some of the things he had said, but checked her thinking by saying to herself, "He was drunk, things a man says when he's drunk don't make sense."

Slowly she undressed for bed, and when she had turned out the light and got between the sheets she lay stiffly on her back with no idea of sleep in her mind. To sleep one must relax, and her body felt as stiff as if it had been set in cement. Then with surprising suddenness she flung round on to her face and once again she was lost in a storm of silent weeping. . . .

At what time she fell asleep she didn't know, but she knew that she was dreaming, she told herself that she was dreaming. It was a habit she had acquired years ago. When in dreams she was being chased by weird animals and her legs suddenly refused to move, she would comfort herself by shouting, "It's only a dream! it's only a dream!" This was likely an echo of her mother's voice when she would wake her from the nightmares and would say, "It's only a dream, darling. There, there, it's only a dream."

The dream that she was now in had taken on the form of a never-ending nightmare. Sometimes it was Great Leader who was chasing her, and just as the bull's hooves were about to come down on her she would regain the use of her legs, and then once more she was running, bounding into the air. Now it was Sep Watson chasing her, and just as he was clutching at her flying hair, Ralph Batley's hands came out of the air and flung him towards the sea and she watched him toppling over and over down the cliff. And then again she was running, from Ralph Batley this time, and she heard his steps sometimes pounding just behind her, sometimes in the distance, coming and going, coming and going. He wasn't trying to catch her, but like a sheep dog he was pressing her forward to the cliff path. Which ever way she darted there were the footsteps to the right, to the left and behind her. And now she was on the actual cliff path, racing towards its narrow end, knowing that when she reached it she would jump to the cliff to escape her pursuer. It's only a dream . . . it's only a dream! But still she ran, on and on, her heart pounding against her ribs as if it was going to burst. The steps were nearer now, close behind her, and then his hand came on her shoulders and she let out a great cry, yelling, "No! no!"

As the cry escaped her lips she woke to reality more terrifying than the dream for a hand was on her shoulder and, there above her, his face alone looking so gigantic that it seemed to fill the room, was Ralph Batley. As she shrank downwards into the bed in terror he said quietly, "Don't be afraid, wake up."

She remained stiff, staring at him, her eyes fixed wide.

"Are you awake?" He gave a gentle shake to her shoulders.

She blinked now and gasped as she said, "Yes, yes, I'm awake."

"There's nothing to be afraid of." He had straightened up and she saw that he was dressed in only his breeches and his shirt, and this was unbuttoned down the front. "My . . . my mother is ill, I need help. Will you come down?"

"Ill?" She was sitting up now, the covers gathered under her chin. "Yes, I'll come down immediately."

The minute the door had closed on him she sprang out of bed. She was still half-dazed with sleep and the terror of the nightmare, and she groped around for a few minutes before she could find her dressing-gown, but by the time she reached the landing she was wide awake.

Hearing her employer's voice speaking softly in the hall, she ran to the head of the stairs and from there she saw him bending over the couch.

When Linda stood by the couch and looked down at Mrs. Batley she was amazed at the change she saw. Her face was the colour of lint and her eyes seemed to have dropped back into their sockets, in fact there seemed to be no eyes at all behind the closed lids. She seemed to have put on twenty years in a few hours.

Glancing up into Ralph Batley's face, Linda saw no

semblance of the man she remembered from yesterday, and when he beckoned her aside from the couch she moved quietly with him and into the kitchen and there, turning slightly towards her but keeping his eyes averted, he said, "I've phoned the doctor. He won't bring his car across the fields, I'll have to go and meet him." Wetting his lips he added, "I'm very sorry I've had to get you up."

"Under the circumstances I don't expect an apology." Her tone was sharp. Then as she watched him pull his duffle coat from the back of the door she asked more softly, "What is the matter with her?"

She saw him give a little shake of his head and pause for a second with his arm half into his coat as he said, "I don't know." His voice had a frightened note, which sounded odd coming from him. Then he went quickly out into the night, and after looking towards the door for a moment, she returned to the room and to Mrs. Batley's side.

The older woman hadn't moved, and if it hadn't been for a slight, slow rise of the blankets that covered her Linda would have imagined that she had already died.

The collar of her blouse hanging over the edge of the blanket showed her to be still dressed, and this made Linda question the time. She couldn't have gone to bed, and it must be the middle of the night, three o'clock at least!

The grandfather clock on the landing began to strike at that moment and Linda, to her amazement, counted twelve strokes. Only twelve o'clock. She felt as if she had been asleep and in that nightmare for hours and hours.

Mrs. Batley made an almost imperceptible movement and opened her eyes. Slowly she turned her weary gaze towards Linda. "Ralph?" the name was just a faint whisper, and Linda, taking her hand and stroking it

128

gently, said softly, "He won't be a minute, Mrs. Batley, he's just gone to meet the doctor. Lie quiet."

"Girl."

Catching the whisper, Linda bent over Mrs. Batley and said, "Yes, Mrs. Batley, what is it?"

Mrs. Batley stared up into her face for a moment and her lips formed words, but no sound came. She was trying to say something but the effort was too great, and Linda said softly, "Don't worry, just lie quiet. Don't try to talk."

Mrs. Batley's lids slowly closed again and as Linda sat looking at her she thought, Oh, be quick, be quick. He's surely had enough time to get to the road and back again. The doctor mustn't have arrived yet. As the minutes wore on she found herself praying rapidly, beseechingly. Then the back door opened and the next minute Ralph Batley came into the room accompanied by a man who in age and build was not unlike Uncle Shane except that he was clean-shaven.

He gave Linda one searching glance as he came towards the couch, then as he stood gazing down on Mrs. Batley he divested himself of his coat and, throwing it with bad aim towards a chair, he lowered himself slowly on to the side of the couch and, taking up the bloodless looking hand, he said, "Hello there, Maggie."

Mrs. Batley opened her eyes and looked at the doctor, then slowly she closed them again.

After a moment of staring down on her the doctor rose to his feet. He took Ralph Batley by the arm and drew him away from the couch and said quietly, "Can you get her bed downstairs? That room of hers is too far away, she won't stay in it, but if she's down here there's more likelihood of keeping her in bed." He paused, then turned his eyes towards the couch. "And she's going to be in bed for some time, I'm afraid," he ended.

"What is it?"

"I'll tell you better when I've examined her, although I've a good idea already. You can't work an engine night and day, it's got to stop sometime."

Ralph Batley's expression remained the same. The only indication that he was deeply affected was given by his hands. Linda watched as he dug into the cushion of one thumb with the fingers of the other hand.

"Shall I bring it down into the hall?" he asked quietly, referring to the bed.

The doctor glanced round for a moment, then said, "No. No, she'd be in the thick of it here, you wouldn't be able to keep her down. What about the front room? Can you get that warmed up within the next hour or so?"

"Yes, yes, I'll see to that."

"All right then, go on about it and leave her to me."

When he reached Mrs. Batley's side again Linda moved away, he did not seem to require her. Ralph Batley had gone into a room across the hall, it was the sitting-room and had not been used during her stay in the house. He would be lighting the fire, so she must get the bedding down. On this she ran upstairs and into Mrs. Batley's room where the bed was still undisturbed, and stripping it she carried as much of the bedclothes downstairs as her arms could hold. . . .

An hour later a fire was burning brightly in the sitting-room, and not far from it Mrs. Batley was lying in bed, looking worse, if it were possible, than she had done as she lay on the couch. They had transferred her with the least possible fuss, and she still remained in her clothes.

Linda was in the hall when the doctor and Ralph Batley came out of the room, and the doctor was saying quietly, "Well, Ralph, this is no surprise to me, I've been expecting it for the last two years."

Linda saw Ralph Batley rub his lips one over the other before he asked, "But what is it?"

"A number of things. Sheer exhaustion for one thing, a tired heart, a very tired heart. She'll have to be careful. . . ." He came towards the hearth and, taking up his stand with his back to the fire and looking about the room, he said, "It's going to put you in a fix for there's no need for me to tell you she's been doing the work of three women for years. But that's past, you'll have to make other arrangements. . . ."

"I . . . I'll see to that." Ralph Batley broke in, speaking hastily. "But . . . but can you tell me if there is any danger?"

"No, not if she remains quiet and isn't troubled in any way. She's had all the worry she can stand. Anyway, there's one thing you can be thankful for at the moment, you've got help." He glanced towards Linda and gave her a quiet smile. "But I'm afraid that, however willing, one person won't be able to do all she did. But then she wanted it that way, she was always a worker . . . oh, yes." And now he added something that brought the colour, not only to Linda's face but also to Ralph Batley's, for addressing her pointedly he said, "She can give you her orders from the bed and teach you to cook . . . you're not old enough yet to be up to her standard." He paused, staring at her, then added, "Well now, I must be off. I've got two babies just waiting to yell at any minute." He nodded to Ralph Batley as he finished with a laugh. "Shouldn't be surprised if there's a message awaiting me when I get back."

Ralph Batley made no comment on this, he was leading the way towards the kitchen door and it was from there that the doctor turned and said quietly to Linda, "Good night."

"Good night, Doctor."

As she walked towards the sitting-room, her face still hot, she repeated to herself, "She will teach you to cook." In the room she looked at Mrs. Batley. The sleeping tablet was having its effect, her breathing was easier and her face was more relaxed and a little less grey.

The room was lit by a central light and the shade was too bright, it needed something to soften the glare. She remembered she had a green silk headscarf upstairs but it was packed in the trunk. In a matter of minutes she was in her room. Scattering her neatly folded clothes from the trunk she retrieved the scarf and ran downstairs again. After pinning it round the light she brought two cushions from the settee and arranged them in the stiff-backed armchair before settling herself quietly by the fire.

After a while a slight movement in the hall told her Ralph Batley had returned. As he came into the room he glanced at the shaded light before going to the bed and looking at his mother. As if compelled against his will, he turned now towards Linda and beckoned her out of the room.

Rising slowly from the chair she followed him, and when they were a short distance from the sitting-room door he said, "I can manage, you must go to bed."

"I'm not going to bed." Her voice was level. "I can sleep all tomorrow if I want to," she laid slight stress on these words before adding, "whereas you will have to work."

There was a conflict raging within her as she stared into his face. Some part of her was still angry with him, but a greater part, a part that was attempting to envelop her mind, urged, Tell him you'll stay, at least for a time. He looks at his wits' end. But the angry section thrusting its way forward said, And be snubbed for your pains.

"That will be my worry."

There, she said to herself, what did I say.

"I'm sorry." His eyes dropped from hers. "You have been very kind, but . . . but I must stay up tonight in case she wakes and needs me." He turned from her towards the fire, adding under his breath, "If you care, you could sleep on the couch."

"Very well, I'll do that." Her own voice was soft now. "Can I get you anything?"

"No. No, thanks."

A few minutes later she was lying on the couch staring across the space towards the fire. She had not bothered to go upstairs and get a blanket for the room was warm, and so she was surprised in more ways than one when he stood before the couch with a travelling rug in his hands.

"It will get very cold towards dawn in spite of the fire." It seemed for a moment that he was just going to hand the rug to her, and then he shook it out and dropped it gently over her. He did not touch her but he looked at her and she at him, and during the space of time their eyes held something leaped the bridge between them. She felt it in the trembling of her hands and the throbbing of her throat, it was as if a live thing had entered her being. And did she imagine in this instant that his eyes were no longer cold, steel grey, but that there was a deep depth of warmth in them, or was it a trick of the firelight?

He moved away and she pulled the rug close about her and lay staring towards the fire.

Although she lay with her eyes closed she did not sleep, there were so many things to think about, so many things. She heard two o'clock strike, then half-past. It must have been near three o'clock when the sullen glow of the fire that was resting on her closed lids was replaced by darkness, and without opening her eyes she knew that Ralph Batley was at the fireplace making up the fire. She heard the hiss and spit of fresh wood on the embers, then, although she had heard no movement whatever, she felt that he was standing by the side of the couch looking down at her. When after a few seconds there was still no movement, she had a strong desire to open her eyes but repressed it . . . he thought she was asleep, otherwise he wouldn't be standing there. Then she had startling proof of his presence for she heard his breathing distinctly and realised with an inward tremor that his face could not be far from her own. The urge to open her eyes wide and surprise him was overpowering . . . she had never yet seen him at a disadvantage, this would be the moment . . . but she did not move. And then her heart seemed to give a loud bounce which reverberated through her body for he was whispering. Very, very softly, he was saying two words and he repeated them. It was only with the greatest possible effort that she went on feigning sleep, for she wanted to reach out her hands to him and give him an answer to his words, she wanted to say, "It's all right, I won't." A few seconds more and she knew she was alone again and she turned her face into the cushions and in a very short time she was asleep. . . .

It was Shane's agonised voice that woke her. He was saying, "God in heaven! what have I done? She looks like death."

"It wasn't anything to do with you, take a hold of yourself." Ralph Batley's voice was low and harsh. "If there's anyone to blame it's me."

"Oh, boy, what have you done, you've done nothing but work and work."

"That's just it, I couldn't see anything else but work, I couldn't see that she was ill. Doc Morgan says that he's been expecting it for the last two years and there was I, letting her get on with it. Working from Monday morning till Saturday night."

The voices were coming nearer the couch now, making their way towards the fire, and Shane's voice had a tremor in it as he said, "But Maggie's always worked, not just this last year or so."

"Yes, and that's the trouble. But I could have made things easier. I should have made her have that washing-machine and floor-polisher last year when we talked about it."

"Aw, boy, it would have been as she said, they would have been a nice couple of ornaments decorating the kitchen, for she wouldn't have used them."

"That was just a bluff, she didn't want me to spend the money on them."

There followed a silence before Shane said, "Aye . . . aye, well, there might have been something in that. Her main idea was that you should plough every penny back. But what's goin' to happen now? How are we goin' to manage without Maggie?"

Again there was a silence. Then Shane's voice whispered, "There's only Peggy Johnstone who would come up this far, and she's expecting a child any minute now. If only the young girl here . . ."

"Ssh!"

Linda knew that the eyes of the two men were on her and it was quite some time before Shane's whisper came again, "She's still asleep." And then, "Would you have it in your heart to ask her to stay a while?"

There was another space before the answer came. "She wouldn't, not after the way I went for her yesterday, hell for leather."

"But why did you?"

"Oh, I don't know. . . . Seeing her with a Cadwell, it looked for the moment like the old pattern over again. She must have thought I was mad, and I was for a time.

She would never understand the feeling between the Cadwells and us."

"What if I were to ask her?"

"No, I did the damage, the rest is up to me. But look, go and get a wash and I'll see about breakfast."

When they moved away into the kitchen she lay for a moment longer savouring a feeling of power, sweet power. She had not dreamed the two words she had heard in the night. She said them to herself, "Don't go, don't go." But could he, the master in the house, the god in this domain, bring himself openly to apologise to her and ask her to stay? Before she had sat upright on the couch rubbing the sleep from her eyes, she knew that she would not put him to any test . . . enough it was for her to know that she was needed.

Before going upstairs she crept towards the sitting-room door. Mrs. Batley was still asleep. She seemed to have sunk deeply into the bed and her face once more was ashen and old looking.

Then she went swiftly to the kitchen. Ralph Batley was at the stove. He had the pan in his hand and his back towards her, and without any preliminaries she said to him quickly, "Leave that, I'll see to the breakfast in a few minutes. I'm just going to change."

He had only time to turn towards her before she hurried from the room.

She stopped for a moment at the head of the stairs and looked at the clock. It said ten past five. So early! She felt as refreshed as if she had been asleep all night.

It was nine o'clock in the morning. Mrs. Batley had been washed and was now attired in her nightdress, and with Linda supporting her head had just finished drinking a cup of tea. And now, lying back on her pillows, she lifted a hand and clutched weakly at Linda as she moved

136

away from the bed. "I . . . I want . . . will you . . . ?" The words were brought out with a painful effort, and Linda, stroking her hand, said reassuringly, "I know what you want to say. But don't worry, I'm not going to leave you, I'm going to stay on and look after you." And then with a smile she stroked the older woman's hair back from her brow and finished, "The doctor said you've got to teach me to cook and do it from here." She now patted the bed and her smile broadened as she saw the look of utter relief come into Mrs. Batley's face. But when painful tears welled from the corners of the older woman's eyes she said hastily, "Oh, don't cry, Mrs. Batley, everything's going to be all right."

"What's the matter, is she——?" Ralph Batley's voice came from behind her, and without turning Linda said, "She's all right, I was just telling her that I had asked you if I could stay on." She straightened the sheet under Mrs. Batley's chin, then turning to the side table she picked up the cup and saucer and left the room.

She was in the kitchen at the sink when Ralph Batley passed through on his way outside and she did not turn her head in his direction until he spoke to her.

"Thank you," he said.

She looked across the table towards him but could find nothing to say, but the colour swept up to her forehead when he came slowly towards her. In this moment he looked different, entirely different from the man she knew as Ralph Batley. Not only his eyes but his whole face had softened, and it was not hard to imagine that at one time here had been a strikingly handsome man. She could almost see what the face had been like before the flesh had left it to its bony contours. There was even a suspicion of a smile on his face as he said, "This is what is known as heaping coals of fire."

"I did not intend it should be." Her eyes dropped

from his and he said quickly, "I know that, and I want to say now that I'm very grateful to you. Also I'm very sorry for my behaviour yesterday."

Her eyes came up to his and she let her smile envelop him as she said, "Mine wasn't very exemplary either." Then a wonderful thing happened. They laughed together, quietly they laughed together, and when their laughter subsided they were still looking at each other. Slowly she turned to the sink and he to the door.

Through the window she watched him as he strode down the yard and disappeared round the dry-stone wall. Outside the sea fret had soaked the land and darkened the sky, but somehow the morning was very bright.

4

Although Linda's first day as a substitute for Mrs. Batley had been filled with every kind of household chore, plus nursing, there was only one duty of which she would have been pleased to be relieved, it was making Sep Watson's break tea. He had come into the kitchen around ten o'clock and, looking at her closely, he had said, "Sad thing about the missus, ain't it? Worked to death I would say. I've thought it for years."

"Do you want something?" Linda had asked him.

"Aye, me tea." He had given her a twisted grin, and as she put the kettle on the stove he went on as if nothing had interrupted him, saying, "Nobody but a fool would take on running this house on their own, no matter what the bribe."

On this she swung round on him, but with an effort she refrained from making any comment. That's what he wanted, that she should talk to him, argue with him, discuss the family with him—well, she wasn't going to be drawn. So she remained with her gaze fixed on the kettle willing it to boil. And then he said softly, "Hear you had an up and downer with the boss in Morpeth yesterday."

She was round at him before she could stop herself, demanding, "How do you know what happened yesterday?"

"Ah, things get around in these parts. Perhaps it's them seagulls that carries the messages, eh?" He gave his thick laugh, and then he said, "Suits you, the blush. You could do with a bit of colour, among other things." He cast his eyes swiftly over her slim figure.

For a moment she was not afraid of him and she faced him squarely, saying, "If I hear any more of that kind of talk from you I'll report you to Mr. Batley. You know what happened last time."

"What kind of talk? What're you gettin' at? I haven't said nowt, nowt out of the way."

At that moment the back door opened and Shane came in. His glance darting between them, he asked, "Anything wrong?"

"No, nothing." The kettle was boiling and she mashed the tea, and when she pushed the jug across the table towards Sep Watson he looked at her and said with quiet civility, "The missus usually gives me a slice of something."

Going to the pantry Linda cut a slice of meat pie and, putting it none too gently on a plate, she handed it to him.

When the door had closed on the cowman Shane said quietly, "Tell me, what was he saying?"

"Oh, it was nothing, just some silly remark." And then her tone changing, she turned to the old man and said quickly, "I don't like him, Uncle Shane."

"You're not the only one, girl. I wouldn't trust him as far as I could toss him. Be careful of him is my advice to you." He was half-turned from her when he said softly, "Before the subject is closed finally let me say that I'm glad to the heart that you're staying with us. God works in very strange ways. He let me get drunk to act as the last straw to break Maggie's back. Don't you think His ways are strange?" His head was dropped to the side now, and he was looking at her with a side-long glance. And for reply she said, "I'm glad to be staying, Uncle Shane."

By the end of the first week Mrs. Batley was showing signs of improvement and the house had fallen into a new routine, a routine that filled every second of Linda's day. But although her hours were long those of Ralph Batley seemed to be longer, for when she rose at six in the morning he was already up, and when she went to bed towards ten at night he was still busy.

As Mrs. Batley began to recover there came a slight feeling of gaiety over the house. The hall had on more than one occasion been filled with high laughter. That the laughter was against her, Linda did not mind in the least. Her first efforts at baking the bread had not been the roaring success that she had imagined it would be. Following Mrs. Batley's instructions it had sounded easy. But the reason why her loaves refused to rise became evident when Ralph Batley picked up a basin from a side table in the kitchen and, after smelling it, he looked over the rim of the basin at her and said softly, "This is the yeast. I think it should have gone in the dough." That was one of the occasions when they had laughed, and Linda thought that the wasted batch of bread was a small payment for the look on Ralph Batley's face, for his laughter seemed to transform him.

There was only one incident that brought a sad note to the new atmosphere. Jess had died and Michael had cried bitterly. Not even the knowledge that another sheep dog, and a retriever pup, were to become members of the farm as soon as his uncle could drive over to Elsdom Farm, which lay beyond Morpeth, seemed to bring him any consolation.

That Linda had not been out of the house for a week did not trouble her. The weather had been vile, squalls of rain and winds that could cut through you weren't any inducement to be about the farm. But the weather today, like a capricious woman, was showing its other side. The sun was bright, even warm where it came through the kitchen window, and Linda had a sudden longing to take a walk just along the cliff.

The sun must have stimulated the same idea in the minds of Mrs. Batley and her son, for some time during the morning Mrs. Batley, looking anxiously at Linda when she brought her a drink, said, "You look peaked, girl, you've lost your colour. Look, the sun's shining, go on out for a while, just a walk round."

"This morning?" Linda looked at her in mock amazement. "And the dinner to see to? Would you have taken a walk round in the middle of the morning?"

Mrs. Batley shook her head slowly. "No, lass, but I can see now things would have been better if I had done. I should have let up a bit."

"Well, things will be different when you get up, you can rest assured of that." Linda bounced her head towards her.

"I feel sometimes that I'll never get up again. It's a dreadful feeling."

"Oh, of course you will, you're much better, so much better."

"I feel so weak"—Mrs. Batley shook her head slowly— "like a child. I wouldn't have believed that I could have lost my strength like this." Then looking towards Linda she said, "What I would have done without you, girl, I just don't know. What would have happened to them?"

"Something would have turned up, it always does. There now, drink your milk."

As Linda was moving from the room Mrs. Batley called after her, "But you must get out, I'll see Ralph."

Linda turned quickly to her. "No, no. Please don't say anything to him. I'll go out if I want to, never worry."

But before Mrs. Batley could see her son, he, too, spoke to Linda on the same matter. She was setting the

142

table for the lunch when he passed through the hall on his way to see his mother, and he stopped and looked at her before saying, "Shane's going to stay in for a couple of hours this afternoon so that you can take a walk."

"But I don't want to walk." And now that she was being pressed she felt that she didn't.

"You've never been across the door this week and we won't get many more days like this. I think you should. I'm merely being selfish as always. If anything should happen to you I'd be sunk."

The look on his face did not match the self-centredness of his words, and Linda, dropping her gaze from him as she moved round the table setting out the cutlery, said, "Very well, I'll go out for a little while."

He stood for a moment longer, his eyes hard on her, before going towards the sitting-room and his mother, and he left her feeling strangely happy.

Although the day was one the northern winter has rarely to offer, with the atmosphere perfectly clear and the air as bracing as spring water, although the view from the cliff path was magnificent, the coastline could be seen for miles winding away in a rugged curve, Linda was finding no joy in it. To the right of her lay the moors, great stretches of land with touches of brown that spoke of past glories of heather. She had passed the Batley boundary some time ago and had been walking for at least an hour, yet had seen no one, not even in the distance. The scenery was grand and rugged, but it was lonely. You needed someone with you to enjoy it, someone to combat the solitariness that cried aloud up here. She had a sudden longing to be back in the warm atmosphere of the farm kitchen, and immediately she began

143

to retrace her steps, taking now a left-hand path which shut out the lonely grandeur of the coastline.

The path led further inland than she had imagined, and when she came in sight of the boundary wires she realised that she wasn't far from the road. It was as she was passing the crop of rock near where the sheep had broken through the wire, which was the only part of this side of the Batley boundary open to the road, that she heard the sound of horses hooves. The rider, she thought, could be anyone from around here, but it could also be one of the Cadwell men, perhaps Rouse Cadwell. She stopped for a moment and remained in the shelter of the rocky hillock. The sound of the hooves came nearer, but slower now. When the rider came into view and she saw the head and shoulders of the elder Cadwell man, she was more than thankful she had kept out of sight. She pressed herself against the rock and from her slanted vision she could see his head. He was looking up and down the road. Then she saw him bend forward towards the high bank as if he were going to pick something up, or put something down. A minute later he galloped off.

When the sound of the hooves had faded away Linda went tentatively towards the bank. She did not trust the Cadwell man, she never had. Above the spot where she had seen him lean forward she examined the wire. It was only a few yards from where Ralph Batley had fixed the new strands, but there was no sign of a break in the wire now. Why had he stopped here at this spot, and what was he picking up from the bank? She leant well over the wire, looking up and down the grassy slope but all she saw, that was not of nature, was a crumpled piece of paper. It was as if someone had thrown it away, but the fact that it was wedged in a small hole at the back of a root of hawthorn she found rather curious. Lying flat now along the bank, she put her arm under the wire and found she could just reach the hole. When she withdrew her hand she was staring in amazement at a crumpled five-pound note. Her eyes moved in the direction the rider had taken. Five-pound notes didn't wedge themselves in holes. Her mind began to race. If what she was thinking was right, this money would be collected later this evening around quarter-past five. But no, Sep Watson couldn't be as vile as that, working for the Cadwells against a family who had employed him for most of his life. But her instinct told her that the cowman could be as vile as that, and she remembered back to the morning when, practically on this very spot, Ralph Batley had questioned the man as to how he had known the sheep were out. She remembered that his answers had made her uneasy then, but she had taken the matter no further in her mind.

Gone now was the idea of sauntering back to the farm. She set off at a run and didn't stop until she came within sight of the farm buildings. But it wasn't these that brought her running to a walk, it was the sight of a burly figure filling the archway in the high brick wall. Although she could not see his face she knew that the man was Sep Watson, and although she had just caught sight of him she knew, too, he could have been watching her for some time, for from where he was standing he could see the hills beyond the valley. She told herself quickly that he could gauge nothing from her running, but even as she thought this she was reminded of his cunning. He might be dull-witted but he was like a fox, wary, and nothing escaped him. She did not go towards the archway but walked now with seeming casualness towards the front of the house and knew a great measure of relief when she saw the jeep in the yard. This meant Ralph Batley had returned from taking the milk down to the bay. Yet, as far as she could see, there was no sign of him

145

about the buildings. But as she made her way up the yard to the farm kitchen she heard his voice, and the high laugh of Michael.

As she opened the kitchen door Michael ran to her with a cry, saying, "Oh! you're back. Uncle was saying he was going to send a search party for you, it's getting dark."

Ralph Batley had his back towards her and he didn't turn and chide his nephew for chattering. He went on pouring the boiling water into the teapot. It could have been that she had never entered the kitchen.

"Can I speak with you a minute?"

He turned his head quickly in her direction. His face had a quiet look—she nearly put the word contented to it. Yet no, that didn't suit his expression. He looked now at the boy and said, "Go and fetch Uncle Shane, he'll be in the shed."

Michael hesitated for a second, and then his desire to be with Linda dared him to make a protest in the form of saying, "But Uncle Shane's just gone out."

To save the boy from the sharp reprimand that was coming to him, Linda said quickly, "I won't be a minute, I just want to have a word with your uncle. There's a good boy, go on." She opened the door and pressed him outside, and when she closed it again and turned to her employer he was standing at the far side of the table, waiting for her to speak. And she did so rapidly, as if she was still running. Without any lead-up she said, "I've seen something. It's very odd, but near the wire where it was cut the other day, where the sheep got through, I saw . . ." She now paused and lowered her gaze from him for a second before continuing quickly, "Mr. Cadwell. He was riding by and stopped near the bank. I was curious. I saw him bend down as if he was picking something up, and when he was gone I looked at the bank and I saw

146

something in a hole, a piece of paper. It was—" she paused again, "it was a five-pound note."

Although her employer was looking straight at her Linda knew he wasn't seeing her, and she closed her eyes for a moment to shut out the changed countenance of the man before her, for it was the face she had seen as he stood on the bank a few mornings ago ready to spring on the elder Cadwell man. She saw his Adam's apple move rapidly twice, and then he said, "You're sure of this?"

"Sure? Of course I am. I had it in my hand, a five-pound note."

"What did you do with it?"

"I put it back. I feel . . . I feel. . . ." She turned her head to the side. She thought that she knew how her employer regarded his cowhand, and yet, what if she were wrong?

"What do you feel?" His voice was hard, as if she was in some way to blame for what she was telling him.

Her head came round. "I feel it will be collected . . . and soon."

"Yes. How soon?"

"About quarter-past five."

He stared hard at her for a moment before swinging away from the table. "My God! He's been in our employ for years. He's a funny customer, I know, but not that bad. And yet." He turned and faced her again, saying slowly now, a puzzled note in his voice, "It would all add up. . . . Everything. But why should he do it?"

"I don't know. Money, I should think, and spite."

"Yes, and spite. It's odd, but for some reason I haven't got to the bottom of, he's always hated me."

She watched him draw in a long, deep breath. Then looking quickly at his watch, he said, "You say it's near the wire?"

"Yes."

"Where were you?"

"Behind that crop of rocks."

He nodded, then said, "Look, carry on as if nothing had happened. Go for the milk. Could you keep him occupied until I get out, just for a few minutes, he mustn't see me. I've got to get to the bottom of this, and if I do I may get to the bottom of everything that has happened to this farm for years. Everything. I may catch the servant of the jinx, and my God, if I do he'll need someone to pray for him." His voice held a deep, threatening quality, his face was dark with passionate anger. And now he added rapidly, "Don't tell my mother anything of this."

"No, no, of course not."

"Go on then. Take the can for the milk, it will be nothing unusual at this time. Try to keep him occupied for a moment or two until I get along the top. Will you do that?"

The last was a question, a little softer now, and it conveyed that he knew how distasteful to her the request was.

For answer she picked up the big shining can from the dresser and went out.

When she entered the dairy there was no sign of Sep Watson, for from the side door she could see the full length of the cowshed. What should she do now? Michael . . . she would pretend she was going in search of Michael. Yet how would she keep the man in conversation? She had never spoken voluntarily to him from the first day she had been here. Wood. . . .Yes, wood. She would ask him if he would bring a load of wood to the house before he left off work, and that should be any minute now. She hurried out into the yard again and towards the byre where Sarah and her calf were housed. But there was still no sign of the cowman or Michael.

It was Michael's voice that at last indicated where Sep Watson was, and she was led towards the big barn. As she stood in the doorway she saw Michael standing in front of the cowman. The cowman was looking down on him, but as Linda came in through the open doorway they both turned towards her. Linda spoke to the boy first as if she hadn't seen him for some time. "I've been looking for you, Michael," she said, "your tea's ready. Did you find Uncle Shane?"

"No, no." Michael's voice was high and excited. "I'm looking now. I was . . . I was asking Sep."

Sep Watson was now looking towards Linda, and not taking his eyes from her, he spoke to the boy. His voice was quiet and ordinary sounding and did not match the look on his face. "Your Uncle Shane was in the store the last time I saw him." Before the cowman had finished speaking Michael had darted away out into the yard and Linda was left alone facing the man.

As he stood staring at her, not speaking, Linda told herself not to be afraid, there was nothing he could do. Ralph Batley had asked her to play for time and that's what she must do. She said, "We're down on wood. I wonder if you'd bring a load in?"

Slowly he stepped towards her until there was not more than two feet between them, and then he repeated her words. "You want me to bring some wood in?"

Linda swallowed and put her hand gropingly behind her and touched the wall of the barn for support, and she endeavoured to bring a coolness into her tone as she said, "Yes, that's what I said. Bring some wood in."

"Why d'you want me to bring wood in? You've never asked me afore."

"Well, I'm asking you now."

"Aye, you are, and why are you asking me? If I didn't know I'd be puzzled. I'd say to meself, 'Why is this hoity-

149

toity madam stooping to speak to me?' That's what I would say to meself, there must be a reason for it. But I've got no need to ask you, I know the reason." As his lips closed on the last word his great hands shot out and gripped her shoulders, bringing an involuntary scream from her lips. "Go on, have a damn good scream, nobody'll hear you. You've settled your own hash. Old Shane went off to the north side after a heifer not ten minutes gone, and you, you know what you've done? You've got rid of your protector. Aye! Aye!" His voice was high in his head, soft and high and terrifying. Linda's eyes were fixed on him with the hypnotic stare of a trapped rabbit. Her limbs seemed paralysed, even the terror that was filling her now could not galvanize her into any action. "He's running hell for leather up to the road to catch somebody out, isn't he? You must have seen something that wasn't meant for you to see this afternoon. You came back running like a scalded cat over the hills, I watched you. I wondered at the time, and then the bairn's just told me the reason. Aye, the bairn was listening in. Bairns are funny things, aren't they? You generally get the truth out of bairns. Michael's just told me his uncle's gone up to the top boundary to catch a man who's going to get some money that's been left there. Bairns cause a lot of trouble, don't they? You!" The cowman's voice suddenly turned to a deep growl. "You sneaking little heifer! For two pins I'd throttle you." His hands were round her throat, she couldn't have screamed now if she had wanted to. His body was pressed against her, his hot, smelling breath was over her face, his squat nose was almost touching hers and his eyes, like pinpoints of fire, were boring through her head. And he hissed at her now, "I'm finished here. I've known it was comin' anyway. It makes no difference, I can get a job anywhere, but I like doin' things in me own way. I don't take to being stumped by a long-legged bitch like you. An' I'm tellin' you now, you're a goner be sorry afore you're very much older that you crossed me. By God! you are. When I'm finished with you, me dear, you'll wish you had kept on the right side of Sep Watson. Come here!" As one arm went round her his other hand clapped over her mouth, and she felt herself lifted bodily from her feet. And at this moment she came to life—struggling, kicking, shrieking life. But the shrieks could not get past the grip of his hand. She fought and kicked as he carried her up the length of the barn and round behind the end bales, and there with a jerk of his arm as if he was throwing a bullock off its feet, he flipped her flat on her back. For a moment she was sickened and stunned by the fall, then in a frenzy of terror she was fighting him, kicking, rearing, struggling. When for a second his hand was pulled from her mouth the compressed screams that were filling her body escaped, but only for a moment, for his hand now gripped her face as if he meant to crush the bones. And a wild terror enveloped her when the wind was knocked clean out of her body with the weight that fell upon it, and for a second everything went black about her. The next moment a light that seemed as bright as the sun pierced the darkness and the weight was lifted from her, and she lay dizzy and sick, conscious only of a struggle and gasping breaths at her side. A volley of curses in a terrible Irish voice told her now that it was Uncle Shane who was fighting like a madman with the cowman. She turned off her back on to her side and was attempting to rise when she was knocked flying across the floor into a bale of straw. And she knew that it was Uncle Shane's body that had been hurled against her. She way lying on her face now, and as she felt the old man struggling gallantly to his feet amid a flood of oaths Sep Watson's voice came to her again, but now it was directed towards the old man.

"Stay where you are, if you get off your knees I'll knock you flat. I'm tellin' you mind." There was a scrambling sound by her side and then Sep Watson's voice crying, "Well, you asked for it."

Drawing her head into her shoulders she waited, expecting the old man to come thundering to the ground, but instead her dazed mind became aware of a new sound, a strange sound, as of feet dancing on the wooden floor of the barn. This was followed by the thick sound of blows, of deep gasping breaths. Uncle Shane couldn't be standing up to Sep Watson like that, couldn't be pounding him like that. She turned slowly on to her side again and there, in the weird light of the lantern that Uncle Shane had stood near the wall of the barn, she saw, with overwhelming relief, the figure of Ralph Batley. He looked gigantic and even terrible as his fists pistoned in and out as they contacted the cowman. Sep Watson, she saw, was returning blow for blow. It seemed that the cowman did not feel the hammering fists. The weirdness of the scene was increased by the silence of the combat, only the sound of the blows and the quick intake of breaths filled the barn. She was aware now of Uncle Shane standing near her, he had pulled himself up and was resting with his back against the bale of hay, the blood was running from the corner of his mouth. Linda now put her hand to her face as she saw Ralph Batley stagger backwards and almost fall as the ox-like arms flayed about him. As she covered her eyes there came the sound of a blow as if a piece of wood had suddenly split. When fearfully she opened her eyes wide again, it was to see Sep Watson lying on the ground.

Like a boxer trying to recover the cowman got to his hands and knees and shook his head, and then slowly pulled himself to his feet again. But he did not put up his fists, instead, with lowered head, he looked upwards at his master and said thickly, "I'll hev you for this, you'll see."

"Get out while you're whole. . . . Go on, get!" Ralph Batley spoke to the man as he would not have done to an animal, and as the cowman stumbled towards the door of the barn he added, "If I see you on my land again . . ." He didn't finish but turned swiftly now towards his uncle and Linda.

"You all right, Uncle?"

"Yes, yes, I'm all right. Just a split lip. Nothing, nothing. Here a minute, here a minute." The old man pulled his nephew aside and said something to him in an undertone.

Linda was now sitting with her back towards the bales. She felt, as she put it to herself, slightly odd. All the strength had gone out of her body; she had a great desire to cry. When her employer's hands came down to her she put hers into them, but was unable to pull herself from the ground. She knew she was beginning to tremble, and again she wanted to cry. Her head drooped forward and when his hands came under her arms and raised her gently to her feet, she said, "It's all right, it's all right." And then she knew it wasn't all right, her legs were going to give way, and she added hastily, "I must sit, I must sit down." But there was nowhere to sit and she hung on to his arm.

"Are you . . . are you hurt?" His voice was quiet.

She did not answer for a moment, she felt sore and bruised all over, and she dare not trust herself to speak. Her one desire at the moment was to cry, cry with relief at the escape she had had.

"Look at me." His voice was soft, even gentle. "Linda,

look at me. Did he . . . ? Uncle Shane said . . . Tell me what happened."

He had called her Linda, but she did not even comment to herself about it. At the moment it had no effect on her, she only wanted to cry and he didn't like crying. She managed to gasp, "No, no," before the storm of tears overwhelmed her. She was hardly aware that she was being held in his arms, her head pressed into his shoulder, or that his voice was saying in the endearing terms he had used to Sarah, "My dear, my dear." She was only aware that she was crying as she had never cried in her life before, and she felt she would never stop.

She knew he was carrying her across the yard, but she felt no wonder in it. And then she was sitting in a chair by the kitchen table, and she didn't seem to care at the moment what happened for she dropped her head on to the table and sobbed into the crook of her arm.

"Drink this. Come along, stop crying. Now stop crying. Do you hear? You'll make yourself ill."

Her head was brought up from the table by his sharp tone, but she did not look at him, nor attempt to take the glass from his hand.

"Drink it up, all of it." He put the brandy to her mouth, and at the first swallow she coughed and spluttered over his hand. It was the spluttering that pulled her to herself—she was being stupid, she must pull herself together. She drew in slow, deep breaths of air, then she lifted her head and murmured, "I'm all right now."

When his hand came out towards her and smoothed the rumpled hair from her forehead she became quiet inside. It was a quiet threaded with a single thread, a thread of wonder, a thread that she recognised must have very gentle handling or it would snap. She tried to clear her mind, to deal with a new situation. She managed to

154

put matters on to a commonplace footing by asking, "How . . . how did you get back so soon? Did you——?"

It was now Ralph Batley's turn to avoid her eyes, and he turned from her as he did so, saying, "I'll never really know. It's strange, but I thought I heard the conch shell."

"The conch shell?" She was looking enquiringly at his back.

"It's a superstition attached to the house. It goes that danger is imminent to one of the family if they hear the sound of the conch shell. Isn't that so, Shane?"

Shane was at the sink dabbing his mouth with a damp cloth, and he nodded towards Linda, saying, "Yes, that's so." Then looking at his nephew, he asked, "You heard it, boy, you sure you heard it?"

"Well, I came back. I was on my way to trap Watson."

"To trap Watson? What about?"

Ralph Batley, speaking tersely and somewhat wearily, went on to explain to Shane what had occurred, and ended, "I think we'd better get cleaned up." He looked down at the tear in his coat, and touched his jaw bone tenderly before adding, "And remember, not a word to my mother." He cast a look between Linda and his uncle, and bringing everything back to normal with a bump, he now said, "We'll have to get out a new schedule, it's going to be time and a half for all of us."

"Yes, aye, it will that. Well, I'd better go into Maggie and tell her I fell over me own feet and greeted a wall." Shane smiled wryly. "I'll have to tell her something to account for this." As he was about to leave the kitchen he turned to his nephew and asked quietly, "Is there anything left in that bottle, Ralph?"

"Help yourself, Uncle." Ralph Batley's voice was quiet and his uncle's reply had a grateful note as he said, "Thanks boy, thanks boy."

They were alone together in the kitchen now and it

seemed to Linda that they both were uneasily aware of the other. She shivered just the slightest when he came and stood in front of her.

"It was strange about the conch shell, wasn't it?"

Her heart began to pound. "Yes, yes, it was strange."

They were looking at each other. She had her head tilted slightly back when his hand once again touched her brow and smoothed her hair. The shiver became a tremble when he lifted a strand of hair behind her ear.

"Sit still while I get the tea."

She sat quite still when he turned away. Even if she had felt like helping him, which she didn't, she would still have obeyed him. The effect of Sep Watson's attack had taken all her strength from her, and now she seemed weakened still further by this feeling. It was as if the thread of wonder had begun to restrict the beating of her heart.

5

It was at the skin-shivering hour of five o'clock the following morning, in obedience to the sound of an alarm clock, that Linda pulled herself out of bed. It was the same clock that had for years aroused Mrs. Batley. With half-closed eyes and chattering teeth she dressed herself, finding as she did so the soreness in her back and her right hip where she had hit the ground when Uncle Shane had been hurled against her.

Although she had still been somewhat unnerved when she came to bed, she had worked out what was to be her routine. She would rise early as Mrs. Batley had done, get through the household chores, then go to the dairy and try her hand at making the butter, and also help in any way she could with the outside work, because she realised that until they got another hand it would be almost a round-the-clock job for Ralph Batley and Uncle Shane. But when, a short time later, she descended the stairs and saw the lamp turned up and a fire blazing high, she blinked her eyes questioningly—she had heard no movement in the house.

When she entered the kitchen Ralph Batley turned from a stooped position over the stove and asked somewhat sharply, "Why are you up at this time?"

She watched him jerk his hand away from the spluttering steam of the kettle, which he lifted on to the hob of the fireplace, before she answered him, and then it was with a question, "Have you been up all night?"

"No, of course not." He put the teapot on the table.

"How is your mother?"

"Oh." He paused as he pulled the cups towards him. "Still asking questions. She doesn't believe uncle hit a brick wall, or that I tore my knuckles on the barbed wire, nor yet that you came back from your walk suffering from a bilious attack. You can hardly expect her to. The fact that something was amiss was clinched in her mind when she saw that Michael had been crying."

He handed Linda her cup, and as they drank their tea there was quiet between them. Mrs. Batley, Linda knew, was no fool. She herself had thought it would have been wiser to tell her the truth, for she would only question Michael later, and he was bound to confess to her his part in the affair of yesterday, as he had done to his uncle last night. The boy had apparently witnessed the fight in the barn and in some vague way had felt himself responsible for it. This had caused him to hide in the byre with Sarah. When Ralph Batley had found him there, it hadn't taken much questioning to make him reveal that he had listened to what Linda had been saying and had run to tell the cowman the exciting news.

Linda was only half-way through her cup of tea when her employer thrust his arms into his coat preparatory to going out. He had his back to her and she expected him as was usual to leave the kitchen without any formal word of farewell, this was five o'clock in the morning, yet she wasn't surprised when he turned towards her. Not only turned, but came towards her, until he was not more than a bent arm's distance from her. Then he said quietly, "I never asked how you were."

"I'm feeling all right, just a bit stiff in the hip."

His hands were hanging by his side, he was looking straight at her and the expression in his eyes was familiar, she had seen it in those of Michael. He said now very quietly, "You must try to take it easy today."

"Yes . . . yes, I will."

They were still looking at each other, then so quick was the movement that she almost jumped back in fright for his arms seemed to spring upwards, and the next minute she was enfolded in them, pressed close to him, hard against him, painfully hard, with her face against the coarse fibre of his coat. If she had wanted to return the embrace she would have found it impossible, for her arms were pinioned. She had no time to think or react for within a second she was back as she was. He had released her as quickly as he had taken her to him, and when she found herself standing alone in the kitchen she put one hand to her throat and with the other supported herself against the edge of the table. Her heart seemed to be bounding painfully and joyfully upwards, she could feel it under her hand as she gripped her throat. It was as if it was trying to escape, bound out into freedom. Minutes passed while her mind went galloping into the future, until with a quick movement of her head and a lifting of her shoulders she pushed the joy down, saying, "Don't be silly," and she remembered, as she spoke to herself, the look on his face that was similar to Michael's. Michael's face expressed loneliness, deep loneliness, and his uncle was lonely too. That was it. With a sudden tired movement she sat down in the chair near the table and, looking towards the fire, she asked herself, Would she pander to his loneliness? She remembered last night he had said, "My dear . . . my dear," and he had also called her Linda. But she also remembered that he had talked like that to the cow. "My dear . . . my dear," he had said to Sarah. Could she take these endearments as a sign of love? She had last night because she wasn't herself, but in her right mind she was no stupid, fanciful girl. A man, and a man of Ralph Batley's calibre, did not love lightly. She had seen his face black with pas-

159

sionate rage, she knew that he could hate, and she felt that his love would be of equal intensity. So, because a few moments ago he had held her in his arms, she would not allow herself to imagine that this was the beginning of a passionate love for her. No, like Michael he was lonely and lost and she was the only young female thing near. She thought of the upper barn, the locked door, the love-nest as Sep Watson had called it, and she rose to her feet. If the loss of his loved one still had the power to embitter him so much, she couldn't see that he would be able to gather even a sediment to offer to anyone else. She looked towards the fire. She liked playing mother to Michael, would she like playing mother to Ralph Batley? If it was to be that or nothing, what would she do? She bit on her lip but did not give herself an answer; instead she started on the chores of the house. There was work to be done, lots of it, and such things would have to wait until she had time to give them thought. At least, so she told herself at this unromantic hour of the morning.

It was five hours and a lot of work later that Linda, pausing to take a breath, said to herself, "Well now, that's all done, the dinner's all ready and everything, I'll just take Mrs. Batley her milk in and then I'll go." Go, in this case, meant to the dairy. She took up the tray and went swiftly across the hall and into the front room, and an exclamation escaped her on the sight of Mrs. Batley sitting up on the side of the bed, her dressing-gown pulled round her.

"Oh, Mrs. Batley, you're not to get up."

"Now girl, say nothing. I'm up and I'm going to stay up. You fetch me me clothes, you know me skirt and blouse, you know me everyday things."

"No, Mrs. Batley, I'm going to do no such thing." Linda put the tray down. "If you don't get back into bed

I'll go for—" she almost said Ralph, but ended with "Mr. Batley."

"It's no good, I'm going to stay up. Things are not right, I know they're not right."

"Everything's going smoothly, Mrs. Batley. Please go back to bed."

Mrs. Batley did not answer, and Linda saw by the expression on her face that she was determined to have her way. She also saw that she looked more ill than she had done yesterday. Leaving the room without another word, she ran across the hall through the kitchen and out into the yard and into the cow byres.

"Mr. Batley! Mr. Batley!" There was no answer to her call. She came into the yard again and called, "Uncle Shane!" But there was no answer to this either. Uncle Shane would be up in the top field. Where Michael was she did not know . . . likely following his uncle. Perhaps Ralph Batley had gone up to the top boundary to test the wire. After last night's business anything could happen. She felt that Sep Watson would stop at nothing in the way of spiteful revenge. She ran towards the high stone wall and the archway, and she had no sooner come through the archway than she saw the figure of a man crossing the field from the main road. But it was neither Ralph Batley, Uncle Shane nor yet Sep Watson. It was with a thrill almost of horror that she recognised the man coming towards her as Rouse Cadwell. Her instinct was to turn and run, but she couldn't, he had seen her, he had even lifted up his hand in salute. She looked behind her into the yard again. This was awful. On top of all that had taken place, if Ralph Batley was confronted with a Cadwell again there would be trouble. It was this thought that drove her towards him. But whatever approach she had expected him to make, jocular or otherwise, she was surprised by the abruptness of his voice when he said immediately, "Where is he . . . Batley?"

She was nonplussed as she stood looking at him and stammered in her reply. "Mr. B—B—Batley? I don't know. I was looking for him myself. He's not about."

She moved her head in the direction of the farmyard but did not take her eyes off him.

"Haven't you any idea? Is he down in the Bay?"

"No, no, he can't be down in the Bay, he's likely on the land somewhere."

He looked behind him towards the valley, and as he did so she moved a step nearer and appealed to him beseechingly as if the Batley family were her own kin and, as such, their concerns dear to her heart. "What is it? What's happened? Mrs. Batley's ill, there's been enough trouble. Is it about Sep Watson?"

He brought his head sharply to her. "Sep Watson" It was a question and she knew he had been surprised by the name. "What about Sep Watson?" She shook her head and said, "Oh! I thought that was why you had come."

"No, I haven't come about Sep Watson. You wouldn't understand, but I must see Batley. By the way, where's old Shane?"

"I don't know, I can't find him either."

He made a tut-tutting sound, then added, "Well, I'd better go and look for one of them."

She was about to say, "No, please, please wait," when her head was jerked round in the direction of the fells to the left, and there coming over the brow of the last hill was her employer. She saw him stop, stop dead. She could not see his face but her imagination gave her a good idea of what its expression would be like, and she almost groaned to herself.

Rouse Cadwell had also seen Ralph Batley but he did

not now move towards him, he simply stood waiting for the other man to come up.

In the comparatively short time that Linda had been at Fowler Hall she had seen a variety of emotions expressed in her employer's countenance, mostly strong, tearing, unhappy emotions, but she had never seen such a look as was on his face now. It was so cold, so full of what could only be described as hate, that she turned her eyes away from him, for although his gaze was now directed at Rouse Cadwell it had been full on her for the space of ten strides, and she was shivering as if from the impact of a blow.

It was Rouse Cadwell who spoke first. His voice was harsh and yet there could be detected a placating note in it as he said, "Don't start, I just want a minute with you. I want to talk to you."

"What can you talk to me about that I don't already know?"

Rouse Cadwell looked at Ralph Batley for a moment and his lips took a rather scornful lift as he said, "You don't let up on yourself or anybody else, do you, ever? There are some things that you don't know and that's why I'm here." He now looked towards Linda, then turning his gaze back to Ralph Batley he said quietly, "I'd better speak with you alone."

Linda watched her employer's eyes lift towards her and the bitterness in his voice hurt her as he said, "Let her stay, by all means let her stay."

Now Rouse Cadwell gave a short laugh as he answered "You're on the wrong tack as always, Batley, but since you don't mind who hears my news, here it is. . . . Our Bruce is home and he's in a dangerous mood, he's looking for Edith."

The look of amazement that swept over Ralph Batley's face seemed to wipe out the dark suspicious blackness for a moment. She saw him mouth a word, perhaps it was the name Edith, but no sound came from his lips.

"Is she here?"

"What!" The word had a cracking sound as if a whip had been flicked.

"Well, she disappeared a week ago. He found out she came north, this way in fact." Rouse Cadwell paused, then went on with harsh quietness, "If you're shielding her, Batley, you'd better think again. Get rid of her if you don't want murder done, for I'm telling you he'll come up. . . ."

"And I'm telling you"—Ralph Batley's voice was thundering now—"let him put a step inside my boundary and there'll be murder done. You tell him that, d'you hear?"

"I came in good faith, I thought you'd better be warned."

"Good faith!" Ralph Batley almost spat in the younger man's face. "Could ever a Cadwell keep good faith? Five-pound bribes left in holes for Watson. Well, you can tell your father he'll have to find other means with which to do me down, for his henchman's gone."

"What are you talking about? The old man may have his faults but he wouldn't pay Watson to do his dirty work."

"No? Ask him then. There was a five-pound note stuffed in a hole in my boundary bank last night, it isn't there this morning. . . . Now get going."

In this moment Linda felt sorry for Rouse Cadwell, she felt he had come as a friend. She watched his jaw tighten, she watched him bite down on the retort he was about to make, she watched him turn swiftly away and stride towards the gate. When she looked back at her employer his eyes were on her but they were no longer accusing—at least he knew that she hadn't come out to meet Rouse Cadwell—but his face was wearing the tight-closed look she had seen on it the first time she met him. She said quietly, "I was looking for you. Your mother's up, she insists on staying up, she doesn't look well. I thought I'd better find you."

He blinked and jerked his head once as if to bring his thoughts back from a far place, and he repeated, "Up?" Then he strode towards the archway and Linda followed him, her eyes on his back. . . .

An hour later Mrs. Batley was sitting propped up in a big chair to the side of the fireplace in the hall, and Linda was once more alone with her employer in the kitchen, but the atmosphere, unlike what it had been at five o'clock this morning, was tense and strained. The kitchen door was closed and he was speaking in a low voice, "You'll say nothing about this; you'll give her no hint of what Rouse Cadwell said."

"Of course not, why should I?" Her voice was cool and impersonal.

"I'm asking you because if she gets wind of this matter she'll become greatly upset." He paused. "You understand?"

She had her eyes on him as she inclined her head slowly downwards. "I understand." There was a sick feeling in her chest, she felt weary, tired. Early this morning, even with a heavy day's work in front of her, she had felt fit to cope, but now all she wanted to do was sit down, sit down and think. Her mind at this point said, Think that he meant something when he took you in his arms? Don't forget you told yourself then that you knew it meant nothing, he was just lonely. Well, nothing has changed, he's still lonely and he's still in love. Get that into your head, he's still in love with that woman, that Edith, and from what Rouse Cadwell says, she's back. She turned from him saying, "You needn't worry, I'll say nothing to distress your mother. I think you should realise that."

"I do, I do." His voice was now deep and unsteady. "But you don't know what it could mean to her if she. . . ." The words trailed off and she turned and looked at him again, saying quickly now, "Your mother won't hear of anything through me that might hurt her, you can rest assured on that point. If that's all you've got to worry about then your mind can be at rest." She knew that her tone was curt, she meant it to be curt. She turned from his troubled gaze and went out of the kitchen and into the hall, thinking that it was a great pity Mrs. Batley had taken ill when she did. If that hadn't happened she would have been gone from this place and would have been saved a heartbreak that was only at its beginning.

The storm came up about teatime, preceded as storms usually are by a stillness and heavy sky, and it was not long before every member in Fowler Hall knew that they were in for a night of it. By eight o'clock the rain was hitting the windows with the force of machine-gun bullets, and the wind screaming round the house seemed bent on tearing it from its very foundations. Uncle Shane, coming into the kitchen on a blast of wind, forced the door closed and stood with his shoulder to it as he pushed home the bolt. Linda, turning from the stove where she had been stirring a pan of broth, looked towards the old man, and it did not need any close scrutiny on her part to see that he was very tired, almost exhausted.

"Do . . . do you think you could come and brave it and give us a hand, Linda?" The old man's voice sounded hoarse and cracked. "The cattle are uneasy. One of us has got to stay with Sarah, we've had to put her calf in a separate box, just in case she might hurt her in her trampling. She never liked storms and now you can hear her almost above the wind. Would you mind very much staying with her for a while, there's a light there. We've got our work cut out in the big byre. It isn't the cattle there, it's the roof, although they are kicking up enough shindy."

"Yes, yes, of course, Uncle Shane. Look, have a cup of soup before you go out and I'll just tell Mrs. Batley. There"—she scooped a bowl of broth from the pan— "you can give yourself a minute to have that." As she left the kitchen she added, "Michael needn't go to bed for a time yet, he's frightened anyway, he'll be much better staying with his grandmother."

Linda was gone from the kitchen for a matter of minutes. When she returned Shane was no longer there, but the soup bowl was empty. Swiftly she got into her duffle coat. Once outside she thrust a piece of wood through the handle of the door to keep it from being blown open. It was when she left the shelter of the wall that divided the house yard from the farmyard proper that the real force of the gale caught her, and she was almost lifted from her feet. The only way she could cross the yard was to turn and, walking backwards, press against the wind.

As she passed the big barn a section of her mind told her that she should have brought Ralph Batley a can of soup, but this was dismissed as she realised it would have been ripped from her hand before she was half-way across the yard. By the time she had struggled towards the door of Sarah's byre she realised that she was more than a little frightened by the ferocity of the storm. She had witnessed storms before but nothing like this. Mr. Cadwell, on that night of her first coming to this part of the country, had sneered at her when she had said she was used to rough weather. There was weather and weather, he had said, and this was what he had meant.

At last she was in the small byre and the sound that greeted her was, to say the least, weird. Coupled with the noise of the storm, it did not tend to calm her nerves. But so agitated were the animals and so pathetic the crying of the little calf that soon her own fears were in the background. She went between the two of them, talking to and soothing them, until at last, like weary children, they settled down. . . .

It must have been about an hour later when Linda, sitting on the box with her back leaning against the stanchion of the byre, felt herself being lulled into sleep by sheer weariness. The thunder of the storm was so persistent that it seemed as if it would go on forever and life would have to be adjusted to it. The byre had a sweet, warm smell, the whole atmosphere, engulfed as it was in the noise from outside, acted as a drug. Not that Linda needed much of a drug to put her to sleep for she had been on her feet since five that morning, and when she felt her head and lids drooping she did nothing to resist the blissful oblivion about to overtake her.

Whether she was asleep and dreaming, or awake and seeing aright she didn't really know, but before her mind's eyes there flashed a picture. It was of the door of the cowshed being thrust open and a dishevelled, wild-looking woman standing framed for a second in the dim light of the lantern.

Then Linda was on her feet, and when wisps of straw began to whirl in the atmosphere around her and the wind, forcing itself up to the roof, threatened to lift it off, she ran towards the open door and forced it shut. She had seen a woman standing here, she hadn't been dreaming, dreams didn't open doors. She had seen a woman. Pulling the hood of her coat over her head and buttoning it under her chin she snatched the lantern from the hook and went out into the yard. Standing with her back to the cowshed wall and lifting the lantern above her head, she peered round the farmyard, and for one fleeting second she saw the figure again. It was just a distorted bulk, a wind-contorted shadow, but Linda knew it was the woman who had opened the cowshed door and that she was now going into the big barn.

She hesitated a moment, her eyes turning in the direction of the main cowshed where Ralph Batley was, and then she was looking towards the big barn and within a second she was making for it. Hugging the walls as far as she could, and then once again pressing her back to the wind as she reached the opening. And there, lifting the lantern above her head, she looked about her. There was no one to be seen. Her eyes lifted to the ladder leading to the upper floor, and as she walked slowly towards it she imagined that above the turmoil of the storm she heard a thud that had no connection with the elements outside. Slowly she mounted the ladder, feeling as she did so that all this had been gone through before. Perhaps in that fleeting second when in half-dream, half-reality, she had looked towards the wild-looking figure standing in the doorway of the cowshed she had known what was to follow.

As she reached the upper storey of the barn and moved slowly towards its end she knew whom she would find there, she knew whom she would see when she turned right to the door of the studio—to the door of the love-nest. Not only her heart but her whole body and mind felt heavy, dull, and sick at what this meant.

She came to where the packing-cases were stacked, and turned right. And now she could see the door, and it was closed. Then she drew in her breath sharply as she saw the prostrate figure lying across the threshold of the studio.

As, with the lantern in her hand, she stood stiffly looking down at the figure at her feet, a feeling of revulsion came over her. She didn't want to touch the woman. And then, the lantern standing on the floor, she was bending over the huddled form and lifting the rain-drenched face. It was a white, dead-looking face, a frighteningly dead-looking face, but a startlingly beautiful one.

Leaving the lantern where it was she turned and groped her way down the barn and scrambled down the ladder. She was out in the yard once again, running now with the wind towards the byre. She unlatched the door, and when it was almost wrenched from her grasp she forced it closed and stood with her back to it gasping. And then she called twice, "Mr. Batley! Mr. Batley!" There came a movement from somewhere high up in the roof. When she saw her employer sitting astride a beam, his hands reaching towards the rafters, she called again, "Mr. Batley!"

His body was twisted round and his face was looking towards her. "What is it?"

"It's . . . it's . . ." She could have said, "It's Edith." So sure was she of the woman's identity, so sure was she of the pattern that life was now about to take, she almost said, "Your Edith. It's your Edith, she's come back."

"What is it, girl? Is it Maggie? You look like a ghost. Is it Maggie?" This was Shane speaking.

"No! no!" She shook her head, aware now that Ralph Batley was scrambling down the ladder near the beam. When he stood before her he, too, said, "What is it?" and then asked, "My mother . . . she's all right?"

"Yes, yes, she's all right. It's . . . There was a woman, she came to the shed. I was sitting with Sarah. I thought I was dreaming, and then I saw her going into the barn. She's there now, upstairs. She's—she's unconscious." She stared at her employer. Did he know without being told who the woman was?

"A woman? What woman?" Shane's voice came in between them. Neither Ralph Batley nor Linda answered the old man, but something equivalent to the tight grip of a fist closed round her chest as she watched him swing round and run towards the door without even thinking of donning his coat.

"Saints alive! What woman would be out a night like this? Are you sure, girl?"

"Of course I'm sure, Uncle Shane." Linda's voice was strangely level now. "I know who she is."

"You know who she is? What d'you mean, child?"

"Did Mr. Batley tell you that young Mr. Cadwell called here this morning?"

There was a flicker in Shane's eyes before he replied, "Yes, yes. Name of God! You don't mean . . ." He, too, was out of the door, and Linda now followed him, but more slowly. She went across the yard, walking backwards once more, and when she reached the barn and went up the ladder her legs felt strangely heavy. As she turned the corner near the boxes she saw that the door to the studio was open. The lantern was standing on the table and on a couch near the wall lay the woman. Both Uncle Shane and Ralph Batley were standing looking down at the inert figure, and as Linda neared the door Shane's voice came to her in an almost fear-filled whisper, saying, "In the name of God! What a predicament. You'll have to get her out of here, boy, and lose no time at all. You understand that, don't you?"

"Where is she to go?"

"Phone them."

"I doubt if she'll thank me for that. We must wait until she comes round, she'll know what she wants to do."

"But Ralph man, think. Think!"

"We can't do anything until she comes round."

Linda, hearing the almost level tones of her employer, thought with painful clarity, He wants her to come round, he couldn't possibly let her go without her coming round. She met his eyes as he turned from the couch and for a moment she imagined that he looked ashamed; and she thought, He is ashamed, ashamed of still being in love with this woman who had been stolen from him. Or did she leave him willingly for another man? And in this moment, too, she thought, Thank God I didn't let this thing get a hold of me. Thank God I realised that it was loneliness, not love. But the thought, like most reasonable thoughts, was devoid of comfort.

Shane was now hanging on to his nephew's arm, gripping it tightly, and his voice held a stern, almost angry note as he said, "Have you thought about your mother? Have you thought about Maggie? This will drive her mad. She's in no state to have any more worry. Look, I'm telling you, boy, phone them, they'll come and take her."

"Perhaps she doesn't want to be taken. Don't you see?"

The old man stared at his nephew for a moment before saying, "Well, if she wants to or not, that's beside the point. Do you want all hell to be let loose? I'm thinking of nobody but Maggie at this moment. She's had enough, she's had enough, boy."

"I know, I know, and so have I, Uncle Shane. I've had enough, too, don't you realise that? D'you think I asked for this?" His voice was hard and bitter. "D'you think I'd have laid myself open to this? But I can't tell them she's here until she comes round. It'll be up to her. If she's running away, who am I to stop her?"

As the grip loosened on his arm Ralph Batley turned to Linda and in his eyes there was a look of appeal, but she was soon made to realise for what the appeal was meant. "She will need some dry clothes, and blankets and a water bottle. Do you think . . . ?"

She did not let him finish but turned hastily away, yet she had not reached the end of the passageway between the crates and the wall before she was pulled to a stop, and in the dim light from the lantern standing in the room behind them they peered at each other. His hand was holding her shoulder as he began rapidly, "She's ill, more ill than Uncle Shane realises. Her pulse is very low, I may have to get a doctor. This is all very painful to me, you can't understand, you don't know what it means. I knew her years ago, she was a . . . a close——"

"A close friend of yours. Yes, I understand, Mr. Batley, there's no need for you to explain." Her voice was cool and level, even to herself it sounded indifferent. When his hand dropped from her shoulder and he said in a flat-sounding tone, "Well, that's all right then," she looked at him a moment longer before turning from him.

As she walked in the darkness towards the end of the loft she warned herself to be careful in case she went over the edge. When a desperate voice deep within her said, "Oh, what would it matter, even if I were to go over the edge of the cliff," she chided it saying, "Don't be a fool, don't let it get you down."

Again she had to force her way across the yard. The rain had stopped now but the wind was still tearing and screeching, still clawing at the buildings as if bent on uprooting them.

When she looked into Mrs. Batley's room she was thankful to find that the older woman was asleep and that Michael, curled up in a chair before the fire, was also asleep. She decided to leave him there until she had taken the things to the loft.

Quickly now she ran upstairs. Taking a warm dress from the cupboard and her dressing-gown from the back of the door, she went to the linen cupboard in the bathroom and gathered some blankets in her arms before again making her way downstairs. In the kitchen she filled a hot-water bottle, and as she hesitated on the thought of filling a can of soup the door opened and Shane came in.

Never had she seen the old man's countenance look so thundery. Without any preamble he said, "We only needed this. Do you know what this means, girl? All the old business over again. He'll go mad again, stark staring mad . . . she bewitched him. I thought when you came . . ." His head dropped and he swung it from side to side in a desperate movement. "Why has God to inflict people with such troubles, people that's done Him no harm? I tell you, there'll be trouble." She did not remind him that he believed that God worked in strange and wonderful ways, but she watched him pull off his cap and scratch his head violently before she said, "Help me over with these things, Uncle Shane, please."

His tone was one of defeat as he replied, "Leave the blankets, I'll be over after you in a minute."

"Do you think you could manage to bring a can of soup?"

"I'd like to bring a can of poison if I had my way."

Sadly she turned from him and went out into the night once more.

The door to the studio was closed and she didn't knock but pushed it open and went straight in, some part of her was hoping, she knew, to surprise him. This part of her should not have been disappointed because there he was, on his knees by the low couch, and the woman had her eyes open and was looking at him. Yet he seemed strangely unperturbed as he rose to his feet and came towards her, saying quietly, "Do you think you could help her off with her things?"

Linda made no answer to this but walked towards the

174

couch and placed the dressing-gown and the dress across the foot of it before turning and looking at the woman.

The eyes that looked back out of the white face were soft, brown, melting eyes, they were frightened eyes, but behind the fear was a quality to which Linda, for the moment, could not put a name. She did not know this woman, only of her, and she was prepared to hate her, but the eyes looking up at her reminded her of Sarah's eyes, they were beseeching and asking dumbly for kindness. She was surprised at the warmth of her own voice as she said, "You must get these wet things off. I've brought you a dress and a dressing-gown. Do you think you could sit up?" When she went round to the other side of the couch to help raise the woman up she found they had the studio to themselves. The woman could barely assist herself, and she did not speak as Linda, with gentle dexterity, stripped her of her wet clothing. But when finally she was arrayed in the dress and dressing-gown, she whispered in a voice that for all its faintness held a warm charm, "Thank you. Oh, thank you."

Linda went to the door now and opened it. Outside, standing with unusual patience, his face almost as white as that of the woman she had just undressed, was Ralph Batley. He was holding the blankets and the can of soup, but Uncle Shane was not to be seen. He came in, and going to the couch, he opened the blankets one by one and put them over the woman. When this was done he poured some soup into the lid of the can. Kneeling once again, he put his arm underneath her shoulders and said quietly, "Come, drink this."

The couch was low and Linda told herself that he would have to kneel. As she stood looking at them she was torn by conflicting desires. One was to run out of the room, the other to stay and witness this scene and what would follow. She saw the woman's hand come up and touch the lid of the can and also the fingers that held it. The moment of contact seemed to act as a spring releasing her emotions, for Linda watched her push the can away and turn on her side and bury her face in the crook of Ralph Batley's arm. As she listened to the shuddering sobs and watched their reaction on her employer she told herself to get away, out of the studio, away from the self-inflicting pain, but she didn't move. Then the woman, between her sobs, began to talk disjointedly. "Oh, Ralph, Ralph. Oh, what have I done? Oh, Ralph, Ralph. I can't go back, I can't. Don't send me back, he'll kill me. I was mad, Ralph, I was mad."

"Keep quiet, keep quiet. Don't excite yourself. Try to rest."

"But, Ralph." Linda watched the slim hand groping up towards Ralph Batley's face. When she saw him disengage himself and get to his feet she felt no relief, he was only embarrassed because she was witnessing the scene.

"Don't leave me, Ralph, don't leave me, please, please." The hand was outstretched to him and Linda saw the muscles of the right side of his face work like pistons under the skin. She waited for him to turn towards her and he did, and she was in no way surprised by his words. "Go and get some rest. Tell Uncle Shane I want him when he has a minute."

She gave him a long, straight look and turned towards the door. When he reached it he was behind her, and when she went out into the loft he was still with her. And now he spoke rapidly and quietly. "Michael mustn't know of this, you understand. He'd blurt it to my mother. Can you keep him with you in the morning?" He paused and swallowed. "She'll be gone tomorrow, some time tomorrow."

"I'll do my best."

"Linda." His hands were lifting to her but the almost imperceptible recoil that she made from them was sensed by him, and they dropped to his side before the gesture had hardly commenced. As he swung round from her and went into the studio again she closed her eyes for a moment before once again groping her way along the loft.

It did not need an alarm to get Linda out of bed the following morning. Last night she had been so tired that she could have fallen asleep on her feet, that was up until she had seen the woman framed in the doorway of Sarah's byre. If she had slept at all it had been in fitful, troubled doses. She had been so wakeful that she knew the exact time the storm had died away.

It was just on five o'clock when she descended the stairs, but no bright fire greeted her this morning, no shining lamp or spluttering kettle on the kitchen hob. As she set herself the task of rectifying these omissions she could not overthrow the resentful feeling that was enveloping her, nor yet erase from her mind's eye the face of the woman who had haunted her all night. It was almost with unseemly haste that she prepared a jug of tea, and when she stepped out into the calm but biting dawn it did not affect her, as did the feeling of apprehension that swept over her when she came within sight of the studio door.

Afraid of what she might see by an unannounced entrance, she knocked on the door, and when after a moment there was no reply she turned the handle. There before her, fast asleep on the couch, lay the woman, Edith Cadwell. She could not think of her as Edith, only as the woman, or that woman. And there, not an arm's length from her, stretched out in the big, old, dilapidated chair, was Ralph Batley. They were both in deep sleep. Their hands hanging, hers over the side of the couch and his over the arm of the chair, seemed to suggest that they had been locked together before sleep had relaxed them. The scene was painfully intimate, it had a nakedness about it that stabbed so deeply into Linda that she was forced to say to herself roughly, "Well, what did you expect?" The lantern she saw was burning low and in a short while would be out if not refuelled. She went and stood by her employer, reluctant to touch him. She did not touch him, but said sharply, "Mr. Batley!"

He stirred, shook his head and opened his eyes, then closed them again before stretching them wide.

"I've brought some tea."

"What?"

It was evident to her that for a moment he did not know where he was, but only for a moment. Then he said, "Oh! Thanks, thanks."

"The lamp needs oil, it'll soon be out."

"Yes." He stood up and stretched himself; then said again, "Yes." Without looking at her he took a mug of tea from her hand and having drunk it he asked her quietly, "Will you stay here until I come back? I'll get the oil first, then do a round. I'll be as quick as I can."

She did not look at him as she answered, "Don't forget there is your mother to be seen to, and Michael."

He did not answer her immediately and she knew he was angered by her words. "I won't forget. I'm sorry I have to ask you to do this, but if she wakes up and finds herself alone she may be——" He paused, then added, "She's in a high state of nerves—very frightened."

The only reply she made to this was to raise her eyebrows slightly and go and take his place in the chair.

When he had gone she looked round the room. It was like something, she thought, that one would see in a ghost picture. Cobwebs were hanging from the rafters.

On the bench running along the length of one wall there were what she judged to be three heads, they were covered with sheets, and these, too, were joined together by cobwebs. The floor was covered with a fine dust. The only other article of furniture besides the couch, the chair and the bench was a bookcase, and this was draped with the clothes she had taken off the woman last night, and in the far corner, piled one against the other, were chunks of wood, pieces of stone, and canvases, and all covered with the netting of cobwebs.

She had hardly made her survey of the room when Ralph Batley returned with the oil, and when he had refilled the lantern the bright glow showed up the dirt in the studio still more. He directed neither look nor word to her before leaving the room again, but the glance he cast swiftly towards the woman on the bed was not lost on Linda.

She had thought of this stranger as a woman, yet looking at her now, at the pale, beautiful face, she knew that here was still a girl, and her intuition told her also that here was a person who could have the word enchanting attached to her. This thought made her vividly conscious of her breeches and rough coat, made her feel gawkish, without confidence. It was at this moment that the brown eyes opened and looked at her, and they remained wide.

"I've . . . I've seen you before." The voice was very low and soft. Like the eyes, it had a far-away, dream-like quality.

"Yes. You saw me last night." Linda made her tone ordinary.

The head turned slowly on the pillow. "I feel very tired—so tired." The eyes were turned on Linda again. "Ralph . . . where is Ralph?"

"He is on the farm seeing to things."

"What is your name?"

"Linda, Linda Metcalfe."

"You . . . you are——" She took in a slow, long breath and eased herself up on the couch and lay for a moment before continuing, "You are staying on holiday?"

"No. I work here. I'm a student, an agricultural student."

The bloodless lips formed the words agricultural student but there was no sound from them. She turned her cheek to the side of the couch and, looking at Linda, she asked slowly, "Do you know who I am?"

"Yes. Yes, I know who you are."

"Oh!" The eyes widened still further, then they were lifted from Linda and she watched them moving around the studio, and when the girl said softly, "I used to know this room very well," she stiffened inside.

"Oh, if only we could see ahead, if only we knew." The great brown eyes were on Linda again and they rested on her face for a while. "You are young, very young," the girl said, in a soft, appraising tone.

"I don't think I'm much younger than you."

"I'll never be young again, I'm old, old, old." As she repeated the word for the third time she put her hand towards her hair, and then added wearily, "I must look a terrible sight. I think I had a bag with me. I'm not sure."

"There's a bag here." Linda walked towards the bench and picked up a leather bag and brought it to the girl on the couch. She watched her open it and take out a comb, but when she attempted to put it through her hair it appeared too much for her, and she lay back against the head of the couch, her long hands lying limp before her on the blanket.

"I'm weaker than I thought. It's just tiredness, it'll pass."

"Let me have the comb."

When Linda stood behind the couch and combed the tangled hair, she told herself she would do this for anybody who was sick. She was combing the last strand of the thick auburn hair down to the shoulders where it turned naturally inwards, when the door was pushed open and Ralph Batley entered, carrying a laden tray. On the sight of this a feeling of resentment welled up in Linda. He had asked her to stay until he had done a round, but he had spent the time preparing a dainty breakfast for the newcomer, for she saw at a glance there was little difference in the setting of the tray from what she herself would have prepared.

She handed the comb to Edith Cadwell.

"Thank you. That was sweet of you."

Linda made no rejoinder to this but, picking up her coat, went out of the room. But she had not reached the end of the packing-cases when she heard her name called. She paused but did not turn.

When Ralph Batley was standing confronting her he spoke in an undertone but briskly, saying, "I want to talk with you, not now, later. I must explain."

"There's no need, there's no need to explain anything to me, but I should have thought that you'll find it difficult to keep this matter a secret from Michael if you are going to carry trays up here."

"Trays?" He screwed his eyes up at her. "There'll only be this one. And Michael isn't up yet."

She raised her brows and jerked her head slightly to the side but kept her eyes fixed on him as she repeated, "Only this one? You think there will be only this one?"

When his gaze moved from hers and she saw his teeth clamp down on to his lip she walked away. She could not trust herself to look at him any longer.

The farmyard was still in darkness but the sky was high and star-filled, and she stood for a moment looking up into it before turning aside and running towards the small byre. It was black dark inside the byre, and although she did not speak to Sarah or the calf they made no uneasy movements. Groping her way to the post between the two pens she stood with her head against it and her hands gripping it. Her throat was tight and her eyes stinging with tears, and she had to let them flow to relieve the awful pressure that threatened to choke her. Her crying was quiet, and when it ceased she felt her way to the box and sat down, and in the darkness, enveloped by the warmth and familiar smells of the animals, she faced the fact that she loved Ralph Batley, she loved this man who, because of his passionate overwhelming love for a woman who rejected him, had become a different being. Over the last few days she had glimpsed what she thought should be the real character of her employer, a character that was not without tenderness. When this woman had thrown him over the tenderness had turned into hatred. Now she had returned. She had sought him out, she had come to him in need, and the tenderness had returned too. She felt that from the moment he had looked down on the prostrate figure he had become the old Ralph Batley, a man who would be like putty in the hands of anyone so charming as the woman who was now lying in the studio. The fact that she herself had been held in his arms for a brief second yesterday morning, the fact that he had called her Linda at least three times since then were as nothing. These facts now took on the appearance of tiny, unimportant incidents, driftwood on the crest of a mighty wave, swept away on the return of an old love, an only love—men like Ralph Batley didn't love lightly.

She rose from the box, wiped her face with her handkerchief, straightened her shoulders, closed her eyes for a moment and said a little prayer, the substance of which was that she wouldn't make a fool of herself. On this foundation she went out and towards the house to start the business of a strange day.

6

It was forty-eight hours later and the studio was still occupied. The repercussions to this were many, and they all held the one element—tension. It filled the house until the atmosphere was almost unbearable to Linda.

Short-handed as they already were, the work was getting more and more behind. Open conflict had sprung up between Shane and his nephew, who, in turn, was treating Michael with unjustified harshness, curtailing the child's movements at almost every step. Mrs. Batley, too, sensing the troubles that enshrouded her loved ones, was not only asking, but demanding, explanations. Her strength of will was aiding her to sit up in the chair by the hall fire, and Linda knew that it was only fear of collapsing that stopped the older woman from leaving the house. And then there was the cause of the tension, the visitor in the studio.

Why hadn't Edith Cadwell gone by now? Was it because of Ralph Batley's desire to keep her? This question kept hammering at Linda every hour of the day. She had paid three visits to the studio yesterday, each time carrying a meal, at the request of her employer—he had not talked to her as he had promised but had merely asked her if she would try to get some food to Mrs. Cadwell. He called her Mrs. Cadwell, and as far as she could see the hated name had now no effect on him. Each time she had gone to the studio she had found it empty except for the woman on the couch. Mrs. Cadwell had remained on the couch all day yesterday, and all day today.

Although, naturally, she hadn't seen her employer entering the barn she was aware that he must have visited the studio frequently, and if she had needed proof of this she had had it only a few minutes ago. When, after some manoeuvering, she had managed to evade Michael and take a meal up to the studio, it was to find Edith Cadwell in a state of agitation. She had clutched at her hand and implored her. "Please! please! don't let Ralph send for a doctor. I'm all right, I only want another day. If he sends for Doctor Morgan he is sure to tell them. He would persuade Ralph to tell them, and then my husband . . . he'd kill me if he were to find me here. I must go, I know I must go, but at the moment I don't feel able." She had released the grip on Linda's hands and, lying back and looking about the studio, she added, "It's so peaceful here. Oh, you don't know, you can't understand. I've dreamed of the peace of this room. It looks neglected now, but it wasn't always like this." The brown eyes were full on Linda, the soft, melting gaze was, in spite of herself, drawing on her sympathy.

"You are a kind person, aren't you?"

"Not more than anyone else."

"Oh, yes you are. You don't want me here. Now don't look like that, it's only natural, but you're still kind."

Linda had found herself taken completely off her guard. She realised as she looked back into the brown eyes that there was an astute brain working behind the soft, melting glance. Edith Cadwell's next words confirmed this.

"You know at one time Ralph and I were very close. We—we were to be married."

"Yes, I know." Linda's voice sounded even and flat and without interest.

"You know? Who told you?"

"Oh, things get about—where there's no other form of entertainment people talk."

Apparently this answer did not please Edith Cadwell, and for the first time Linda saw a look of sharp annoyance on the white, thin features, and she knew that the annoyance had gone deep when Edith Cadwell allowed her to leave the studio without further words.

And now Linda was standing at the kitchen table preparing the supper, she was so tired and weary that she felt she could have fallen asleep where she stood. She was telling herself that no matter what happened, as soon as she had washed-up she was going straight to bed. She couldn't keep her head up another hour. And her thoughts were finishing philosophically: Anyway, I can do nothing, what has to happen, will happen, when she heard Uncle Shane's raised voice coming from the yard, calling, "Ralph! Ralph!" The next minute the kitchen door burst open and the old man stood gasping as he looked towards Linda. "Where is he?" he cried. "Have you seen him?"

"Yes. He went into Mrs. Batley not more than a minute ago."

Uncle Shane was supporting himself with his two hands on the table now, and he said between gasps, "Go and get him for me. Make some excuse, say you thought you heard me call." He nodded sharply. "That's the truth, anyway. Go on now, quickly."

Bemused, Linda went out of the kitchen across the hall and to the front room, and she looked to where Ralph Batley was standing near his mother's bed. Going no further than the door she said, "Uncle Shane's needing you a moment, Mr. Batley. I think it's one of the cows."

A few minutes later when he came into the kitchen Ralph Batley looked in surprise from his uncle to Linda, but as he was about to speak Shane cut him short, saying, "There's someone about the place, I saw him at the bottom of the studio staircase. Did you know the light was coming from under the door there? I thought for a moment it was yourself, and when I crossed towards you I knew my mistake, for whoever it was scuttled away. I thought he went into the barn but didn't go after him, I hadn't a light with me, and anyway, I didn't want a clunk on the head from behind. You'd better come, and come quick. What did I tell you? I can't help saying it, I told you this would happen."

Linda looked at Ralph Batley's face. It had turned a dirty grey colour and his eyes had darkened considerably. When he made a sharp movement towards the cupboard in the corner of the kitchen, Uncle Shane's hand came out as his voice rapped, "No! no! boy, no guns."

Linda watched her employer hesitate for a moment before swinging through the door, the old man at his heels.

She stood staring at the closed door. Uncle Shane was right, of course he was right. But what if the other man had a gun on him? What if he shot . . . ? Her harassed thoughts at this moment were interrupted by a tinkle coming from the vicinity of the hall, it was the recognisable tinkle of a telephone bell, but it was the first time she had heard the telephone ring since she had come to this house. Taking into account that it had been out of order for the first three days after her arrival, to her knowledge it hadn't rung since. She went quickly into the hall and towards a dark little cubby-hole of a room under the stairs that Ralph Batley used as an office. The bell ringing again directed her to the instrument, but when she picked it up and said "Hullo" no answering voice came to her. She was repeating the word when she heard what could have been a quick intake of breath on

187

the wire, and then a voice said, "I want to speak to Mr. Batley." It was a woman's voice and she recognised it.

"I'm afraid . . . he's not in."

"Is he on the farm?"

"Yes . . . yes, he's just gone out into the yard."

"Will you take a message?" The voice paused. "It is important. Will you tell him to phone me . . . Mrs. Cadwell?"

"Yes, yes, I'll tell him that, Mrs. Cadwell."

"You'll find him as soon as you can?"

"Yes, yes, I'll go right now."

"Thank you." There was the click of the receiver being replaced and then Linda slowly put down the phone.

When she entered the hall again it was to see Michael running out of his granny's room, and he cried to her, "Who was on the phone? Granny says, who's on the phone?"

"It was a wrong number. Someone . . . someone thought this was a school . . . a boy's school in Morpeth." The glibness of her reply had a somewhat disturbing effect on her—the situation in this house was such that she always had to be thinking a step ahead to soothe Mrs. Batley's fears, or, to be more correct, to hoodwink her and the boy. The thought wasn't pleasing, and as Michael ran from her again to give the news to his grandmother she went hastily into the kitchen. She had no desire to go outside, no desire to meet whoever it was prowling about the buildings. Her encounter with Sep Watson the other evening had frightened her and she felt that if she met up with him again the effect would be more than unnerving. But as she stood hesitating, she knew that Mrs. Cadwell hadn't had Sep Watson in mind when she came on the phone to the Batleys. It was her son she had had in mind. She herself could almost tell her employer the message Mrs. Cadwell was going to give him, that her son was looking for his wife and he was coming to find her in Fowler Hall. With a gesture that was a mixture of impatience, weariness, and desperation, she pulled her coat from the door and, thrusting her arms into it, went out.

From the main yard she saw the light from a swinging lantern. It was near the barn and, going towards it, she called, "Mr. Batley! Mr. Batley!"

It seemed that Ralph Batley leapt towards her, so quick was he at her side, and before she could speak he said, "Yes? What is it? What's the matter? Have you——"

"I've just come to tell you," she broke in on him, "there's been a phone message. It's from Mrs. Cadwell, she wishes you to phone her immediately." She could not see what effect this had on him as his face was in shadow, but he was some time in answering her, and then he said rapidly, "Will you go up to the studio and stay for a while." He paused. But when she made no answer he added, "It'll just be for a short while. And you need have no fear, we've been all round up there, there's no one about, only . . ." He left the name unsaid. "Will you . . . please?" His tone was hurried and urgent, yet he was speaking as if asking a favour of her, and she felt that much as she had tried to hide her reluctance to visit the woman in the studio, he was aware of it.

"Very well."

"Here, take this light." He thrust the lantern into her hand and for a moment their fingers came in contact. His felt cold and hard.

She was shaking slightly as she entered the big barn, she did not deny to herself that she was afraid, and although she had the light with her and swung it backwards and forwards, she expected at any moment to feel herself thrown to the ground. On the upper floor she walked quietly and cautiously towards the end of the barn, and it was as she turned right to go towards the studio door that she halted. She had imagined for a moment that she had heard a voice, a male voice, and it brought her to petrified stillness. After some seconds while she held her breath she swung the light along the passage towards the closed door of the studio. Then it came to her again, a thick murmur that could only mean a man's voice. She had the desire to turn and flee back down the barn. Ralph Batley had said he had searched up here. He knew his own barn, and there would not be a corner he had left untouched . . . and would he have missed out the studio? No. Of course not. It would have been the first place he would have made for. And yet she could hear a man's voice coming from there. No one could have entered the studio by the staircase door, that was locked, and to her own knowledge there was no key in the lock. Anyway, it would have to be opened from the inside to allow someone to enter.

Her curiosity and a form of high indignation set her moving towards the door. The murmur was still going on, yet not audible. It wasn't until she stood to the side of the door, her ear pressed against the lintel, that she could make out any words at all, and these were disjointed. "One good turn . . ." These were followed by a mumble, and then after some more murmurings, "I'm as good as me word——"

She now heard the soft, rapid tones of Edith Cadwell's voice, but so low was it that she could make out none of the words. And then again she heard the man's voice, saying this time on a low, surly note, "O.K." and again the soft tones of Edith Cadwell's voice. There followed a longish silence which was broken by the man saying, "I'm no hand with a pen."

Linda knew that voice, and she felt that she could endorse that its owner would be no hand with a pen.

Although she strained her ears now no further sound came through the door. She told herself that she should thrust it open and surprise Sep Watson, but her common sense warned her that her efforts would be useless. She was checked by the thought, too, that perhaps Edith Cadwell was trying to save Ralph Batley from an underhand attack by the Cadwells. No, no, her mind rejected this. There was something fishy here to say the least. Why had Ralph Batley not been able to find the cowman when he searched this place a few minutes ago? Should she go for him now and tell him Sep Watson was in the studio, talking to Edith Cadwell, an evidently unafraid Edith Cadwell? But what good would that do? By the time he could reach here the bird, in the shape of Sep Watson, would have flown. What she could do would be to thrust open this door and scream her loudest. Both Ralph Batley and Uncle Shane would be about the buildings, they were bound to hear her. This was an idea that if dwelt upon would have to draw on courage for its action. She knew she was very low in courage at this moment, and it could only be done if she didn't stop to think. She turned from the wall and, grabbing the handle, thrust at the door. When it merely shuddered under her impact, she felt the amazement covering her face. It was locked.

"Who's that?"

It was some seconds before she could find her voice to answer.

"Me, Linda Metcalfe."

It seemed a long time before the door was opened, and Linda found herself standing on the threshold stock-still, looking at the pale, haggard face of the girl. Neither of them spoke, but after a moment Edith Cadwell, her steps almost tottering, made her way back to the couch, and the voice Linda now heard bore no resemblance to the crisp whispering she had listened to a few minutes earlier.

"I was so afraid when Ralph told me about Watson being on the prowl I . . . I felt I must lock the door."

Linda came slowly into the studio; there was no place for anyone to hide except . . . her eyes moved down to the couch, low as it was a man could hide under that. The blankets were trailing on to the floor covering the front. She went slowly towards the couch, trembling now from head to foot. Bending down she lifted the blankets from the dusty floor and put them further over Edith Cadwell's legs. She looked at the girl as she did this, but there was no protest from her, no quick movement of the hand to stop her, and when she stepped back from the couch she could see for quite a way under it. There was no one there. She asked herself, had she been dreaming or was she a little mad? But no, she had heard Sep Watson's voice coming from this room. And now she looked towards the door that was never opened, the door that led to the outside staircase, and from it to Edith Cadwell again. She was lying with her eyes closed and she asked in a weary voice, "Have they found him? Has Ralph found him?"

Linda forced herself to answer calmly, "No, not yet." Then she added, "Did he say it was Watson he was looking for?"

"Yes. Yes, I suppose so, or how would I have known? He . . . he told me there had been trouble with him. Anyway, I . . . I do hope it is Watson, if it isn't it could be . . ." She broke off and closed her eyes, and Linda, after gazing at her steadily for a moment, moved away. She walked round the head of the couch towards the door, but it wasn't at the lock she looked but at the floor.

The room was still dusty, the floor very dusty, no attempt had been made to clean it up, there had been no time. There were footmarks about two feet from the door, and the light grey dust, mostly seepings from the barn, should have remained intact to the skirting board or to the bottom of the door, but it wasn't intact. The door fitted flush to the floor and there were the tracks where it had scraped the surface. The door that always remained locked had been opened, but there was no key in the lock. To make sure that her surmise was correct she looked along the floor to each side of the door. The dust here for some way from the skirting board was quite undisturbed.

When she turned from the door to go back to the couch it was to find Edith Cadwell's eyes on her. She was twisted round and looking over the head of the couch, and her eyes were no longer brown and soft, they were black and almost fierce.

"What's the matter, what're you looking for?"

"Nothing. I was just wondering if anybody could get in this way."

"No, they couldn't, that door's locked; it's always locked."

Linda came to the foot of the couch again and stared at the pale face. She wanted to say, "You're lying, you've just let him out through that door. You've got a key to that door. You must have kept it all those years. You've got keys to both these doors, duplicate keys." And she might have said it if she hadn't, at that moment, heard the quick step of her employer coming along the barn. She turned hastily away from the staring eyes and went out, for she couldn't trust herself to witness the play-acting that would take place when Ralph Batley came into the room.

She was halfway along the passage when they met, and

to his quick enquiry, "Everything all right?" she could only incline her head before moving on. But she had hardly turned the corner near the boxes when a rapid, quick-firing sound of his voice drew her to a halt. He must have cut short some words of Edith Cadwell's for he was saying, "Now, you listen to me, Edith, this can't go on. It's got to end and right now for everybody's sake. I'm taking you into Morpeth into an hotel—you'd better get . . ."

"What! You can't, you can't. Oh, Ralph, I'm not well enough to go, you know I'm not. Give me until tomorrow morning, please. Please, Ralph."

"Now, Edith, don't get het up like that, it's no good. I've just had a phone message—from . . . from Mrs. Cadwell, she's in a dreadful state. She says that . . . that he's been out walking the countryside for the last two days because he feels that you're here, he knows that you're here. He's given you until tomorrow morning to go back. All right, all right"—the words were sharp—"I know you're not going back, I know you can't go back. But you can't stay here. Edith, I've told you, anything more to upset my mother and I dread to think of the consequences. Doctor Morgan warned me . . ."

"Oh, your mother, your mother, always your mother. Don't you realise that all that's happened and what's happening now is because of your mother? Don't you realise that? Don't you know that it was because of her that I did what I did? I felt that I couldn't stand her for another day, and the thought of spending a life-time in this place with her was too much. Just waiting for her to die."

"Be quiet, Edith! How dare you say such things." His voice came as a growl to Linda.

"I dare because they are true, and you know they are true."

"You went with Cadwell because you thought he could give you more than I could. Not in money, oh no, you had plenty of that, but you thought he would lavish on you the whole of his time to the exclusion of everyone, and everything. You thought that he would profess his love for you every hour of the twenty-four, and he didn't, and you found he was just a man and took you for granted. That's the truth and you know it. My mother had nothing to do with it."

"It isn't. You are changed . . . cruel. But it doesn't matter, nothing matters except one thing and you know what that is, Ralph." There came a pause now and Linda waited for the next words. They came, soft and clear. "I still love you, Ralph. I've never stopped loving you. I knew I'd made a fool of myself the first night. Come here, Ralph."

"No, Edith, you made your choice three years ago, you'll have to stand by it, and him. I've had to stand by it. You affected a number of people's lives when you took Cadwell and what is done is done."

There was a silence now in the whole of the barn and Linda could imagine that it was empty of human beings until Edith Cadwell's voice came again. Her tone was quiet and flat, but her words were startling. "You think you're in love with that girl, don't you?"

"Be quiet, Edith, I'm not discussing any——"

"You think you're in love with her," the flat tone persisted, "but you're not. You can't be in love with any other woman, Ralph, there's been too much between us. Anyway"—there came a light touch into her voice— "you'll never really be a farmer, there's just a tiny fraction of you a farmer, and I can't see the sculptor in you ever going over the brink for anyone like her. She's pretty and healthy and she appeals to the farmer side of you—the cow girl, a female Sep Watson."

By this time Linda was standing clutching the front of her coat, her head bowed down, and her heart jumped under her hand as Ralph Batley barked, "Be quiet! Do you hear? If you dare make such comparisons . . ."

The barn was once again lying under a silence. It went on and on until suddenly it was broken by a low moan, followed by the faint sound of weeping, painful weeping.

When Linda heard the dull thud which meant that the studio door had been pushed to, she raised her head. He had not denied Edith Cadwell's accusation, nor had he admitted it. But a cow girl, a female Sep Watson. If he hadn't seen her in this light before, the picture Edith Cadwell had painted was too vivid for him not to see it now. And the door of the studio was closed and Edith Cadwell was crying.

Slowly Linda made her way to the end of the barn. She had been jealous of Edith Cadwell, yet she had seen that one could like the woman, more than like her. At least these were her feelings up to a moment ago, now she felt she hated her. That anyone could liken her to Sep Watson. . . . Sep Watson, the name brought her to a halt at the top of the barn steps. She could go back now and accuse her of hiding Sep Watson and letting him out the side door, of having a key to the side door. She could say to her, "You were talking to him, planning something," but where would it get her? She had no proof. Ralph Batley had searched this barn only minutes before she herself had entered the studio, and there was no place in the studio for anyone to hide but under the couch. Should she accuse Edith Cadwell of hiding the cowman under her couch? Even if she did, she couldn't see Ralph Batley believing that. The question would be, for what purpose? There seemed no purpose.

As she reached the floor of the main barn Uncle Shane came from the yard saying, "Is that you, girl?"

"Yes, Uncle Shane."

He came close up to her and, lifting the lantern, looked into her face. "You sound tired. You are tired, go on to the house. Go on now and get yourself to bed, and don't worry. Whoever was here has made off. We've combed the buildings. Away to the house now, and I won't be long after you, I'm dropping with sleep meself. Where is he now?" He did not leave Linda time to answer but added, "Is he up there?"

"Yes."

"God in heaven! there'll be trouble, there'll be trouble. I can smell it. Ah well, we can do no more, only pray, eh? Go along now, go along. There's a good girl." He patted her shoulder as he shoved her forward, and Linda went, across the yard and into the house where slowly she finished setting the supper.

When she went to see to Mrs. Batley the older woman was strangely quiet, asking none of the usual questions about the house or its running, or yet the farm, but after a while she looked at Linda closely and said, "Don't bother about anything more, I'm all right. And I'm quite able to get up and get what I want. Go on now, get yourself to bed, you look dead beat. It's too much for you. . . . Now don't say anything"—she lifted her hand— "we'll talk about this tomorrow. Good night and God bless you, girl."

Her tone was such that Linda found herself crossing the hall blindly. As she passed the big couch near the fire she felt she would have liked to throw herself full length on it and give way to the pressure round her heart.

She was surprised in the act of drying her eyes by the kitchen door opening, and more surprised still to see the form of Ralph Batley standing there. She had expected Uncle Shane to come in long before her employer. She turned her back on him and went to the cupboard, but before her hand had turned the latch he was confronting her. His hand on her shoulders, he pulled her round to face him, and the tenderness in his tone threatened to bring the tears to her eyes again. She did not look at him as he said, "Mrs. Cadwell is leaving in the morning. When she is gone I want to talk to you, you understand?"

She wanted to lift her eyes to his and say, "Yes, yes, I understand," but with the picture in her mind of the studio, and the sound of weeping behind the closed door, she said, "You're always asking me to understand."

There was a pause before he spoke again. "Yes, yes, I suppose I am, and I want you to go on understanding until tomorrow."

She felt his fingers moving gently in the flesh of her shoulder. From her downcast eyes she saw him come nearer and she felt that in the next moment she was going to rest against him, but he released her. When she raised her head he was standing near the door, taking off his coat, and from over his shoulder he said, "Go to bed now. I'm going too, and Uncle, we'll all have an early night."

It was out before she could check it: "What about——?"

"She's well enough to be left. I've locked the door, no one can get in."

She looked at him and, as she thought, "No one can get in, but someone can get out," she had the desire to tell him all she knew. But would he like her any the more for blackening Edith Cadwell further? And apart from the disturbed dust on the floor, what could she prove? Wearily now she said, "I've seen to Mrs. Batley, and Michael is in bed. There is a hot dish in the oven if you want it. Good night."

"Good night . . . Linda."

As she went out of the kitchen and into the hall her

body felt warm. She knew that he was standing looking at her. As she ascended the stairs she saw him come from the kitchen, and as his eyes lifted to hers their gaze held for a moment. Then she was in her room, leaning with her back against the door, her eyes closed, until she chided herself harshly, saying, "Get yourself into bed, before you freeze or drop."

At some point in her dreaming Linda heard a bell ringing. It went on and on until she got the idea of lifting her hand and stopping it. Then she went into a deep, quiet sleep again.

"Linda! Linda! Wake up."

"What? What is it?" She was leaning on her elbow, looking into Michael's smiling face.

"It's time to get up, it's seven o'clock."

"Seven o'clock!" She was sitting bolt upright now. "But the alarm?" She looked to where the clock lay on its face and she remembered faintly putting out her hand and switching off the bell. "Oh, Michael. All right, go on, I'll be down in a minute. Is everybody up?"

"Yes."

"Oh dear. Not your grandmother?"

"No, she's still in bed. She said you hadn't to be wakened but Uncle Shane sent me."

"All right, I'll be with you in a minute. . . . Dear, dear, dear." All the time she was dressing she kept repeating, "Dear, dear, dear. Fancy, oversleeping like this." She was still in a daze and talking to herself as if it had been her habit to rise at five o'clock every morning.

When she reached the hall Michael was trotting back and forward between the kitchen and the table. The breakfast she saw was set after a fashion, and the boy called to her, "I've set the table and washed-up the supper things. I'm going to the top field with Uncle Shane

199

and if the mist clears when the tide goes out, he says I can go down to the boat. Are we going to have bacon?"

Linda realised that Shane was doing his utmost to keep the boy away from the buildings.

"Yes," she said, "yes, we'll have bacon. Thanks for setting the table, I'll see to the rest. Where's your uncle, your Uncle Ralph?"

"I don't know, about somewhere. I haven't seen him since I got up."

Linda did not see Ralph Batley until half an hour later. When he came into the kitchen his face was stiff, and he did not address her with any preliminaries but said immediately, "Things never go according to plan, do they? I've got to make a decision, I've to send for either Doctor Morgan or the Cadwells."

"Why the doctor?" Linda's voice was low.

"She's running a temperature, well over a hundred, she's feverish."

She wanted to say, "I'd phone the Cadwells." but she didn't. Instead she said, "Have you talked it over with Uncle Shane?"

"No. Is he in?"

"Not yet."

They were seated at breakfast when Shane came in. The old man had no light patter these days and he had just taken his seat at the table when his head, in fact all their heads, were turned in the direction of the front door.

During the time Linda had been in this house she had never heard the front-door bell ring. Since she herself had come in the front door on the night of her arrival she couldn't remember seeing it being opened.

"Will I go?"

Ralph Batley, rising from the table but looking towards the door, answered Linda, saying, "No, no, I'll see to it." They all watched him open the glass door, then go into the porch. They listened to the sound of the bolts being drawn and the chain being lifted, then there was nothing more until he opened the glass door again and, holding it back, allowed the regal figure of Mrs. Cadwell to step through into the hall.

As Shane got sharply to his feet, Ralph Batley, stepping aside from his visitor, went softly to his mother's door and closed it. Taking no heed of the sharp enquiry that came from within the room, he now approached Mrs. Cadwell again and said quietly, "Take a seat." As he turned the chair round for her, the tall, grey-faced woman shook her head and looked straight into his face. "I am looking for my son, Ralph."

Linda watched her employer's eyes flick downwards for a moment before coming to meet Mrs. Cadwell's piercing glance again.

"Have you seen him?"

"No, Mrs. Cadwell, I haven't seen him."

"He was coming here last night."

"I didn't see him."

"But he didn't come back. He was in a state when he went out. We waited up and when he didn't come back his father went out looking for him. He and Rouse have been out most of the night. If you know anything, for God's sake, Ralph, tell me. He wasn't himself, he was near mad because of——"

"What's this?"

They all turned towards the voice of Mrs. Batley. She was standing in the doorway of her room, her dressing-gown hugged about her, and now she walked slowly towards Mrs. Cadwell and again she said, "What's this?"

"Hullo, Maggie. I'm . . ." Mrs. Cadwell's voice was

very low, "I'm sorry to find you ill. I . . . I came about Bruce."

"Bruce?" Mrs. Batley flashed a look of enquiry towards her son, then bringing her small, bright eyes back on to the tall woman she demanded, "What about Bruce? Why have you come here?"

"Sit down. Sit down, Mother." Ralph Batley had taken his mother's arm with the intention of leading her to a chair, but she shook it off, saying almost roughly, "Leave be. I knew there was something going on, I want to know what it is."

"Just this, Maggie." Shane spoke for the first time. "Bruce Cadwell is looking for his wife, he thought to find her here."

As Mrs. Batley exclaimed, "God in heaven!" Ralph Batley's head lifted sharply, and his eyes flashed a warning towards his uncle, and the old man stopped and turned himself about and went towards the fire place.

"Have you known of this?" Mrs. Batley was now looking towards her son and he hesitated before answering her. "Yes. Rouse came the other day and told me, and Mrs. Cadwell"—he inclined his head towards the visitor —"phoned me last night. But I haven't seen . . . Bruce." He seemed to have difficulty in speaking the name and Linda wondered if Mrs. Batley's next question would be, "But have you seen her?" But it was Mrs. Cadwell's remark that caught the attention of the occupants of the room when she said, "He went out without a coat. It was when he got the letter, it was put through the door late on, I . . . I thought it was from you." She was looking again at Ralph Batley, and now he answered her sharply, "A letter from me! To . . . to Bruce? I've written him no letter. If I had anything to say to him it would be face to face. Why did you think it was from me?"

Mrs. Cadwell remained silent for a moment then she

202

answered hastily, "I don't care who it was from, I only want to find him. He has been distraught for days. He had quarrelled with . . . with Edith. They were always quarrelling but they made it up again. He followed her here from London—he knew she was here, she got off the bus in the Bay. Mrs. Weir saw her, spoke to her. She came this way all right, there's no doubt about it."

"Mrs. Cadwell." Ralph Batley was speaking again, his voice deep in his throat now. "I want you to believe me, Bruce and I have not met, you can rest your mind on that. It's the truth."

Mrs. Cadwell's head was bent. "Very well," she said. Slowly she raised her eyes and looked towards Mrs. Batley and her voice was sad. There was a painful, lost sound about it as she said, "I'm sorry, Maggie. I'll go now. They are still looking, I've got a dread about me, you know, Maggie."

Now Mrs. Batley answered and her tone, too, was soft and quiet. "I know, Beatrice. Try not to worry. You'll find him, he's likely just walking."

Ralph Batley led the visitor across the hall and they all listened as they had done a few minutes ago to the front door being opened and closed again. When he returned Linda waited for Mrs. Batley to start firing questions at him, but she didn't, and Linda realised that so deep was the understanding of this woman for her son that she could restrain her own feelings in consideration for him. She sat quietly in her chair for some moments, and then it was Michael she spoke to.

"Will you bring some wood in, Michael, the fire's going down, I see."

"Yes, Gran."

As Michael reluctantly left the room Linda made to follow him, but Mrs. Batley's voice checked her, saying, "Stay." And when the kitchen door had closed on the boy she looked at Linda and said, "I feel you know all about it, whatever there is to know. Your face is too frank and open to hold dark secrets." Now she turned and looked towards the stiff, dark countenance of her son and she spoke one word and that quietly, "Well?" she said.

"I haven't seen Bruce Cadwell."

"I believe you . . . but have you seen her?"

Linda could not bear to look at her employer's face.

"Now, Maggie, don't worry yourself, he's told you." It was Shane speaking.

"He hasn't answered my question, Shane. Ralph, look at me."

Ralph Batley looked at his mother and Linda felt something twist inside of her when he said, "I haven't seen her, Mother."

She watched the mother and son stare at each other for a long moment, then Mrs. Batley's eyes dropped to her hands, and Ralph Batley turned sharply about and went out of the hall.

When the sound of the outside door banging shook the house, Mrs. Batley, looking towards Shane, said quietly, "I don't believe him, Shane, and you won't tell me the truth either, will you?"

"Now, Maggie."

"All right, all right, say no more, don't sin your soul."

"Aw, woman." Shane could find nothing to add to this and with a jerk of his head he lumbered away. And Linda was left alone with Mrs. Batley, who sat in silence now gazing down at her hands as if to probe from them the extent of the trouble weighing on the house.

As she was about to lift the laden tray and go into the kitchen Mrs. Batley said, "Why are men such fools?" Linda cast her eyes swiftly towards the older woman and

Mrs. Batley, raising her head, added, "You wouldn't know, not yet, but they are fools. Come here, girl."

When Linda was standing in front of her, Mrs. Batley, looking up into her face and shaking her head slowly, said, "And you're so bonny."

"Oh, Mrs. Batley." It was with some difficulty that Linda kept her voice steady.

"You are, you are a bonny girl. But away and above that, and what is more important, you are a nice girl." The worn hands came out and caught Linda's and there was unusual strength in the boney fingers. "Beauty without a kind heart is worthless. There, there—" she patted Linda's hand gently now, adding softly, "don't upset yourself, what has to be will be."

Linda put the tray down on the kitchen table, and she closed her eyes for a moment as she repeated to herself Mrs. Batley's words, "Don't upset yourself." She was so caught up in the emotions of this house that even without the feeling she had for its master she wouldn't have been able to remain untouched by the hate and love that threaded the Batleys together. She glanced at the clock, it was just turned eight, the routine of the day had hardly begun and yet she felt weary already, and as she stood for a moment looking out of the kitchen window a most oppressive feeling of dread enveloped her. It was like a premonition of evil and she tried to shake it off by saying, "Don't be silly, don't go looking for trouble." But fifteen minutes later when she had apparently thrown off the feeling, it returned with startling intensity.

She was at the sink when she saw Uncle Shane, he came at a staggering run across the yard. She saw him halt for a moment and look towards the farm buildings before making his way towards the kitchen door, but she was out in the yard before he reached it.

"What is it, Uncle Shane? What's happened?"

The old man's face was blanched and his eyes staring wide as he gripped hold of her arm to support himself. "Is he . . . is he indoors?"

"No, Uncle Shane, he's about the farm somewhere."

The old man was about to speak again when he turned quickly aside and to Linda's astonishment vomited in the yard.

"Oh! Uncle Shane, Uncle Shane, what is it?" She went to support his head but he thrust her roughly away with his hand and stumbled into the kitchen. Grabbing a towel from the rail he sat down by the table and wiped at his mouth as he gasped, "Find him. Find him quickly."

Linda stared for a second at the old man before turning and dashing out of the room. As she ran across the yard calling, "Mr. Batley! Mr. Batley!" she thought that she had done nothing in the last three days but run here and there calling "Mr. Batley, Mr. Batley." At any other time she would have given a wry smile to this thought, but not now. Whatever had frightened Uncle Shane was something that was going to frighten the other occupants of the house.

It was Michael who shouted to her, "Uncle's in the bull pen."

When she got round the corner of the buildings it was to see Ralph Batley coming out of the pen, and without any preliminaries she shouted to him, "Will you come? Something's happened to Uncle Shane, he looks dreadful. He's in the kitchen." Before she had even finished speaking she turned round and was making her way back to the house with Ralph Batley hurrying at her side.

"What's the matter with him?"

"I don't know, he looks dreadful. Something awful must have happened, he was sick in the yard."

He now sprinted ahead of her, and when a minute

later she entered the kitchen he was holding his uncle by the shoulders and the old man was looking up into his face and saying pitifully, "It was up at the end of the valley, just inside where the gate used to be leading into the Cadwell's. I saw it lying in the ditch, the dark thing, and I went and looked. He was face downwards, the back of his head was all blood and the back of his coat, too, was soaked in blood. He was dead cold, he must have been lying there all night. Oh, my God! What does this mean? Tell me, boy, what does this mean?"

Linda saw her employer slowly raise himself up now, his face the colour of a piece of lint, dirty lint. He did not answer his uncle but stared over his head and said softly, "God Almighty!"

"You know what this means, boy, don't you?"

"What?" The word was muttered dazedly as if he was emerging from a drugged sleep.

"I said, you know what this means, don't you?"

"Uncle"—his gaze fell heavily on the old man—"I didn't kill Bruce Cadwell. Could I have faced his mother this morning if I had?"

As Uncle Shane's head drooped and he made no reply, Ralph Batley suddenly cracked at him, "I tell you I didn't do it."

"Ralph!" Mrs. Batley's voice came calling from the hall and the sound of it startled her son. Looking down at his uncle again, he whispered, "Come on."

"Ralph!" The voice was coming near, but before Mrs. Batley reached the kitchen her son was well out into the yard. But the old man was not so quick, and Mrs. Batley's voice halted him as he was going through the door.

"What is it, Shane?"

When he turned his white, shaggy, whiskered face to her and didn't speak, she said, "Oh, what is it? Tell me, man, what is it?"

Shane did not answer, he simply turned from her and walked drunkenly after his nephew.

"What has happened?" Mrs. Batley was leaning against the table looking towards Linda now, but Linda did not answer her either. She, too, felt that at any moment, like Uncle Shane, she could be sick.

"It's Bruce Cadwell, isn't it?"

Linda turned her back on the older woman and Mrs. Batley said quietly and fearfully, "They've found him. . . . is he dead?"

Linda bit into her lip and lowered her head, and after what seemed a long time, Mrs. Batley spoke again. "I knew it," she said. "I've been waiting for it for a long time, years in fact. . . . And the things they dreaded came upon them."

When Linda heard the soft shuffle of Mrs. Batley's slippers she turned slowly about. She was in the kitchen alone now. Groping her way towards a chair she sat down, and putting her elbows on the table she pressed her face into her hands, her eyes were dry and burning. There were some tragedies that went beyond tears. In the picture behind her closed lids she saw Ralph Batley going towards the gun cupboard last night. He hadn't taken the gun then, had he taken it later? He had said he hadn't killed Bruce Cadwell, and she knew that every farmer in the vicinity carried a gun, but she felt sure that there was only one farmer who hated Bruce Cadwell enough to shoot him.

7

It was lunch time for other people, but not for the Batleys, nor yet the Cadwells. Linda was standing in the hall facing the police inspector and for the third time he asked her the same question in a different way. "You have seen no one suspicious about the farm?"

"No, no. I told you." How could she mention Edith Cadwell? How could she mention Sep Watson without incriminating her employer, and what was more, making him out a liar? She knew that everyone, without exception, suspected Ralph Batley to some extent, and some, the Cadwells primarily, were adamant as to his guilt.

Questions had arisen at the beginning of the enquiry concerning the whereabouts of Mrs. Bruce Cadwell. Politely and tentatively the inspector had asked Ralph Batley if he had come across Mrs. Cadwell of late, and the reply he had received had been a curt no.

Everyone in the room, with one exception, had their eyes on Linda—Mrs. Batley, Uncle Shane, the two policemen and the inspector, all but Ralph Batley were looking at her, but she knew that not one of them was waiting for her answers with the trepidation that he was. As she lied to the inspector, the very core of her being was bruised with the knowledge that her employer would swear his life away, and let her do the same, to shield Edith Cadwell. If that wasn't love, what was?

The inspector had finished with her for the moment and was again addressing Ralph Batley. In a polite, quite impersonal tone, he asked. "There is no place anyone could hide around the farm buildings, Mr. Batley?"

"No, none that I don't know of."

"But it wouldn't be impossible for someone to hide here?"

"I suppose not, but there's only the big barn."

"You wouldn't object to us looking around?"

"No, not at all."

Linda put her hand to her throat and she could not help staring at her employer, but he did not meet her eyes. His answer to the inspector told her plainly that Edith Cadwell was no longer in the studio. But hadn't he said she was ill and had a temperature? Where was she? She couldn't be roaming the countryside, she would soon be recognised. He must have worked fast between the time they came and took the body of Bruce Cadwell from the ditch and an hour ago when the inspector arrived from Morpeth.

"That'll be all for the present. Thank you. . . .Thank you." The inspector nodded to one after the other. His voice was such that he could have been a friend who had dropped in and was now taking his leave. As he made to move out of the room he turned to Ralph Batley, saying pleasantly, "Don't bother to come, we'll find our way around. By the way"—he had reached the door leading into the kitchen now and he turned once more to him, saying casually this time—"you said you only have the two guns, the twelve-bore and the four-hundred and ten?"

"Yes. Yes, those are all I have."

"And you said you dismissed your man a few days ago. Did he have a gun?"

"Not to my knowledge."

"Very good. Thank you." The inspector smiled and went out.

Linda looked at Mrs. Batley now, and Mrs. Batley was looking at her son and in a voice edged with trembling was asking him, "Do they know what gun it was?"

"It was a twelve-bore." Ralph Batley's voice was thick and it deepened as he added, "But I didn't use it. I didn't do it, Mother."

"No, son, I know you didn't do it. At first I thought you might have, but you'd shoot no man in the back, not twice in the back. I know you didn't do it. But what I feel strongly"—now her voice rose to a trembling pitch—"is that you know who did do it."

"How should I know who did it?" They were confronting each other.

"Is she about the place? I'm asking you: Is she about the place?"

"If she's about the place they'll find her, won't they? If I were hiding her here would I let them search?"

"You wouldn't be able to stop them."

"No, I don't suppose I would, but I'd be worried, wouldn't I?"

Mrs. Batley's eyes were the first to drop away.

"Maggie . . . Maggie"—Shane's voice came at her now, like a thin reed pipe—"have you a drop of anything by you?"

"You are having no drops today, Shane. There are enough troubles on the house, God knows, without you going mad. Have a strong cup of coffee." She looked towards Linda. "Would you mind making a pot of coffee, Linda, please?"

Compassionately Linda glanced at Uncle Shane's bent head. If she had her own way she would have given Uncle Shane a bottle of spirits at this moment, for the old man was in deep distress. But Mrs. Batley knew best.

She kept her eyes averted from the master of the house as she made her way into the kitchen, but it was only a

211

short time later as she was putting the coffee pot and cups onto the tray that he came in and stood by the table.

"Do you believe I've done this?" His voice was deep, almost guttural.

She answered him after a perceivable hesitation. "No, not now." Then her eyes flicked away. "I did at first, before I knew he had been shot in the back. I . . . I think like your mother on that point."

"Thank you." Across the table they stared at each other for the space of seconds. "I'm in trouble, Linda." His voice was still deep and thick but now gave evidence of the riot of emotions he was clamping down on. "They think I did this, they're out to prove I did it. The Cadwells will help them every step of the way, naturally."

Linda did not answer this confidence with any sympathetic words, instead she asked a question. "Where is she?" she said.

"Up in the rafters."

"The rafters?"

"There's a ledge where the big beams meet at the side opposite the studio. It's high up and doesn't look broad enough to hold anyone, they'll never look for her there."

"I thought she was ill."

"She is. In many ways she's a very sick woman."

"Does she know what's happened?"

"Yes. I had to tell her. She became terrified; she thinks"—he paused, and his eyes were veiled from Linda's gaze—"she thinks they might blame her."

"Mr. Batley"—she was leaning across the table towards him—she had wanted to say "Ralph" but she couldn't—"Mr. Batley, I think you should know that she has a key to the staircase door, or . . . or is that no news to you?"

His eyes were on hers now, hard and penetrating. "It is news. What more do you know?"

She swallowed. "I should have told you this before . . . Sep Watson was about the place last night. When I went up to the studio after meeting you, and you said you couldn't find anyone, I heard his voice. It was—he was—he was in the studio talking to Mrs. Cadwell."

She watched his lower jaw slowly sink downwards, then snap closed.

"You're sure of this?"

"Yes, I heard them. I heard them talking. I—I meant to surprise them but the door was locked, and when she opened it there was no one but herself there. Then I saw that the staircase door had been opened, the dirt on the floor was scraped where it had been pulled back. She knew that I knew."

"Is—is that all you know?" He was still looking intently at her.

"Yes."

"Are you sure?"

"Yes, yes, if I knew anything more I would tell you."

When he swung round from her and went towards the door she said quickly, "You can't go to her now, they're still about the place."

He paused. "I'm not going to her, I'm going to see if I can find Watson. If they ask where I am, say I've gone to see to the sheep near the top boundary."

"Yes, all right, I'll do that." She stared at the closed door for some time before lifting up the tray and going into the hall. And it was as she stood pouring out the coffee before the still-bowed head of Shane and the silent, gravely troubled woman that Michael came dashing into the hall crying, "Gran! Gran! Grandfather Cadwell is coming along the cliff path, he's very angry. He pushed Grandma Cadwell away, and she fell down and she's limping."

Both Shane and Mrs. Batley rose to their feet together,

and Mrs. Batley, in a low tone said, "Now, Michael, listen to me. I want you to go and stay with Sarah and the calf, stay there until Linda comes for you. Go now."

"But, Gran . . ."

"Go, Michael, do as I bid you. And don't come back until I tell you."

"Yes, Gran."

The boy went slowly out of the room, and Mrs. Batley, turning to Linda, said quickly, "Where is he . . . Ralph?"

"I think he has gone to look for Sep Watson."

"Sep Watson? Why Sep Watson?"

"He was about the place last night, I heard him, Mrs. Batley."

"You heard him?" This was Shane speaking now. "Why didn't you say so afore?"

"Well, I . . ."

"It doesn't matter, it doesn't matter. Ralph's out of the way and thank God for it. Go and open the front door, Linda. Quickly now, for they may get round into the yard and meet up with the inspector and the others."

"That's the best thing that could happen in my opinion."

"Quiet, Shane! I'll deal with John Cadwell."

Linda almost ran to the front door but her fingers fumbled at the bolt and chain and when she had the door open there was no sign of Mr. Cadwell outside. Then she almost left the ground as his voice came from behind her in the hall crying, "Where is he? It's no use, Maggie Batley, you won't be able to hide him under your skirts any longer."

She was on the point of closing the door when she caught sight of Mrs. Cadwell coming from the cliff path and approaching the end of the house, and the change, even over the distance, in the smart, austere woman drew her immediately outside and towards her.

"Are you hurt, Mrs. Cadwell?"

"I—I've hurt my knee. Is my husband . . . ?"

"Yes, yes. Let me help you." She took Mrs. Cadwell's arm and helped her towards the front door and in through the lobby. Then they were in the hall under the thunder of Mr. Cadwell's voice.

"He'll hang, Maggie Batley. I'll not rest easy until he's got his deserts. If I don't get him, they will, and when they have him if they don't finish him off I'll wait until my last day, but I'll get him."

"Stop bawling, John Cadwell, I don't want to fight with you. You're in trouble, deep trouble. Whether you believe it or not, my heart bleeds for you at this moment, but my son isn't the cause of that trouble, he didn't kill Bruce. You've never liked Ralph, John, but in your heart you know he's not the type of man to crawl up behind another and shoot him in the back. You'd know that if you'd stop to think. There are others who wanted Bruce out of the way, I don't need to name them, and you'll likely find out soon enough who shot your son."

And now with a composure that simply amazed her Linda watched Mrs. Batley turn towards Mrs. Cadwell and say, "Sit down, Beatrice. Get off your legs. Are you hurt much?"

Mrs. Cadwell did not answer but slowly tried to lower herself into a chair, groaning as she did so with pain of her knee, and Mr. Cadwell's voice came at them all again crying, "You can talk until you're black in the face, Maggie Batley, I know your whelp."

"Don't call my son a whelp. And you don't know him." Mrs. Batley was facing him again. "You've always thought what you wanted to think, not only about him but everybody else. Now you listen to me"—she raised her hand at him—"and stop waving that gun about, hasn't there been enough gun play? All right, all right, I

215

know what you're going to say, but think man, think. If Ralph had wanted to kill Bruce he would have done it three years ago, he knew where they both were at the time and his blood was hot against them. He's had time to cool down quite a bit in three years, don't you think?"

"No, I don't. He still wanted Edith. You can't tell me that a man who is deprived of a woman ever forgets her. Love might cease but hate takes its place, and in hate, or love, he would have her if he got the——"

"Shut your mouth, John Cadwell."

As Mrs. Batley rapped out this command Linda's eyes were drawn towards Mrs. Cadwell. She was sitting with her hands clasped tightly on her knees and her head bowed, and Linda's sympathy and understanding went out to this woman, for hadn't her husband just said that he had never forgotten Maggie Batley, or Maggie Ramshaw, that was. Whether in hate, or love, it would be hard for anyone to decide at this stage, but Mrs. Cadwell's drooping attitude seemed to point to a certain knowledge. Linda had thought of Mrs. Cadwell as a dignified, rather haughty individual, now she saw her as just another woman, hiding behind a façade.

"Go home, John Cadwell, and wait, and I have a feeling it won't be long before you know the truth of the matter. But I tell you here and now, you are barking up the wrong tree when you are hunting my Ralph. And finally, listen to me, John." She did not add Cadwell this time, and it was as if she and the tormented man before her were in the room alone, for she said, quietly now, "If you do Ralph an injury in any way you'll have me to deal with, whatever you do to him I'll do to you, that is a promise, John."

Not only the tone but Mrs. Batley's whole attitude made Linda shudder. She was amazed at the strength of this sick woman. She turned her face away and looked at

Uncle Shane. He had his head bowed as if the scene was too painful for him.

"Could I ask you to phone, Maggie, and get them to bring the car?"

All their eyes were turned now towards Mrs. Cadwell, and Mrs. Batley, her attitude changing again, answered quietly, "Yes, Beatrice, yes."

"I'll do it." Linda hurried away to the room under the stairs, glad to escape for a moment from the terrible raw emotions.

When she got through to the Cadwell house it was Rouse Cadwell's voice that answered.

"Mr. Cadwell, this is Linda Metcalfe. Will you please bring the car? Your mother is here and has hurt her knee."

"What . . . what's happened? Is my father there? Has he . . . ?"

Linda answered the racing questions briefly and calmly, saying, "Yes, he's here."

"Has he . . . is Batley . . . ?"

"Mr. Batley is away in the top field. Your father hasn't met him."

"Thank God for that." There came a sigh on the wire, then Rouse Cadwell's voice, changing suddenly, said, "But why I should thank God for his safety I don't know, because if I meet him myself I won't be accountable for what might happen."

"You'd be wrong, Mr. Cadwell. Mr. Batley didn't do this thing . . . I know he didn't."

"Personal opinions won't help much in this matter. My brother is dead, and the police are not fools, they'll find the proof they're after. Anyway, I'll bring the car over at once. If Mother can't walk I'd better bring it along the cliff road."

"Yes. I'll tell them."

When Linda re-entered the hall she was surprised and apprehensive to find that Mr. Cadwell had already gone and Shane was helping Mrs. Cadwell towards the glass door. Mrs. Batley was standing in the middle of the room looking after them. When Linda came up to her she did not look at her, but taking hold of her arm held it firmly until Shane had pulled the door closed, then she turned to her. "You said he went to find Sep Watson. Did he go to the house?" Her words were running one into the other.

"I don't know, Mrs. Batley."

"Do you know where Sep Watson lives?"

"No."

"You know the place where the sheep got out? Take that road. It's a little cottage standing back on the right, you can't miss it, it's the only one thereabouts. Tell him that Mr. Cadwell has been here. Tell him to be careful and not run across him if he can help it." Mrs. Batley now looked downwards as she said, "I thought I could manage John Cadwell but this is beyond me. He's beside himself, and he won't rest until he meets up with Ralph. . . .Go! Go and warn him. Hurry now."

Linda ran out of the hall and through the kitchen, whipping her coat from the back of the door as she did so, but she had the sense to draw to a walk as she was crossing the yard. And she kept to a walk until she had left the farm buildings. Now, taking the cliff path, she ran swiftly until she came to the valley, then down it and up the other side and through the narrow, winding path to the outcrop of rocks that were near the boundary. She was passing the largest of these when the soft hissing of her name brought her to a dead stop, and there, standing well within the shelter of a rock and almost hidden by scrub, was Ralph Batley. Silently he beckoned her towards him, and when she came up he cautioned her to

218

silence. As she looked at him enquiringly he bent his head and whispered, "Watson, he's down on the road. Twice he's got under the wire, then gone back again. I don't know what his game is, but wait."

As they stood tense and close together, his face only inches away from her own, she could not but comment to herself on the almost drastic change in his appearance. It was, she thought, as if she were looking at a different man, an elder brother to the man she knew. True, most of the time his countenance had been stiff and forbidding, but now his face looked so much older. He looked weary, and his eyes had a sad, defeated look. Compassion for him rose in her. She had the strong urge to put her arms about him and comfort him. Even the knowledge that he might love another woman didn't matter at this moment, all she wanted to do was to give him some measure of comfort. But as she couldn't bring herself to do this she delivered to him the message that had brought her here. "Your mother sent me." She had her lips near his ear. "Mr. Cadwell has been to the house. He had his gun with him and was very threatening. Your mother begs you to be on the look-out and take care."

He turned his head and looked at her, but what reply he was going to make was checked. With the quick pressure of his hand on her arm he warned her to silence. She watched him now look cautiously round the rock, then stretching quickly upwards he gripped a jutting piece of stone with his hands and, finding a foothold about three feet from the ground for his foot, he hoisted himself up over the edge of the rock. He stayed in this position for only a few seconds, before dropping to the ground again. "He's gone, that was his bike I heard." He moved further into the open now and it was with his back to her that he gave her an answer to the warning. "I'm not afraid of meeting up with Cadwell," he said. "He's a rough, uncouth swine, and he's not above hiring others to do his dirty work. I know where I stand with him. At a pinch he'd fight it out, clean, according to his lights."

"He didn't talk so generously of you."

"No. Well, that's beside the point, but if I'd only him to fear at the moment, I wouldn't worry, but I'm up against someone more dangerous than Cadwell. At one time I thought there couldn't be anyone worse than he is, but you live and learn. . . . Come on, we'd better be getting back."

There was now no chance to keep up a conversation, for he did not suit his steps to hers. She had almost to trot to keep pace with him. But just before they came in sight of the farm buildings he slowed his walk, and turning to her, he said quietly, "If they've gone, I want you to help me . . . will you?"

"I'll do whatever I can."

"Have you a spare breeches and jacket?"

"Breeches and jacket?" She screwed her eyes up at him. "Yes."

"Good. Can you get them out, do you think, without being noticed? Wear two pairs at once, or something like that." He shook his head. "It's this way, I've got to get her out . . . Edith. She must get away, and if she was wearing your things, and that scarf you sometimes have over your head, she could go in the jeep with me, as if we were going to the Bay with the milk. I must get her as far as Morpeth, once there she can look after herself."

"But I thought you said she was ill, she had a temperature. You were going to get the doctor."

"I know, I know what I said." His voice was terse. "She was feverish, and she is ill, but now, ill or well, she must get away. Do you *mind* giving her your clothes?" He paused. "I'll see that you don't lose by it."

"That won't be necessary," she said sharply. Then

went on, "I keep a spare coat hanging in Sarah's barn. I doubt if I could get another pair of breeches over these, but there's a pair I put out for cleaning. They're in the bottom of the cupboard in the kitchen."

"Good. You can easily get them from there, but whatever you do don't let my mother see you. You'd better go now, round the front way, I'll go through the arch. I expect the police will have gone by now. But if by any chance they've gone back into the house do nothing for the moment. Wait." His hand went out as she turned away—his fingers were touching lightly on her shoulders —"I want you to know how grateful I am."

"That's all right, it's nothing. Anything I can do to help, you know I will."

"Yes. Yes, I know that. You're so good."

Their eyes held, then almost simultaneously they turned from each other. . . .

When ten minutes later Linda entered the big barn, Ralph Batley was waiting for her, but he was not standing idle, he was hosing out the pens. And she knew as she watched his quick, nervous movements that this too must be a worry to him, for the work schedule had gone completely adrift.

"I've got the things."

He turned off the tap and hung up the hose before speaking. "There's nobody about the yards, how about the house?"

"They're gone, your mother says they left about ten minutes ago. She said the inspector wanted to see you again, he's going to ring and tell you what time he's coming out."

"Is he?" He made a deep obeisance with his head. "Well, I hope he finds me at home."

She could make very little out of this remark. She followed him now towards the big barn and watched him pick up a ladder from the floor and hoist it up on to the first storey. When she herself had ascended the steps he was at the far end of the barn, and when she reached the line of boxes he had already set the ladder up against the beams. She watched him mount upwards and heard him say softly, "Edith . . . Edith."

When the white thin face appeared like a blur over the side of the beam the effect was eerie to say the least. It looked, Linda thought, like a disembodied thing floating near the roof.

"Come down."

"Have they gone?"

"Yes. Can you manage? Here, take my hand."

"I'm all right, I'm all right."

It was with amazing alacrity that Edith Cadwell descended the ladder, and when a moment later she stood in the passageway Linda could not help commenting to herself that there wasn't much sign of illness about her now. Fear, yes, because the girl's face was almost livid with fear.

"Linda has brought some of her clothes for you, I want you to get into them. You won't be noticed dressed like this in the jeep. I'm taking you to Morpeth." He did not look at her as he spoke but pulled the ladder from the beams and laid it on the floor.

"No. No, Ralph, I'm not going, I'm safer here. They won't come back."

"They will come back, Edith." He was facing her now and his voice sounded strangely flat to Linda, weary and flat, as if he hadn't just made this statement but had been pressing it home for some time.

"I'm not going, I tell you I'm not going, Ralph. What would I do? Where would I go?" There was a note of panic in her voice.

"You said last night you had friends in Morpeth and

222

you would go there today, that you'd be safe there. . . ." He paused here for a long moment before adding, "He wouldn't find you there, you said. Well, there's no need to worry now, is there, Edith?"

Her lips were trembling and the muscles of her face twitching. "I'm not going, Ralph."

They were both quiet, staring at each other, their wills warring.

"This is the last place they would think of looking for me." Her voice was low now. "Anyway, why should they bother, it was only . . . only Bruce that was out to find me, not anyone else?"

There followed a silence while the eyes of each probed the other. So lost in their searching did they become that it was borne home painfully to Linda that they were momentarily oblivious of her presence.

Then Ralph Batley's voice cut into the spell, saying, "They will want to question you, they will want to know where you have spent your time during the last few days. . . .There are a lot of things they'll want to know, Edith."

"Ralph! Ralph!" On a sudden she flung herself against him, her arms round his neck, her composure broken, pleading now like a child. "Ralph, don't send me away. Please! Please! you can't send me away. Please, let me stay here, I feel safe with you. I always felt safe with you. This will pass over, they will forget all about me. I don't mind your mother, I don't, I don't. I'm sorry I said the things I did. I'll put up with anything. . . .Oh! I didn't mean that, I only meant . . ." Her head sank on to his shoulder. "Don't send me away, Ralph."

Linda turned away. She felt that both of them had entirely forgotten her existence, but in this she was wrong, for she hadn't taken more than a couple of steps when Ralph Batley's abrupt tones stopped her, saying, "Let me have those things."

As she picked up her coat and breeches from where she had placed them across one of the empty packing-cases and handed them to him, Edith Cadwell moved swiftly forward. Her voice a faint hissing whisper now, she said, "I won't put them on, I won't. I'm not going, I tell you I'm not going."

"Listen to me, Edith"—he rounded on her quickly—"if you were yourself you would know that this has got to come to a head some time. You have either got to get right away or face up to the Cadwells. What is it going to be? I can't keep you here any longer."

"Face up to the Cadwells? Why should I face up to the Cadwells? I have nothing to do with the Cadwells any more. I am free! Ralph, I'm free, don't you realise that . . . free."

Gently he removed her clawing hands from his coat, but he held them within his grip as, continuing to look at her, he said, softly but insistently, "Edith . . . Edith, get this into your head, if you don't get away now you'll *have* to face the Cadwells. And what is more . . . the inspector."

"The inspector?" Her mouth hung open for a moment before her whole body jerked and she tried to pull her hands from his. "I know nothing, what could the inspector have to ask me?"

"Don't get excited. Now don't get excited, Edith. Edith, listen to me." He shook her. "Everybody is under suspicion until this matter is cleared up, everybody. Me, you, everyone. But most of all me . . . and you. Don't you understand? It's for your own good, your own good, I want you away."

Linda now watched the great brown eyes slowly turn on her, and something in their depths startled her, and for the first time she thought that what Ralph Batley had said about this girl was true—she was ill and not just physically ill.

The next second the eyes were jerked away from her and all three of them had turned their gaze towards the end of the barn, and the sound of footsteps.

"Are you there, Batley?" The voice, unmistakably that of Rouse Cadwell, brought their eyes together. Ralph Batley now using both hands simultaneously pushed Linda forward while at the same time he thrust Edith Cadwell back in the direction of the studio.

When Linda reached the edge of the upper floor and looked down she could not help an exclamation escaping her, for there below her was not only Rouse Cadwell but with him was Sep Watson.

There was no exclamation of surprise from Ralph Batley when in the next second he came to her side, but Linda, glancing quickly at him, guessed that he was momentarily taken off his guard by the sight of the cowman, yet his voice gave no indication of his feelings as he asked gruffly, "Well, what d'you want?"

The question could have applied to either of the men standing below, but it was Rouse Cadwell who replied, "I want to talk to you, it's important."

After a moment of staring at them Ralph Batley turned round and descended the ladder. When Linda, following him, reached the foot he was saying menacingly to Sep Watson, "I told you what would happen if I found you on my place again, didn't I?"

"It's that very threat that kept him away"—it was Rouse Cadwell speaking—"so he came to me. He has something to tell you. Do you want to hear it?"

"That will depend, won't it?" Ralph Batley was staring at the cowman when Rouse Cadwell said, "It might mean the saving of your neck."

This statement seemed to make no impact on him but,

still looking at Sep Watson, Ralph said, "Well, go on, I'm waiting."

Linda would have said that no circumstances could have changed Sep Watson, but the man standing before his old employer did not look the thick-set, dull-witted, gossiping bully that she remembered. It seemed to her that the wave of fear that enveloped the farm had reached him, for his face was drawn and his voice when he spoke was neither bumptious nor whining, but the voice of a man in trouble.

"I . . . I came round last night." His eyes dropped away from Ralph Batley's at the next words. "I was after gettin' me own back, I came to do you a mischief. Well . . . not you yourself, your things. I meant to get one of the cattle, say Sarah, or set this here alight." He now lifted his head and moved it in a wide circular movement above his thick shoulders. "I saw a chink of light coming from the studio door, the outside door, and it set me wonderin' as I knew you didn't use it no more. It was when I was goin' up the stairs that old Shane came on the scene and I bolted. I made for up there." His head jerked towards the upper platform of the barn. "I knew it wasn't you in there 'cos I'd seen you go into the house, but I thought it might be . . ." He paused and once again his eyes dropped, and Linda shivered, knowing that it was herself he had imagined would be in the studio.

"Go on, we know who you thought was there. Go on." Ralph Batley's voice had a rasping sound.

"Well, I pushed the door open and then I got the gliff of me life when I saw it was Mrs. Cadwell. She was frightened for a minute, and then when she heard you comin' she acted funny like. She told me to get under the couch and keep mum, an' I did. And then you came in and she played on that there'd been nobody near her,

226

and when you was gone she said a funny thing. She said
. . . well, that I was the answer to her prayers and would I
take a note to her husband? Then she said she had no
paper, there was plenty of pencils 'bout the place but no
paper, an' would I just write and say would he meet her
at the gate in the valley? I told her I wasn't much hand
with a pen but I'd do it. . . . I thought it was one way of
getting me own back. Then she let me out of the top
door, she had a key. And it wasn't until I was half-way
cross the first field that it dawned on me I hadn't me gun,
she had taken it off me when I got under the couch."

Again the cowman's eyes flickered downwards and
Ralph Batley said, "I didn't know you had a gun, Watson. You always professed to have no use for them."

"Aye. Well, that's what I told you. But I've always had
a gun. I did a bit of poaching on the side."

"What is it?"

"It's a twelve-bore." Now the cowman's eyes were looking straight into Ralph Batley's and his voice took on an
agitated earnestness. "I went home and scribbled out the
note and took it up to the Cadwells"—he motioned to
where Rouse Cadwell was standing silently listening to
the story he already knew— "and then I came on back
here. I went up to the studio again. It was round about
midnight, and I tapped on both doors but couldn't get
an answer. I kept at it for a while but couldn't make her
hear. Then I decided to give it up and come back the
night. And then . . . well . . . and then I heard the news,
the news that Mr. Cadwell had been shot in the back,
twice, and that it was a twelve-bore that done it. And I
knew if they found the gun . . . well, they only had to
take finger-prints and they'd know it was mine. You see
. . . you see"—he turned his head away now and looked
towards the wide opening of the main barn, as he went
on—"that couple of years I was away just after the war I

was doing a stretch. I broke into a shop and was caught and beat the bloke up afore they got me." Now his head jerked towards Ralph Batley again as he gabbled, "But I didn't do this, I'm no murderer. Not that many a time I didn't feel like conking you off 'cos of your high and mighty airs and graces, but I'd never have been able to bring meself to do it. Set the barn alight, aye, or put a bullet into a beast, aye, or lay poison an' do the dogs in, but not murder. I tried to come this mornin' when I heard, but knew what kind of reception I'd get. So I went to Mr. Cadwell here, for I'm not takin' the rap for nobody, her or nobody else. When she took that gun off me she held it gingerly, as if she was frightened of it, and I remembered after, she had her hanky in her hand when she pushed it behind her on the couch. She must have known what she was goner do then, for she wasn't frightened of any gun, she was a good shot, you know she was."

The truth seemed terrible to Linda, staggering, yet she felt she had known it all the time. But she had to admit she had only surmised it. Nevertheless, someone else had been aware of it, vitally aware of it, and this was proved true when Rouse Cadwell said in a quiet tone, "You knew this all along, didn't you, Ralph?" The very fact that he hadn't added Batley, or just used her employer's surname, spoke volumes for his changed opinion.

Ralph Batley did not answer, but he turned slowly about and looked up the ladder towards the studio door. Then without looking back he said to no one in particular, "Wait here." Slowly he ascended the ladder, and when he disappeared from view Linda continued to listen to each heavy lagging step he made towards Edith Cadwell, and she wondered what he was thinking, what agony of mind he was enduring. Some seconds later his voice came faintly to her, calling, "Edith! Edith!" then louder, "Edith! Edith!" She heard him running the width of the barn. She was with him in her mind as he looked here and there between the bales and she knew the exact moment he would make his reappearance at the edge of the upper loft.

"She's gone, There's no sign of her." He scrambled down the ladder, and before any of them had reached the opening of the barn he was past them, but when his eyes turned towards the staircase leading from the studio her eyes were on it too, and the open door.

"She's desperate, and ill." He was speaking to Rouse Cadwell. "The cliffs, she'll likely make for the cliffs." Like missiles from a catapult the two men covered the yard, then Linda was running, racing after them towards the cliffs, and the oddness of the situation could not help but penetrate her thoughts, for here she was running almost side by side with Sep Watson.

"There she is." Ralph Batley's shout came back to her, and the next instant her heart missed a beat as she saw Edith Cadwell seeming to leap into the air from the cliff edge. Then noting the point at which she had disappeared she knew that Edith had not jumped over the cliff but was descending to the beach by the steps.

Linda was away ahead of Sep Watson now, and just behind the two men when they reached the cliff top and there, looking down through the veil of sea fret she saw the ghostly outline of Edith Cadwell walking into the water.

"My God, she's taking the boat out." Ralph Batley followed this by a yell, "Edith! Edith! That's no good, wait a minute. Do you hear? Wait a minute!"

She watched him now as he sprang down the cliff steps, expecting him at any moment to lose his balance. On his heels went Rouse Cadwell. Her own descent had to be more cautious. She remembered that Ralph Batley had told her to be very careful if she ever descended to the beach this way. It was strange but this was the first time she had used these steps, and as she tried to move more swiftly down their slippery surface she realised that his warning hadn't been unnecessary. As she stepped on to the beach Rouse Cadwell's voice came to her now, shouting, "Edith! Don't be a fool, Edith! You'll never make it, the tide's going out, you'll never get through the gap."

When, panting, she reached the water's edge it was to see Ralph Batley tearing off his coat and kicking off his shoes. He was already in the water when he discarded his trousers. Rouse Cadwell too was standing in the water, and he appealed to Ralph, shouting at him, "It's no use, you'll never do it, you'll be carried out by the current. She must take her chance, man, don't be a fool." And he put out his two hands to restrain his one-time enemy, but at that moment Linda saw her employer drop into the shivering cold water and she shut her eyes tightly.

The trembling that now filled her body was a mixture of fear and shock from the cold water, for she was standing beside Rouse Cadwell, and they both gazed helplessly to where the two objects were being swept towards the narrow gap. Ahead was the slim little sailing dinghy, without sails now and being tossed like a cork on the turbulent, churning water as it rushed on its way back to the open sea.

"He'll never make it, he'll never reach her, he's mad."

Linda's mind echoed Rouse Cadwell's words as she watched the threshing arms now hardly perceivable against the white froth of the water.

"My God! She's . . . she's over, she's over. . . . Oh, Edith!"

Linda herself was speechless. She could voice no cry, utter no words. She could just make out the dim black outline of the upturned bottom of the boat, and it said to her, what chance has a man in those waters if a boat could be heeled over like a matchstick? Her heart was like lead within her when Rouse shouted, "He's got her, he's got her!"

"Where?" She strained her eyes through the fret, trying to pick out the figures that evidently Rouse was seeing.

"He has, he has, he's got her. Look there! If he can only make those rocks, the tide's going down. If only he can reach them he could hang on."

"But for how long?" Linda was asking the question of herself, because even with the tide out these rocks would still be surrounded by deep water.

"Yes, look! He's made them. Oh, thank God! Now if he can only hold on."

Linda found that she was clinging to Rouse Cadwell and he to her, but when in the next moment he thrust her away she had her work cut out to retain her balance. When she saw him run towards the cruiser at the end of the bay she yelled, "You can't use that, the engine's broken." For answer she got a backward wave of his hand which drew her swiftly out of the water and along the beach. He was tearing at the rope attached to the mooring stage when she reached him, and again she cried, "The engine's gone, Uncle Shane . . ."

"There's a quant pole, I've quanted this across the bay dozens of times. Where's Watson?" They looked along the beach but could see no sign of the cowman. Linda was raising her eyes to the top of the cliff when Rouse Cadwell said sharply, "Come with me, I might need a hand."

"Yes, yes." She was already lumbering her way through the water, and as she pulled herself up the three steps attached to the stern of the little cruiser, she wondered vaguely for a moment if she was in the middle of a

231

nightmare and would soon happily wake up. But when Rouse Cadwell hoisted himself aboard and, grabbing the quant pole from its rest on the top of the cabin, thrust it into the water, she knew this was no dream nightmare, but a terrifying live one.

"Go to the bows, yell if you can see them."

Hanging on to the cabin rail she went round the narrow deck. When she reached the bows she could see the two figures clinging to the rocks and she shouted back, "They're holding on, he's . . . he's trying to pull her up." She gazed towards the rock and the two bobbing heads, but one minute they were in front of her, the next they seemed to be swept away, but this she knew was the erratic movement of the boat as Rouse Cadwell wielded the pole.

The tide was carrying the cruiser as it had carried the sailing dinghy, rapidly towards the gap leading to the sea, and she wondered nervously, what if Rouse Cadwell couldn't control the boat and the current actually took them through the gap, what would happen to them?

The bobbing heads were now in front of her, and she called anxiously back over the cabin top, "More that way," gesticulating wildly with her arm. "Hurry! He's having to hold her up. Hurry!" It was just as she made this second demand that she was almost knocked over the bows and their progress stopped abruptly.

"What . . . what is it?" She went halfway along the deck hanging on to the cabin rail and looking to where Rouse Cadwell was pushing madly at the pole. "We've struck a sandbank . . . good God! She's heeling. Look out! Here"—he turned and made a grab at Linda—"come up this way, on to the top."

When she clutched at his hand she saw with amazement that he was up above her and the cabin top looked like a sloping roof. As he pulled her to his side it was with horror that she realised that the boat was heeled right over.

"Her bottom's like mush. Must have hit a rock. Look, can you swim?" He had to shout above the noise of the rushing water.

"Yes, yes, I can swim."

"Go back to the beach then, I'll go on to them."

"No, no, I'll come with you, I'm a good swimmer, a strong swimmer."

"Have it your own way, there's no time to argue." He was throwing off his things and Linda did the same, and as she dropped into the water a second after him she felt she would die with shock, so cold was it. She had said she was a strong swimmer, but she had judged her ability by calm waters and the public baths. Here the fight was not to swim but to resist being carried away on the outgoing tide. The crawl was her best and strongest stroke and at one stage, as she lifted her head for air, she glimpsed to her intense relief that the two figures were now lying prone on the rocks ahead. He had made it, he was safe. Thank God for that.

As she felt the tug of the current she had to urge herself on to greater efforts. Then never again in her life was she to experience greater joy as when she lifted her head upwards and saw, a few feet away, lying flat above her, with his arms stretched downwards to her, the beloved face of Ralph Batley.

With a heave and the agonising feel of the skin being ripped off her knees, she was pulled up on to the rock where she lay for a moment coughing and spitting out the sea water. She wondered rather dazedly why his hand had released her so suddenly and why he had said no word to her. She turned slowly on to her side—pressing the salt water from her eyes, and the explanation was given to her and she cried out against it. "Oh, no! oh,

233

no!" When she saw him slip into the water again she had no need to ask what was the matter now.

The way Rouse Cadwell had asked her, "Can you swim?" seemed to point to himself being an excellent swimmer, but it had been proved to her only a minute ago that you could not judge your prowess against such a current. To her horror now she saw that Rouse himself was in difficulty, grave difficulty, for he wasn't swimming, just keeping himself afloat and being swept with the current towards the gap. She saw, too, that it was a tired swimmer that was going to his rescue, for there was no fight now in the flaying arms of Ralph Batley. After long agonising moments she saw the two men meet, crash together would be a better description. Their arms were about each other and they seemed to be whirling in a mad dance. It was agonising minutes later that she realised they were not struggling to return to her and Edith Cadwell, but were swimming towards a sharp black point away from her, and then she saw the reason for this. They were making for the calmer water, away from this rock which was in the main stream of the current. When at last she saw them both clinging to the black point she took in a great intake of breath, yet at the same time she asked the question, how long could they hope to hang on there? But anyway, they were out of the pull of the current. Her mind, released for the moment from the anxiety concerning them, turned to the inert figure at her side, and she bent over the twisted form of the woman who was the cause of their present plight, the woman who had killed her husband and might yet be the means of destroying two other men. Her heart was bitter against this woman until the moment when her fingers touched the sodden face and turned it towards her. Her hand came slowly off the cold flesh and her head turned from the wide staring eyes, larger now and more deeply brown

234

than ever. She thought of artificial respiration, but she had never given artificial respiration. Yet she knew that had she been most proficient in this matter it would have been of little use. She shuddered violently and looked desperately towards the two men again, and she saw now that Rouse Cadwell was no longer clinging to the rock, and Ralph Batley was hanging on to it with one hand only, he was using his other arm to hold Rouse Cadwell to him.

She was on her feet now. Should she swim to them? It was evident that something was wrong with Rouse Cadwell and that Ralph Batley was very tired. Desperately she looked towards the shore where she could just make out the figures of Mrs. Batley, Uncle Shane and Michael, and two other figures, male figures, whom she didn't recognise, for neither of them had the bulk of Sep Watson.

It was as she thought frantically, I must go to them, perhaps between us we can get Rouse Cadwell to the beach, that the faint chunk-chunk-chunk sound came to her, and it brought her eyes swiftly to the gap. . . .The coastguard? No. . . . A lifeboat could never get through that narrow gap. The little cruiser that was now lying half submerged might have made it in its heyday with its engine full throttle, but anything the size of a lifeboat could never get through that slit in the rocks. But there it was again, the chunk-chunk-chunking, coming nearer and nearer. She could hear it clearly now above the surge and gurgle of the water. . . .When the little red object shot through the gap in the rocks and forged its way steadily into the bay she found she was laughing, yet her face was wet, and not with the salt water, and she chided herself saying, "Stop it, pull yourself together."

Linda was past feeling surprise when she saw that the man at the tiller of the little outboard motor dinghy was Mr. Cadwell himself. As he came nearer she saw him glance first towards the men and then towards her, but before she could shout anything to him he had made his way towards the point of black rock.

As she watched the precarious business of hoisting Rouse Cadwell into the little boat she realised what the trouble was with him . . . cramp. And she shuddered at the thought of what might have happened had not Ralph Batley acted when he did.

As the boat and its three occupants came towards her Linda thought how strange life was. Only that morning Mr. Cadwell had threatened to kill Ralph Batley, yet here he was rescuing him. But Ralph Batley had saved him from losing another son, that was certain.

There was no talking when the craft reached the rocks. Linda bent down and held it steady while Ralph Batley and Mr. Cadwell got out. The older man stood for a short time looking down at his daughter-in-law. Linda could not see his face so she could not gauge his feelings, but whatever he was thinking his hands were gentle as he lifted her with the help of Ralph Batley into the dinghy.

The boat was now very low in the water and Mr. Cadwell, looking up at Linda, said gruffly but apologetically, "It won't take us all."

Before she could say, "It's all right, go ahead," Ralph Batley had pulled himself back up on to the rock again and, looking at his old enemy, said quietly, "She's overloaded as it is, we'll wait."

Mr. Cadwell, his face grey and harrowed looking, with none of his usual bumptiousness evident, inclined his head. Then dragging off his coat, he threw it up towards Linda before starting up the engine again.

As she watched the boat move away from the rock Linda wondered how this miracle had come about, for it was nothing short of a miracle that Ralph Batley and Rouse Cadwell had been saved. And then she remembered that there had been one figure missing from those on the beach. If Sep Watson had been there his bulk would have identified him. It must have been he who had informed Mrs. Batley and Shane, then run to the Cadwells for help. Perhaps his knowledge of Mr. Cadwell telling him that word of mouth would be more effective in this case than a plea over the phone. Anyway, however Mr. Cadwell had been urged to take out the dinghy in this fast-running sea was no matter. The wonder of it was he had done it.

Thankfully she pulled her knees up into the warmth of the coat.

"You're cold."

"Ye-es." Her teeth were chattering but she looked up at him with a wry smile as she said, "You don't look very warm yourself."

Slowly he lowered himself down beside her. His face looked tired and sad but in a way relaxed, like a man who had come through a severe operation.

"You've been very brave." He was looking at her and she said on a cracked note, "Me? What have I done?"

"What have you done? Well"—he shook his head slowly—"the time isn't now, but later I'd like to tell you, when this business is all over. . . .You understand?"

"Yes, yes, I do, Ra-Ralph." There, she had spoken his name for the first time and had to stammer it.

"You're very cold."

"No, no, I'm not really." And she wasn't, for through her shivering body was coursing a warm, comforting glow. She knew as he did, that it wasn't the moment for expressing joy, but she could not stem this radiance that was flooding her as swiftly as the tide was running out to the sea.

His arm was about her, holding her tightly as they sat side by side looking towards the bay. They watched the

237

figure of Edith Cadwell being lifted from the craft, they watched Rouse Cadwell being assisted on to the beach, and then Mr. Cadwell was heading towards them again. As the dinghy chunked nearer, the pressure of Ralph's arm about her tightened and his large hand covering hers brought her fingers slowly and unobtrusively towards his lips. As the kiss spread across her fingers she did not look at him but towards the shore, and the oncoming boat, and her heart became strangely quiet. He had said, "The time isn't now," but he had given her all she required at the moment, other things could wait. There was a lifetime stretching before her at Fowler Hall and it would be filled with . . . the other things. The tender embraces, the passionate embraces, the giving . . . the taking. Laughter around the fire in the hall when the day was done, when the work was done, for there would be work, endless work. But it would be all part of living. . . . living to the full. No, the time was not now, but it would come, she could wait.

Slowly she relaxed against him, and she had the idea that she was being drawn into his body, held fast within the portals of strength, tenderness and yes . . . arrogance, that went to make up this man. She was no longer Linda Metcalfe, she was already Linda Batley, and the joy of it was almost pain.

THE END

CATHERINE COOKSON

THE BLACK VELVET GOWN

There would be times when Riah Millican came to regret that her husband had learned to read and write, and then shared the knowledge with her and their children. For this was Durham in the 1830s, when employers regarded the spread of education with suspicion. Now Seth Millican was dead and she was a widow with the need to find a home and a living for herself and her children.

Chance led to Moor House and a scholarly recluse obsessed with that very book learning that could open so many doors and yet create so many problems; especially with her daughter. Biddy, who was not only bright, but wilful . . .

0 552 12473 7 £2.50

CORGI BOOKS

A SELECTED LIST OF
CATHERINE COOKSON NOVELS
IN CORGI

WHILE EVERY EFFORT IS MADE TO KEEP PRICES LOW, IT IS SOME-
TIMES NECESSARY TO INCREASE PRICES AT SHORT NOTICE. CORGI
BOOKS RESERVE THE RIGHT TO SHOW NEW RETAIL PRICES ON
COVERS WHICH MAY DIFFER FROM THOSE PREVIOUSLY ADVERTISED
IN THE TEXT OR ELSEWHERE.

THE PRICES SHOWN BELOW WERE CORRECT AT THE TIME OF GOING
TO PRESS (JULY '85).

☐ 12473 7	THE BLACK VELVET GOWN	£2.50
☐ 06700 9	THE BLIND MILLER	£1.75
☐ 11160 0	THE CINDER PATH	£1.25
☐ 08601 0	COLOUR BLIND	£1.75
☐ 09217 7	THE DWELLING PLACE	£1.95
☐ 08353 4	FENWICK HOUSES	£1.95
☐ 08419 0	THE FIFTEEN STREETS	£1.75
☐ 10450 7	THE GAMBLING MAN	£1.95
☐ 12451 6	HAMILTON	£1.95
☐ 10267 9	THE INVISIBLE CORD	£1.95
☐ 09035 2	THE INVITATION	£1.75
☐ 08251 1	KATE HANNIGAN	£1.95
☐ 08056 X	KATIE MULHOLLAND	£2.50
☐ 08493 X	THE LONG CORRIDOR	£1.75
☐ 08444 1	MAGGIE ROWAN	£1.95
☐ 09720 9	THE MALLEN STREAK	£1.95
☐ 09896 5	THE MALLEN GIRL	£1.95
☐ 10151 6	THE MALLEN LITTER	£1.95
☐ 11737 4	TILLY TROTTER	£2.50
☐ 11960 1	TILLY TROTTER WED	£2.50
☐ 12200 9	TILLY TROTTER WIDOWED	£1.95
☐ 08561 8	THE UNBAITED TRAP	£1.75
☐ 12368 4	THE WHIP	£2.50

*All these books are available at your book shop or newsagent, or can be ordered
direct from the publisher. Just tick the titles you want and fill in the form below.*

CORGI BOOKS, Cash Sales Department, P.O. Box 11, Falmouth, Cornwall.

Please send cheque or postal order, no currency.

Please allow cost of book(s) plus the following for postage and packing:

U.K. Customers—Allow 55p for the first book, 22p for the second book and 14p for
each additional book ordered, to a maximum charge of £1.75.

B.F.P.O. and Eire—Allow 55p for the first book, 22p for the second book plus 14p
per copy for the next seven books, thereafter 8p per book.

Overseas Customers—Allow £1.00 for the first book and 25p per copy for each
additional book.

NAME (Block Letters) ....

ADDRESS ....

....